P9-DEB-073

THE REAL MINERVA

BOOKS BY MARY SHARRATT

Summit Avenue

The Real Minerva

THE
REAL
MINERVA

MARY SHARRATT

Houghton Mifflin Company

BOSTON   NEW YORK

2004

For information about permission to reproduce selections from
this book, write to Permissions, Houghton Mifflin Company,
215 Park Avenue South, New York, New York 10003.

Visit our Web site: www.houghtonmifflinbooks.com.
ISBN-13: 978-0-618-46232-2
ISBN-10: 0-618-46232-5

Library of Congress Cataloging-in-Publication Data

Sharratt, Mary, date.
The real Minerva / Mary Sharratt.
p. cm.
ISBN 0-618-46232-5
1. Women — Minnesota — Fiction. 2. Mothers and daughters — Fiction.
3. Physicians' spouses — Fiction. 4. Women domestics — Fiction.
5. Pregnant women — Fiction. 6. Single mothers — Fiction.
7. Minnesota — Fiction. I. Title.

PS3569.H3449R43   2004
813'.6 — dc22   2004040525

Book design by Anne Chalmers
Typefaces: Janson Text, Copperplate Gothic

PRINTED IN THE UNITED STATES OF AMERICA

MP 10 9 8 7 6 5 4 3 2 1

For Joske

PROLOGUE

HERE ARE SOME pictures of Minerva, Minnesota, in the early twenties, when my mother was a young woman. This aerial shot shows the tracks of the Northern Pacific Railway that ran through town, parallel to Main Street, bringing in commercial travelers, hoboes and migrant workers, even the occasional jazz piano player. Here's a photograph of the Minerva skyline. The tallest building isn't the water tower or the grain elevator but the steeple of Saint Anne's Catholic Church, followed by that of Mount Olive Lutheran, and First Presbyterian. Here is a hand-tinted postcard of the Hamilton Creamery and Pop Factory, the biggest employer in town. Before Prohibition it had been Vietzke's Brewery, but in January 1920, Mr. Hamilton, Presbyterian that he was, moved his creamery business in from its old location and started up the soda-pop factory. "If there's no beer, people will just have to drink pop" was one of his more famous quotes.

Although it's not as easy to find their pictures, Minerva also had its bad women. Some of them merely slept with the wrong person or had a child or two out of wedlock. Then there were those whose crimes were truly shocking. More than one woman in my mother's town committed the unthinkable and then disappeared. Minerva earned its notoriety for producing the rarest of creatures — a female outlaw.

Only a handful of people ever found out the true story concerning Penelope Niebeck. Here is a photograph of her, taken before she vanished from Minerva and embarked on her long journey. In the snapshot she is fifteen, her long dark braid pinned around her head. Her eyes are large, her nose and cheeks dusted with freckles. In those days most people looked solemn and slightly bewildered in front of a camera, but this girl is beaming with an outlandish happiness that completely transforms her face. She is holding a baby.

This photograph hung over the mantelpiece of my childhood home in the small Mexican town where my mother and I were the only foreigners. Penny Niebeck's image is woven into my earliest memories. When, as a seven-year-old, I asked my mother about my guardian angel, she pointed to the photograph and said, "She's your angel. She saved us both."

THE REAL MINERVA

1

THE DAY BEFORE the heat wave began, Penny Niebeck cleaned Irene Hamilton's room. Stooping to her knees, she picked the strewn stockings and underwear off the floor, and the dress that had been worn only once since its last washing and was now crumpled and stained. She was stuffing it all into the laundry bag when Irene marched in, pale and plump, white-gloved hands clenched. Penny struggled to her feet and steeled herself, sweat beading under her armpits as she met Irene's colorless eyes. Irene's hot breath, smelling of breakfast bacon, fanned Penny's cheeks. Both girls were fifteen, their birthdays five days apart. For the past eight years, Penny's mother had worked as the Hamiltons' cleaning woman. For almost as long as she could remember, Penny had clothed herself in whatever Irene had worn out and cast away.

"You want to know something?" Irene let out a swift exhalation that lifted the hairs on the back of Penny's neck. "Your mother named you Penny because she's cheap, and so are you."

Penny took a step backward, nearly stumbling over the laundry bag. "You have to go catch your train," she said. Irene and her sisters were leaving for summer camp that day. "Doesn't it leave at noon?" A glance at the porcelain-faced clock on the dresser told her that it was nearly half past eleven.

"I forgot something." Irene turned to snatch her mother's photograph from the lace-topped vanity and clutched it to her chest, her arms carefully folded around it. The photograph had been taken before Mrs. Hamilton fell ill from the sleeping sick-

1

ness. For the past four years, Mrs. H. had been an invalid in the Sandborn Nursing Home. Her face was frozen up like a statue's. She didn't talk anymore, didn't do anything but sleep and let the nurses feed and change her like a baby. The doctors couldn't say how long she would live or if she would ever get better.

"You know why Daddy's sending us away." Irene spoke accusingly.

Penny breathed hard. "No, I don't." But her voice faltered and blood began to pound at her temples.

"You *know*." Irene spoke so vehemently that her spit landed on Penny's face. "Even someone as dumb as you could figure it out."

"I'm not dumb."

"Oh, yeah? Then why aren't you going to high school this fall?"

Penny looked down at her cracked old shoes, the color of potatoes left to rot in the cellar. When she had finished ninth grade that spring, her mother had told her it was time to leave school and earn her own keep. High school was for people from well-off families or children whose parents cared about education and that sort of thing. At fifteen, Penny had hands already as swollen and red from all the cleaning as her mother's were.

"Your mother's too *cheap* to keep you in school," Irene said, sticking her face into Penny's so that she couldn't look away. "She's as cheap as they come."

"Is that so?" Penny shot back. "Well, your *father* seems to think she's just fine." She watched Irene's face go from flour white to chicken-blood red. "You better hurry," she said, "or you'll miss your train."

Downstairs Mr. H. was calling for his daughter. "Your mother's a whore," Irene whispered, something glinting in her eyes, which had suddenly gone pink. She hugged her mother's photograph tighter. "You don't even know who your father is," she said, her voice breaking as she dashed out the door.

. . .

After the Hamilton girls left for horse camp in Wyoming, the hot sticky weather moved in — the kind Penny hated most. Those nights the back bedroom she shared with her mother seemed far too cramped, the sloping ceiling about to collapse on them. At least winter, for all its bleakness, was pristine, the glittering snow covering everything, even the manure on the road, making the world look immaculate. But in the heat of late June, everything stank and decayed — the garbage pail near the back door with the trail of ants marching up its side, the reek of her sweating body as she scrubbed floors and heated the iron on the stove. With the windows wide open, she heard every noise at night — the raccoons knocking over the garbage pail, the laughter of lovey-dovey couples walking up the street. The sound of Mr. H. pacing in the master bedroom while her mother rolled in her narrow bed, the springs creaking beneath her.

Penny and her mother were hanging laundry on the clothesline when Mr. H. appeared without warning, home from the pop factory at eleven in the morning. Without more than a hastily mumbled hello, he ducked past them and disappeared inside the back door. A furious pounding filled Penny's head like someone hammering away on scrap metal. Her mother, her beautiful mother, turned, chicory-blue eyes narrowing against the sun's glare.

"I s'pose he forgot something."

Clothespins clamped between her lips, Penny grabbed a wet bedsheet from the laundry basket and was about to pin it up on the line when her mother yanked it out of her hands and threw it back into the basket. Penny stared at her, too furious to speak.

"We need bleach," Barbara Niebeck told her daughter, forcefully but quietly. "Go get some bleach." She pulled two dimes out of her apron pocket.

Spitting the clothespins out of her mouth, Penny fisted the coins her mother thrust at her.

"Go on," she said, squaring her shoulders and using the tone Penny knew better than to argue with. Her mouth trembling,

Penny shot out of the yard. She hid behind the lilac bush in the alley and watched her mother head toward the house, watched her skirt swing from her slender hips like a bell. There was nothing hesitant in her mother's gait.

As Penny stumbled off in the direction of the store, she didn't hear the dogs barking or the whistle of the train pulling into the depot four blocks away. She heard only her mother's voice, as hateful as a stranger's. *Go get some bleach*. Afterward her mother would try to disguise the odor by dribbling lily-of-the-valley toilet water all over her bed. The smell was enough to make Penny gag. With Mr. H. of all people. Mr. H. with his wife in the nursing home. How could her mother possibly find him attractive, with his sissi-fied New England accent and his high balding forehead? Penny understood without wanting to what he saw in her mother's firm body, in her thick, lustrous hair that wasn't dark brown like Penny's but blue-black — exotic coloring in Minerva, where most people's hair was blond or mousy brown. Once Penny had over-heard Mr. Wysock from church telling someone that her mother looked like Mata Hari. If people said unkind things about Barbara Niebeck, they all agreed she was a stunner.

Penny had been very fond of Mrs. Hamilton, who in the days before her illness had been kind to her. Mrs. H. had baked short-bread, which she cut into delicately pointed triangles called petti-coat tails. When it was fresh from the oven, she had invited Penny to join her daughters at the table for shortbread and sweet milky tea. Mrs. H. had made her daughters be nice to her, had told them to let her join their games. Penny remembered going to bed pray-ing that Hazel Hamilton was her real mother, but that was four years ago, before Mrs. Hamilton's illness. Penny told herself she was too old for such games of make-believe. Her mother always said that no one could get away with being too soft in life, and Mrs. H. had been as soft as a big hortensia bloom. Look where it had gotten her. The Hamilton daughters would do much better for themselves. They were prickly little porcupines trundling along, knowing that no one would ever lay a hand on them.

4

Turning onto Main Street, she could feel the heat of what would be another merciless day, the humidity coating her skin like grease. When she walked into Renfew's Grocery and Mercantile, loudly jangling the bells on the door handle, Mr. Renfew didn't glance up from his crossword puzzle. His two customers, Mrs. Deal and Mrs. La Plant, were too caught up in their conversation to look her way.

"Oh boy, it's gonna be a hot one today," Mrs. La Plant told her friend. "Supposed to get up to ninety-nine degrees. And with this humidity!"

Inside the store, it was almost bearable. An electric fan whirled from the high, pressed-tin ceiling. Positioning herself to get the most of the circulating air, Penny rubbed the sweat from her forehead with the heel of her hand. She crossed to the shelf where the chocolate bars were displayed and fingered the illustrated wrappers. Her favorite showed a fancy city lady walking a Scottish terrier. Raising the bar to her nose, she smelled the rich chocolate through the layers of colored paper and foil. In the heat, the chocolate had lost its firmness and went limp as butter in her hands. Her fingers sank in, leaving indentations on the lady's face.

Taking a quick look around to make sure no one was watching, she returned the misshapen bar to the shelf before slinking to the water dispenser in the corner. During the summer months, Mr. Renfew set out a big tin canister of ice water and a tray of glasses beside it. Often farmers came in, dry and dusty from the fields. Some farm hands and hired girls walked all the way into town. Sipping from her glass, she read the handwritten ads on the notice board. One in particular made her smirk: WEDDING DRESS, WORN ONCE, CHEAP, FIVE DOLLARS. How was it, she wondered, that girls spent a month or more — and all their savings besides — sewing their wedding dress, decorating it with ribbons, lace, and fake pearls? Why put so much work and expense into a dress they wore only one day? Once it was used, they were lucky if they could sell it for a few dollars.

Mrs. Deal and Mrs. La Plant wilted in the heat. Their carefully crimped hair went lank. The sweat rolling down their faces left snail tracks in their powder and rouge. When Mrs. Deal raised her hand to order another glass of Hamilton's strawberry pop, Penny couldn't help noticing that the armpit of her georgette blouse was dark with perspiration.

But before Mrs. Deal could get Mr. Renfew's attention, the screen door opened and a farmer strode into the shop. The two women looked over at once. Even Mr. Renfew lifted his eyes from his crossword puzzle. Penny stared at the farmer's manure-crusted work boots, his patched overall legs, and the buttoned overcoat he wore in spite of the heat. He was not anyone she recognized. His smooth young face, shadowed by a dusty Panama hat, was guarded and expressionless. When the farmer approached the main counter, she saw in profile the burgeoning belly the overcoat was meant to hide, that belly curving out like a firm ripe melon. Even she knew it could not be the belly of a fat man.

The Maagdenbergh woman. Of course, Penny had heard the rumors about her, but until this minute they had seemed like tall stories. Yet there she was, digging her grocery list out of her pocket and reading it to Mr. Renfew, who pulled the items down from the shelves and packed them into an orange crate for her.

"Insane," Mrs. Deal muttered to Mrs. La Plant. "That creature is insane."

Penny inhaled sharply, wondering if the Maagdenbergh woman had heard. She saw her stiffen, but the woman just went on reading her shopping list. "Two pounds of coffee beans . . . four bars of Luna white soap . . . a bar of Castile soap." Her tone was smooth, resonant. "A quarter pound of brick cheese . . . two pan loaves . . . a pound of rice . . . a box of Ralston crackers . . . two pounds of Cream of Wheat . . . a dozen cans of tomato soup."

"How's the farm?" Mr. Renfew managed to ask.

"The price of wheat has dropped so low, it's a sin." A spark of emotion crept into the Maagdenbergh woman's voice. "I've heard some farmers are switching to potatoes. At least the mills can't fix the price of potatoes, but what can I do? The wheat's already planted. Let's hope the weather will hold for the harvest."

After paying Mr. Renfew, she hoisted the crate of groceries and made her cumbersome way to the door. Penny winced, not willing to believe that such a hugely pregnant woman would carry such a load.

"Ma'am!" Mr. Renfew cried. The *ma'am* must have slipped out before he could stop himself. He leapt out from behind the counter and attempted to wrest the crate from her arms. "That's awfully heavy."

The Maagdenbergh woman trundled right past him. "I'm perfectly capable of carrying my own groceries, Mr. Renfew."

He held the screen door open for her as she hauled her load out to her pickup. As soon as she was gone, he turned shakily to Mrs. Deal and Mrs. La Plant, opening his mouth as if to comment on what had just transpired, when the Maagdenbergh woman marched back in and handed him a piece of ivory-colored letter paper.

"Mr. Renfew, would you mind putting this up on your notice board?"

He pinned it beside the scribbled ad for the used wedding dress.

"Thank you." The Maagdenbergh woman's voice was as smooth as that ivory paper. "Goodbye, Mr. Renfew. Goodbye, ladies," she added, turning to Mrs. Deal and Mrs. La Plant. The look she gave them spoke loud and clear. It was as if she had shouted in their faces, *Don't think I didn't hear what you were saying about me.*

Then her green eyes sank into Penny, fixing her in place so that she could not look away. She felt as though the Maagdenbergh woman could see right inside her, right to the bottom of her humiliation. As though she knew her mother had sent her to the store so she could have a dirty tumble with Mr. Hamilton. Penny shrank, the cheap tumbler falling from her hand. At the sound of the glass striking the floor, everyone turned to her. Mr. Renfew, Mrs. Deal, and Mrs. La Plant looked at Penny in startled confusion as if seeing her for the first time.

"Goodbye, miss." The Maagdenbergh woman stepped out the door. Only when she was gone could Penny take a deep breath and meet Mr. Renfew's eyes.

"Indestructible, that glass," he said as she picked it up, still in one piece, and set it back on the tray. Mrs. Deal and Mrs. La Plant smiled at her a little too sweetly. At least none of them seemed to notice her terrible shame. Only the Maagdenbergh woman had seen that.

"Penny?" he said. "Is everything all right? You look kind of pale." It was true, she was shaking.

"It's the heat." Mrs. La Plant sighed. "A person can't even think straight in this heat."

"You better sit down," Mr. Renfew said. "Why don't you eat something? How 'bout a piece of pie?" Penny edged her way to the counter and took a seat, leaving an empty stool between herself and Mrs. La Plant. Mr. Renfew cut her a slice of his wife's rhubarb pie. "Want some ice cream with that?" Penny offered him one of the dimes her mother had given her, but he shook his head. "This one's on the house."

"I can't believe her nerve," Mrs. Deal whispered to Mrs. La Plant. "Going around dressed like that and in her condition." She glanced at Mr. Renfew. "Did she have the rifle along in her pickup again?"

He nodded glumly. "It was there in the gun rack. I don't like to see a pregnant lady riding around with a gun."

"Heard she took a shot at the Nelson gang the other week," Mrs. La Plant said. "They drove by her place looking to stir up trouble —"

"She's *asking* for trouble," Mrs. Deal cut in.

"— and she shot clean through their windshield."

"The Nelson brothers are no good," Mr. Renfew said. "Serves them right. I just wish she'd try a little harder to stay out of harm's way. Nothing good can come of her living alone on that farm. I don't know how she'll manage when the baby's there."

They went on talking, their three faces a closed circle. Penny ate her pie in silence, grateful to be invisible once more.

"What was that notice she wanted you to put up on the board?" Mrs. Deal asked.

"She's looking for a hired woman."

"God almighty!" Mrs. Deal slapped the counter and laughed. "No one in their right mind would work for a creature like that."

"Now, Edna," Mrs. La Plant said. "Don't be so uncharitable."

"I don't see why she doesn't go back to where she came from."

"Back where?" Mrs. La Plant asked. "Back to her husband in Evanston?"

Mrs. Deal didn't say anything.

"I don't understand," Mrs. La Plant continued, "why you can't feel a little more sympathy for a lady who had to run from her own husband."

"Is it true she tried to shoot him?" Mr. Renfew lowered his voice to a murmur.

Penny listened to them hash out the story, pieced together from so many different scraps of gossip that it was hard to sort out the truth. The Maagdenbergh woman's real name was Cora Egan. She was the wife of Dr. Egan of Evanston, Illinois, a man who had served as a military surgeon in the Great War. That was where they had met — supposedly she had gone to France as a Red Cross nurse. People said Dr. Egan came from money and owned a big house a few blocks from Lake Michigan. As a young wife, Cora Egan had been a celebrated beauty, renowned for her charity work, her picture all over the Chicago papers. Then the previous November she had appeared at her grandfather's farm outside Minerva and asked if she could stay. Roy Hanson, the hired man, claimed she had gone straight for the kitchen shears and hacked off the thick and wavy chestnut hair that had garnered her such praise in the society columns. She had burned the shorn tresses in the stove along with the dress she had traveled in. From that day onward, she had worn only men's clothes, straight from her grandfather's closet. Then one night her husband showed up. First he acted all gentle and nice, but when she cussed him out and said she'd never go back to him, he started to get mean.

"Roy told me he tried to protect her," Mrs. La Plant said. "Threw himself between her and her husband and got a punch in the gut. Said he was all doubled up on the floor."

"Now *that* I don't believe," said Mrs. Deal. "Who ever heard of a doctor knocking down a hired man?"

Mrs. La Plant ignored her. "Roy ended up on the floor and old man Van den Maagdenbergh was too frail to do anything but shout. So she got her grandfather's rifle and shoved it in her husband's face. Told him to get out, and if he ever came back, she'd shoot him dead."

For a moment no one spoke.

"Roy said she was all shaky and white in the face." Mrs. La Plant fiddled with her handkerchief. "But she wasn't bluffing. Her finger was on the trigger. One false move and her husband's brains would have been all over the kitchen."

Penny looked down at the sticky red remains of the rhubarb pie.

Mr. Renfew cleared his throat. "I remember when she and her brother used to come visit their grandpa in the summer. In those days she seemed like a nice enough girl. I went to school with her mother," he added. "Theodora Van den Maagdenbergh." A distant look passed over his face. "She was a tomboy but nice to look at. Sharp as a nail, too." He wiped the counter meditatively. "Went to Chicago on scholarship money and met some swell rich fellow. They ran off together . . . to Argentina, I think it was. She must have broken her old man's heart."

"*Argentina,*" Penny broke in. Startled by her voice, they turned to her. "Why would somebody from here go all the way down there?" She thought of the globe in the Hamiltons' study. Argentina was at the bottom of the world.

"A lot of people were going to Argentina in those days," Mr. Renfew said. "It was after the Wild West closed up. Down there they still had a frontier. They had mining and cattle ranches bigger than the ones in Texas. People thought they could strike it rich."

"Argentina's where the tango comes from," Mrs. Deal said knowingly.

"I think Roy said her parents ran a hotel down there," said Mrs. La Plant. "They died when she was twelve. She and her brother came up to live with the Chicago grandparents. They're dead, too, now. She doesn't have anyone."

"What about her brother?" Mr. Renfew asked.

Mrs. La Plant shrugged. "I don't know anything about the brother. She had Roy, though, but then she fired him. Right after her grandpa died and everyone was ready to feel sorry for her and help her out. Told Roy he didn't show her the proper respect." She laughed in disbelief. "Can you imagine? He took a punch in the stomach for her sake, and she tells him he doesn't respect her." She rolled her eyes. "None of this trouble with the Nelson gang would have happened if she'd had a man with her on that farm."

"It would be a lot easier to feel some sympathy if she let her hair grow back," Mrs. Deal said, "and put on a dress."

"Things are never that simple." Mr. Renfew let out a sigh. "You have to keep up with the times. Harriet cut her hair as short as a boy's." His daughter Harriet lived in Minneapolis. "She wears trousers sometimes. Smokes cigarettes and drives her own car. All the young gals in the Cities are cutting their hair. It's the new fashion."

"Fashion?" Mrs. Deal snorted. "You know darn well the Maagdenbergh woman doesn't give two hoots about fashion. She wants to be a man."

Mr. Renfew blinked and took away Penny's empty plate. Mrs. La Plant plucked a hair off her skirt. Silence settled over everyone, stifling as the heat. Penny slid off her stool and slipped away.

2

AFTER SENDING her daughter off to buy bleach, Barbara Niebeck headed for the kitchen, where she unknotted her apron and folded it over the back of a chair. She prided herself on never doing anything in a slovenly way. No rush, she told herself as she climbed the stairway. No excitement now. Making him wait was part of the game. When she stepped into the back bedroom, they would trade places: she would be the lord and he her servant. She enjoyed taking the role of the man, enjoyed opening him up and making him submit to her. Of course, he paid for it, and quite handsomely — he could afford to — and afterward he was so grateful. She knew what she was doing, knew she was exactly what he craved: an experienced woman, not some hysterical young thing who might foster false hopes or make unreasonable demands. The notion of romance had been beaten out of her a long time ago, starting at the age of fourteen when her father had pushed her down in the woodshed, his hand clapped over her mouth. Having given birth to Penny at fifteen, she knew more than anyone the importance of averting pregnancy. A few weeks ago, she had gone to a special doctor in Sandborn who had fitted her for a diaphragm. She'd waved her fake wedding ring in his face and bribed him, and in the end she'd gotten what she wanted. You couldn't rely on the man to take precautions. You had to go all the way to Sandborn to buy condoms, and Mr. H. could never do that. The way people talked, the rumors would spread through the entire county.

Barbara slipped into the bathroom and took the diaphragm

from its hiding place behind the can of Borax Abrasive Cleanser. The thing she hated most about Minerva, she decided, was that everyone thought they knew you. They thought they knew all about you, but they saw only what fit their own notion of a person, what they were comfortable seeing. People looked at Laurence Hamilton and thought he was some kind of paragon of decency, when anyone with half a brain would be able to figure out the mystery behind his coming home in the middle of the day. People thought that she was a hussy paying the wages for her sins, hiding her disgrace behind the lie of being a widow, but they didn't know a thing.

For an instant, as she held the tube of spermicidal cream over her diaphragm, she allowed herself to remember Mrs. Hamilton in the days before her illness. Squeezing cream out of the tube, she recalled Mrs. Hamilton's lace-edged handkerchiefs, her jeweled brooches, her fading gold hair. Eight years ago, Mrs. H. had hired her. She was one of the few people who had believed Barbara's story about being an unfortunate widow left alone with a child. Previously Barbara had slaved away as a chambermaid at the Commercial Hotel, where she spent her years between the ages of fifteen and twenty-two dodging the traveling salesmen who had tried to grope her in the dim hallways. She supposed Mrs. H., in a way, had been her savior. Mrs. H. had been too noble to hold Barbara's reputation against her. She hadn't considered the consequences of hiring a cleaning woman who was young and pretty.

As Barbara shoved the diaphragm into her vagina, she told herself she wasn't being heartless but merely clear-headed. Sentimentality was not a luxury she could afford — not after having Penny at fifteen and then having to run away from her own father, who had tried to drown her newborn baby in the rain barrel. After all she had been through, bringing up her daughter on a cleaning woman's wages, she had systematically rooted out and destroyed every naïve impulse. As long as Mr. H. wanted her, she would let him have her, but she would be sure to get as much out of him as she could. She was no fool. When Hazel finally got around to dying, he would dismiss Barbara, then find some respectable woman to marry, someone of his own station, a fellow Presbyterian like that Miss Ellison, who gave his daughters their piano lessons and couldn't take her eyes off him. Wasn't Miss Ellison already training for the role of stepmother, judging from all the attention she gave his girls? Those heart-to-heart talks she had with Irene? By the time Mr. H. was ready to marry again, Barbara planned to be long gone. At the end of summer, she hoped to have enough saved so that she and Penny could get on a train and head out to some place like California, where it was always warm and where she could imagine a much easier life.

Appraising herself in the bathroom mirror, she brushed her black hair. Her life was far from over: she was thirty and looked younger, especially if she compared herself to the farm wives her age who had already birthed a whole litter of brats and had to squeeze their sagging flesh into rubber corsets before going to church. With the money she'd made so far from these odd mornings and afternoons with Mr. H., she had bought kidskin gloves to hide her work-roughened hands. In a pair of good gloves she could pass as a lady. She had bought silk stockings and a smart black crêpe de Chine dress. For the time being, she wore them to Mass. Every Sunday, she took her daughter to Saint Anne's Catholic Church, not out of any hypocritical notions of piety, but so all those biddies and stuffed shirts who thought they were better than her could see how respectable she looked in her new clothes. She knew what irked them most was that if she had the right clothes, there was no telling the difference between *her* and *them*. She wanted Penny to sit up and notice her mother wasn't any old drudge. She wanted the girl to take a good look at the way men stared at her while their wives seethed. *This is the way you do it*, she wanted to tell her, *so they don't grind people like us into the ground.*

Honestly, she didn't know what to do with that girl. Penny could be so nerve-racking with her drooping shoulders and mournfully accusing eyes. But sometimes her daughter looked at her slyly, as though she knew things she had no business knowing.

There were times Barbara saw something in that girl's sharp and merciless stare that reminded her, against her will, of her father. Sometimes — God forgive her — she wanted to take Penny by the shoulders and shake her until her bones rattled. Once, in a moment of rage, she had even told her daughter about how her grandfather had tried to drown her in the rain barrel. Although she had never meant to do it, she had spit out the words. "Show me some respect! I'm the one who saved you." But she had never told Penny that her grandfather was also her father. She would jump off a bridge before she revealed that to anyone.

Stepping out of the bathroom, she thought of Hazel Hamilton's daughters: pasty, second-rate miniatures of their mother. Once she had caught Irene cornering Penny on the stair landing and taunting her. "What's a penny worth? Nothing — that's what you're worth." Barbara had rushed up from behind and told Irene in her chilliest voice, "My daughter's name is Penelope, if you please, and some would consider it a nicer name than Irene."

When Barbara entered the back bedroom where Mr. H. lay waiting, she tried to forget that this was also her daughter's room. The drawn curtains made it dim enough for her to pretend not to see Penny's bed in the far corner. On Barbara's own iron-framed bed, he stretched out naked. She heard his breath catch as she began to undress. He was so eager, she nearly pitied him. His whole life he had been obliged to be so correct, so upright, a pillar, but only here in her bed could the man inside him unfold. Straddling him, she loosened her long black hair so that it swept down and touched his yearning face. As she kissed him and drew his hands to her breasts, she imagined the weight of his world dropping away.

3

PENNY WAS HALFWAY down Main Street when she remembered that she hadn't bought the bleach. She paused for a moment, reaching in her pocket for the two thin dimes. Then she bit her lip and kept walking until she reached the Bijou Motion Picture Theater. The matinee had already begun. In the shadows near the screen, Mrs. Jensen played piano to accompany the silent pictures as Penny found her way to an empty seat, sticky with spilled lemonade. Houdini's face hovered before her in the darkness. Her heart beat fast. The heat made her half faint as she watched them bind him with chains as thick as his arms. His eyes leapt off the screen and locked with hers. She winced as his face contorted, her fingers kneading the armrests as he struggled, his muscles chafing against the chains. She leaned forward, her stomach tight as she watched him wriggle like a powerful fish straining against a net. Mrs. Jensen's triumphant chords drowned out Penny's gasp as Houdini finally broke free.

When she returned to the Hamiltons', it was nearly three o'clock. She braced herself as she marched in through the back gate. Just let her mother ask her where she had been all afternoon and what she had done with the bleach money. She lifted her chin in defiance. But her mother, busy taking the laundry down from the line, didn't appear to notice the time Penny had spent away. Her face was set and fixed, with no trace of shame.

"I'm nearly finished here," she said. "Take these sheets in and get started on the ironing."

The sheets to which her mother was referring were the real linen sheets that went on Mr. H.'s bed. Something grew so tight in Penny's throat, she thought it would burst. When was she going to wash her own stinking sheets? Penny remembered the look the Maagdenbergh woman had given her in the store.

"Penny! Did you hear what I just said?"

She tried to stand her ground, the way her mother always did, to hold herself as tall and proud as the Lombardy poplars in front of the public library. "I'm not ironing his sheets." Her voice was strong even though it took all her courage to meet her mother's gaze.

"Pardon me? I don't think I rightly understood what you just said."

"I said I'm not ironing his sheets." Penny raised her voice and prayed there was no tremor in it. "You can't tell me what to do anymore," she added, astounded by her own nerve.

"Very well then, Miss Smarty Pants." She could tell her mother could just manage to rein in her temper. "If you're too high and mighty to do your work around here, then you can pack your bags and go someplace else."

"Maybe I will." If she broke down now and allowed her mother to bully her into ironing those sheets, she thought she would die inside. "Maybe I'll just go."

"Any place in mind?" The corners of her mother's mouth twisted into a smirk. "The Commercial Hotel? Spend ten hours a day cleaning out those rooms while the traveling salesmen try to paw you? Or maybe you want to sweep under the benches at the railway station."

The sarcasm in her mother's voice made Penny want to hate her. Reaching deep inside herself, she summoned up the thing that would shock her mother most, that would shut her up and knock her out of her complacency. "No. I've got something better than that. The Maagdenbergh woman." She felt a cold surge of satisfaction to see her mother frown and take a faltering step sideways. "She's looking for a hired girl."

"If this is some kind of joke," her mother said, "I don't think it's very funny."

"I'm not joking." Penny spoke so rapidly, she hardly knew what she was saying. "She's desperate for a hired girl. Alone on that farm with harvest coming and a baby on the way. She'll pay me any wages I ask."

Her mother shook her head. "Are you crazy or just trying to be smart with me? I don't think you're stupid enough to think you can just go off and work for somebody like that. Come on, let's get started on those sheets."

"I don't see why I shouldn't go work for her. Isn't her money as good as Mr. Hamilton's?" She willed her mother's shame to rise to the surface, longed for some word of embarrassment or regret. An attempt at an explanation, perhaps. One thing was certain — she had managed to get her mother completely flustered. For the first time in her memory, she saw her searching for words.

"You think you're pretty smart," her mother said, this time hesitantly. "But there's an awful lot about this world you just don't know." She stepped toward Penny and rested her hand on her shoulder. "That Maagdenbergh woman is not exactly what people call decent."

Closing her eyes, Penny allowed the hard thing inside her to soften. But before she could accustom herself to the warmth of her mother's hand on her shoulder, the grip toughened, her mother's fingers digging into her flesh hard enough to bruise.

"I have heard *enough* of this foolishness," her mother snapped in the same tone she had used when ordering her to go buy bleach, a tone of such cold authority that Penny wanted to scream.

She had not meant to do it, had not meant to go this far, but before she could stop herself, the words shot out of her mouth. "You know, you're not exactly what people call decent, either."

Her mother's hand flew off her shoulder and smacked her hard across the face.

"Ma!" she cried, eyes brimming.

"You little shit!" She had never heard her mother shriek like that before. "If that's what you think of me, then get out. *Get out!*"

She grabbed Penny's arm and hauled her into the kitchen. As hard as Penny struggled, she could not yank her arm free. She had never guessed her mother was so much stronger than she was. As she dragged her up the back stairway, Penny tried to pretend that none of this was really happening. Then they reached the back bedroom, reeking of lily-of-the-valley toilet water and the other, ranker smell, which the toilet water could not completely mask.

"I can smell him!" Penny cried, rubbing her stung cheek. "I can smell him," she sobbed.

"Shut up."

Her mother grabbed a small wicker suitcase and started hurling Penny's clothes into it. She shoved the suitcase at Penny, grabbed her by the hair, and tried to force her down the hall. Before she could march her down the stairs and out the back door, Penny broke free. The flimsy suitcase banged against her thigh as she burst out of the house. Flying into the shed, she grabbed the battered old bicycle her mother used for running errands. Fast as Houdini, she threw the suitcase into the bicycle basket and started pedaling, her calf muscles straining as she pumped down the alleyway. The garbage pails and the boys playing marbles streaked into a blur. Before she turned onto Lilac Street, she heard her mother shouting her name, but she just pedaled faster. She told herself that Houdini would never look back.

4

THE VAN DEN MAAGDENBERGH FARM was twenty-one miles out of town on a dirt road. The old bicycle jerked over each rut and stone. Penny banged down on the springless seat, rubbing her thighs raw. Flying pebbles bounced off her bare legs. On both sides of the road, corn rose six feet in the air, blocking her view of everything but the road before her. To relieve the monotony, she counted the telephone poles. High overhead she made out the black outline of a hawk circling.

When she first set out, she had expected some farmer to come barreling down the road in his pickup, roll down the window, and yell, "Penny Niebeck, what do you think you're doing out here?" Then he would take her back to her mother. Not a soul had come her way. Now that she was sunburnt, parched, her calves aching and her butt sore from the hard seat, she made herself face the fact that no one cared enough to stop her from doing this. It would be entirely up to her to turn around and go groveling back to her mother. But her face still burned from that blow. She tried to imagine what would happen when the news spread that she had gone to work for the Maagdenbergh woman. It would look bad, her taking off and leaving like that. It would make people wonder. Mr. H. would be embarrassed. He would question her mother, maybe even put an end to their dirty episodes.

The sun inched behind the wall of corn, throwing the road into shadow. Penny pedaled faster, following the tracks made by the Maagdenbergh woman's pickup. She wondered how many miles were left and if she would make it before dark. Finally the corn gave way to a field of wheat, still tinged green but shimmering gold in the sun, which hovered above the flat horizon. Her breathing quickened when she saw the mailbox and then the hand-painted sign marking the entrance of the driveway. PRIVATE PROPERTY. KEEP OUT. ALL TRESPASSERS WILL BE SHOT. For a moment she hesitated, remembering the stories she'd heard. She imagined the Maagdenbergh woman glaring at her down the barrel of a rifle. Mrs. Deal's voice reverberated in her brain. *That creature is insane.* But it was too late to turn back. Slowly she pedaled forward.

Oak and cottonwood trees arched overhead, turning the long drive into a shadowy place where crows hopped up the branches and flapped their ragged wings. Their caws assaulted her ears. There was no uglier-sounding bird, she thought, imagining her mother turning into a crow, picturing the harsh glint in her eye as the crows followed her progress through the tunnel of trees. When she emerged on the other side, an apple orchard came into view and then an old brown farmhouse. Everything was as it should have been. The barn, the outbuildings, the woodlot, the pasture with the single Holstein cow grazing, the kitchen garden fenced with chicken wire to keep out the rabbits. On the back lawn, white geese nestled in the grass, their feathers blinding in the slanting rays of the sun. As she approached the house, they rushed at her, flailing their clipped wings and hissing, but she kicked at them and yelled *shoo*, plowing right through their midst with her bicycle until she reached the back porch.

Leaning the bicycle against the outer porch rail, she climbed the steps, legs stiff from the long ride. The door was ajar, swinging idly in the breeze. Standing at the threshold, she was sweating hard, even though the worst heat of the day had ebbed. She rapped on the doorframe. Three loud knocks. "Ma'am?" she called, not knowing how else to address her. She knocked again, her heart pounding. No one came.

"Ma'am!" Could the Maagdenbergh woman be off in the barn? Out in the fields somewhere? Something about the silence was not right. Her stomach clenched when she heard a noise halfway between a cry and a moan. It seemed to come from overhead. Backing away, off the porch and onto the lawn where the geese hissed, she saw that one of the upstairs windows was wide open with ghostly white curtains fluttering loose. Then, as the geese surrounded her, she heard the cry again, the cry that pulled her inside even as her heart raced in panic. Flying into the kitchen, she saw a narrow staircase. The voice called.

Swallowing, Penny climbed the stairs and reached a hallway where all doors except one were closed. Forcing herself forward, she looked inside that room, and then she was the one who cried out, her fist crammed against her mouth. Some unspeakable crime had taken place. On the floor lay a bloody pair of kitchen shears. What lay on the bed was too awful to look at. How could that half-naked body be the same person she had seen that very morning, the same person who had fixed her with that stare? The Maagdenbergh woman's rifle leaned against the wall in the far corner. A voice inside Penny told her that she would never reach for it again.

Beneath the Maagdenbergh woman's body was a sheet of red-and-white-checked oilcloth where dark red blood puddled. Some of the blood had run off to stain the sheets. The Maagdenbergh woman's face was the color of a dead fish. The only thing she had on was a man's faded flannel shirt, not long enough to cover the part of her that was gaping and bleeding. Her unmoving arms cradled something bloody. At the sight of it, Penny started sobbing. Only when that thing began to cry did she realize it was alive. The sound was as feeble as a kitten mewing.

She did not think but only moved forward. Something beyond reason and free will made her reach for it, determined to rescue it from the dying woman's embrace. But before her trembling hands could touch the baby, the Maagdenbergh woman opened her eyes and stared at her. Penny froze, her hands clutching empty air. The woman gasped. Covering her mouth, Penny prayed she would not be sick.

"I'll get a doctor," she breathed.

The woman's face seemed to split in two. She lifted her head from the pillow. "No. No doctor." Then she collapsed back into the bedclothes. Her husband was a doctor, Penny remembered, thinking back to the conversation at the store.

"We need to get help! Do you have a telephone?" Her voice rose and cracked.

The woman's eyes seemed to cloud over, then they fell shut. Doctor, Penny thought, bile rising in her throat. Telephone. Surely the woman must have one. Hadn't she seen those telephone poles along the road? Racing down the stairs, she found it in the kitchen, mounted on the wall. She pulled the crank, then got through to the operator in town.

"Send a message to Dr. Lovell right away. This is Penny Niebeck out at the Maagdenbergh farm. She just had her baby. I think she's going to die."

When she returned to the room where the Maagdenbergh woman lay gray-faced and mumbling, Penny noticed for the first time the preparations she had made for this event. An old-fashioned cradle lay at the foot of the bed. On the bedside table there were neatly folded diapers, clean white tea towels, and a yellow baby blanket. A tiny nightgown and booties. She saw the bar of Castile soap the Maagdenbergh woman had bought at Renfew's that morning — soft white soap for washing the baby's delicate skin. The bloody scissors on the floor — she must have used them to cut the baby's cord. They had probably slipped from her hand and fallen. The baby was alive and breathing, so she had known what to do. The room grew dim around Penny, the last of the sun gone.

She found the light switch, then took one of the linen tea towels and placed it between the Maagdenbergh woman's legs to stanch the flow, but the blood saturated the cloth in seconds. The Maagdenbergh woman was silent now, her eyes closed, her body unmoving. Penny drew a deep breath and then reached for the baby, staining the front of her dress with the blood and mucus that coated its skin. It was so tiny, gazing up at her with unfocused eyes.

All she could think of was the story of how her grandfather had tried to drown her in the rain barrel when she was a newborn. This baby, too, was a little girl.

Glancing back at the unconscious mother, Penny decided that if she couldn't save the Maagdenbergh woman, she could at least try to save the child. She would wash her. She drew water from the bathroom taps, taking care that it was tepid enough for her to stick her elbow into. With a clean cloth, she gently sponged the baby's skin, holding her carefully, terrified she would slip beneath the water. By the time Dr. Lovell arrived, she had the baby dried, diapered as best she could, and wrapped in the soft yellow blanket.

"Penny!" Dr. Lovell exclaimed when she opened the door to him. "Did your mother send you to check on her?" Before she could reply, he nodded to himself in a businesslike fashion and went to wash his hands at the kitchen sink. "I was telling Laurence just the other week that someone better go check on her, her time being so near. You're a good one, Penny."

Dr. Lovell was a close friend of Laurence Hamilton, and like Mr. H., he was thin, balding, and Presbyterian. He was older than Mr. H., though. Penny paid close attention to his age-spotted hands, which were steady and didn't tremble like hers did when he went upstairs with her to look at the Maagdenbergh woman. But when he saw all the blood, he shook his head and muttered, "Damn." He turned to her. "Penny, I want you to go down to the icebox, take out the block of ice, put it in a scrubbed-out washtub, and break it up with an ice pick. Break it so the pieces are the size of gravel. I need you to work as fast as you can."

It all passed in a blur, her hands frantically scouring the galvanized iron washtub she had found in the kitchen, then hacking the ice with the pick and mallet. As she worked, she heard the Maagdenbergh woman come to life and yell at Dr. Lovell. Penny couldn't make out the words — Dr. Lovell must have closed the bedroom door — but her fury was unmistakable. Penny's hand on the ice pick slipped. Bringing the mallet down, she hit her thumb.

Dr. Lovell opened the bedroom door. "Hurry up!" he shouted down the stairs. "We need that ice."

Hoisting the washtub, she struggled up the stairs, then nearly dropped it when she heard the Maagdenbergh woman scream. When she entered the room, she saw her thrash on the bed, her hands lashing out as she tried to push Dr. Lovell away.

"Mrs. Egan," he said sternly. "How can I help you if you behave like that?"

What came from her was a stream of curses so livid, they made the doctor's face go white. He turned to Penny, as though to seek out a witness for what he had to endure. "I need you to hold her down."

Setting the ice tub on the floor, she shook her head.

"Penny!" he snapped. "We don't have any time to waste."

So she sat on the edge of the bed and took her hands, squeezing them nervously. "Shh," she whispered, bracing herself for a stream of abuse. The Maagdenbergh woman clutched her hands with what seemed to be her last strength.

"Jacob," she said softly. "Jacob, please. Don't let him take the baby away." Her hands were so cold, they made Penny shudder. "Be good to me, Jay." Now she wept, her tears far more alarming to Penny than her curses had been. Penny smoothed back the woman's damp hair, her movements clumsy and faltering. She'd never stroked anyone's hair like that before.

"It's all right," Penny told her. "The baby's safe. She's over there in the cradle. That's only Dr. Lovell. He's trying to help you."

Penny glanced at him, then looked away. He was thrusting his hairy arm right inside the Maagdenbergh woman, who shrieked. Then her hands went limp and she lay unmoving, her eyes closed and mouth slack. Penny could still feel the faint beating of the blood inside her wrists. Pulse, she told herself. That was called the pulse.

"She fainted," she said, unable to look at the doctor while he had his hand inside the woman.

"She's still got some placenta in her." He spoke calmly, like a schoolteacher giving a lesson. "The placenta's the sac the baby comes in. If I don't clear away this tissue that's stuck to the inside of her womb, she could die of infection. Of course, she tore herself, too. She'll need stitches. I can't imagine how she cut the cord by herself. Damn lucky she didn't kill herself and the baby with her."

"I heard she used to be a nurse," Penny said after a pause.

He laughed curtly. "Then what she's done is truly unforgivable. A nurse should have known better. Just imagine if you hadn't found her."

After sponging away the excess blood, he applied the broken ice, which Penny helped him wrap in clean oilcloth and cushion with sterile gauze. He kept sending her down to his car to bring him fresh bundles of gauze and cotton padding. Then he gave her a baby bottle, and instructed her to sterilize it and prepare sugar water. "For the first two days, you can give the baby sugar water, sterilized cow's milk after that."

Why was he telling her this, Penny wondered. She wasn't the mother.

"You know how to give a baby a bottle, don't you?" he asked, but when she shook her head, he didn't appear to notice.

It was hard to hold the bottle steady. The baby was so little and helpless, Penny feared she would choke on the sugar water or that something else would go awry. She considered her own misbegotten birth. How had her mother, weakened from labor, been able to save her from the rain barrel? How had she summoned the strength to take her and run away? But she couldn't bear to think about her mother.

"I've got another job for you," Dr. Lovell announced a while later, handing her an enamel pan filled with something that looked like raw liver. "The placenta," he informed her. "Go out and dispose of this. You might want to dump it in the chicken coop. Some swear it makes the best chicken feed."

"It's dark out there."

"Dark? The moon's nearly full." He turned Penny around by

her shoulders and nudged her in the direction of the door. "Throw it behind some bushes if you have to, but far away from the house, because it'll attract animals."

Trying not to look at what she carried, she hurried out the door. The doctor was right — there was the moon, a hard bony face hovering over the barn. As she made her away across the back yard, she awakened the geese, who closed in around her, honking and hissing, pecking at her shins. Something awful ran up her spine.

"Go away!" She hurled the afterbirth to ward them off, but the afterbirth was what they wanted, what they pounced on and devoured, snapping at each other to get at it. In the moonlight, she saw the blood darken their feathers. She fled back to the house and slammed the door behind herself. For several numb minutes, she stood at the sink and washed her hands over and over.

"Penny!" Dr. Lovell called. "Where are you? Can you find this woman a decent nightgown?"

Penny turned off the tap and dried her hands. "Nightgown?" she echoed as she trudged up the stairs. What could he be thinking? Of course this woman had no decent nightgown.

"This thing she's wearing now," he said as Penny stepped into the bedroom, "is soiled." He pointed at the flannel work shirt. "I want to clean her up, change her into something decent, and get some clean sheets on this bed before I leave." He mopped his bald forehead with a folded handkerchief. The ice was gone from between the Maagdenbergh woman's legs, and in its place was what looked like a huge cotton-wool diaper pinned to a rubber belt. Dr. Lovell told her it was one of those new Kotex sanitary napkins. "More hygienic than old rags."

The Maagdenbergh woman stared at the ceiling, her eyes blank, her mouth and palms open. She lay there like a spent thing, a broken doll flung away, no fight left in her, not even the strength to glare at the doctor.

"Is she going to die now?" Penny couldn't keep herself from bawling, her hands clutching her face.

"Don't cry, honey. Everything's dandy. While you were out of the room, I gave her some ether. Just to calm her down and help her rest."

The only nightgown in the house was Penny's, which her mother had hurled into the wicker suitcase along with her other things. She went down to the kitchen to get it, then brought up a basin of warm water.

"We can't move her from the bed with her stitches," the doctor said, so they gave her a sponge bath where she lay. It seemed obscene that she was so naked and exposed. Suddenly Penny understood Dr. Lovell's insistence on the nightgown, even though her nightie was small on the Maagdenbergh woman, tight across the chest. Carefully turning her over in bed, they stripped off the oilcloth and stained sheets, and made up the bed fresh. Penny brought up a bucket of hot water with vinegar and disinfectant, and went at the floor. At least this was something she knew how to do.

When she was finished, Dr. Lovell called her down to the kitchen. "Penny, sit down for a minute. There's something I need you to sign." He handed her a form. "Tomorrow you can show this to Mrs. Egan and tell her this is a signed statement saying that you and I witnessed the birth of a live female infant. Here is today's date. Here's the mother's name and address. Now, I want you to sign at the bottom, under my name." He unscrewed the cap from his fountain pen and handed it to her. The silvery pen was cool and smooth in her hand. She summoned her best handwriting as she wrote out her full name — Penelope Maria Niebeck. Except she wasn't used to writing with a fountain pen. She pressed the nib too hard, and the ink clotted and smudged.

"Oh, Dr. Lovell. I'm sorry. I . . ."

"That's fine, Penny. Now I want you to sign here, too." He opened a black clothbound book. The heading at the top of the page was BIRTHS. Inside there were columns listing the date, the sex of the child, the parents' names and address, the father's profession. "This is my record of all the births I've attended this year," he said. "Now would you please sign here as my witness and attendant?" He spoke kindly, as if they shared some important secret.

When she signed her name, it occurred to her that he must also have another clothbound notebook titled DEATHS. And the statement he had made her sign wasn't true. They had not witnessed a live birth, only what had happened afterward. She wanted to remind him that the Maagdenbergh woman had birthed her baby alone, but who was she to contradict a doctor?

"What you've signed is very important," he said as he screwed the cap back on his fountain pen. "If that woman tries any funny business, she won't get away with it, because there are two witnesses to a live birth. It's all on record now."

"What kind of funny business?"

He fixed her with a rueful smile. "When babies are born on backwater farms, all kinds of things can happen. You're too young to know the half of it. Let me just say that some women will do all kinds of things to hide their bellies from everyone. Then, when the baby's born, they make it disappear."

Penny's stomach lurched. "You think she would try to kill her own baby?" That didn't make sense. The Maagdenbergh woman had cut the cord and made sure the baby was breathing. She had begged Penny not to take the baby away. Upstairs the bedsprings creaked and the Maagdenbergh woman cried out, her voice jumbled and slurred.

"She probably wouldn't do that," the doctor conceded. "On the other hand, she's an eccentric character, don't you think?" He scratched the back of his neck. "But let's move on to more practical matters. Tomorrow you'll want to make her beef bouillon. I see she has some bouillon cubes in her cupboard. At least she had sense when it came to buying provisions. Make her weak tea with plenty of sugar. Tomorrow I'll bring some cow's liver and you can cook that for her. She needs iron to build back her blood."

"I can't stay here." Penny's voice rose in panic. "I thought you would drive me home, Dr. Lovell."

The doctor rose from the table and laid his hand on her shoulder. He let it rest there gently and smiled at her, making her blush. "I'm very proud of you, Penny. That woman's crazy as a coot, but you might have saved her life. She'll be all right now as long as you keep feeding her and changing the napkins. Remember, those are disposable napkins. Don't try to wash them out and reuse them like the kind you get from Sears Roebuck." He stopped short. "Don't look so peaked, dear. You did a wonderful job. The baby would have most likely died, too, if you hadn't found them."

She could not believe she had saved anyone. "I can't stay here."

"Don't worry, Penny. I'll talk to your mother." He spoke with authority, leaving no room for argument. "I'm sure your mother's very proud of you. Mrs. Egan needs to stay in bed for at least two weeks. Do you understand how important that is? Doctor's orders." He smiled in a way that invited her to smile with him. "You'd make a good nurse," he said. "Now, I'm not one to interfere in family decisions, but I think it was a shame your mother took you out of school. If it were up to me, you'd go to high school and then on to nursing school. You have *nurse* written all over you."

Penny blinked, her throat too tight to speak. High school, nursing school? The house was so quiet, she could almost forget about the woman and baby he had ordered her to take care of.

"Tomorrow or the day after," Dr. Lovell said, "I'll come back and check on her. I need to fill out the birth certificate and have her sign it. She wasn't much good for that today, was she? That woman," he added, his voice going flat, "hasn't done much in the way of making friends here, so if anyone's going to look after her, it has to be you, Penny." He shook his head sadly, then gave her shoulder a reassuring squeeze. "She'll pay you for your troubles, though. I'll see to that. You know that her grandfather had over ten thousand dollars in the bank?"

Before Penny could think what to say, he picked up his black doctor's bag and wished her a good night. Penny listened to his car engine start up, listened to him drive away. Leaving her alone with this stranger and her baby. Responsible for them. She turned on the tap in the kitchen sink. Holding a washcloth under the stream of cold water, she stripped down and scrubbed every inch of her body, scrubbed her legs, grimy from the long bicycle trek. She washed away the sweat under her arms. Wincing at the chilly water, she washed her hard flat chest and told herself she was nothing like the Maagdenbergh woman with her swollen breasts and torn body. She hardly had any hair on her crotch, didn't even bleed down there yet. What happened to the Maagdenbergh woman didn't have anything to do with her — she was completely removed from that whole chain of female suffering. She vowed she would never have a baby, never put herself through that.

Off the kitchen, she found the spare room, which must have been Roy Hanson's when he was the hired man — it still smelled of cigarettes and men's hair pomade. When she turned down the quilt, the sheets looked clean. Opening her suitcase, she looked for her nightgown before remembering she had given it to the Maagdenbergh woman. You're stuck, she told herself, putting on clean underwear to sleep in. Stuck with her. She could just imagine her mother cackling like a crow.

Crawling into the strange bed, she tried to sleep, but the events of the day kept parading through her mind. *Nurse written all over you.* Rolling over, she pictured herself in a clean white uniform, working in some immaculate city hospital, far away from geese that ate placentas and women who gave birth all alone.

5

PENNY'S PILLOW was damp with sweat when the noise wrenched her awake. Glancing around the strange room, filled with the faint glimmer of sunrise, she wondered where she was. But as that inhuman bawling tore through the open window, she remembered. In seconds she was dressed, then dashing out the door, across the dew-damp lawn where she nearly tripped over the enamel pan she had left there the night before. The geese slept soundly, their heads tucked beneath their wings, as she bolted to the edge of the pasture. The Holstein pressed against the gate, the boards creaking against her bulk. Left in the pasture all night and aching to be milked.

"I'm coming, girl," Penny called out before slipping into the barn to hunt for the milking pail and stool.

"Easy now." She set the stool down and positioned the bucket under the udder. Her mother had taught her to milk cows, had told her not to be afraid of them. Honestly, the animal frightened her less than the woman in the farmhouse.

The memory came back to her of shattered sleep, charging up the stairs in the night to the screaming baby, who needed to be fed and changed. She didn't want to think about the look the Maagdenbergh woman, still groggy from the ether, had given her when she had burst into the room, switched on the light, and tended to the baby.

After carrying the milk to the kitchen, she fired up the stove and set water on to boil so she could sterilize the baby bottle. Dr.

Lovell had told her to keep the baby on sugar water for a second day, yet it seemed a shame when there was such an abundance of milk. Outside the geese awoke and the chickens squawked, wanting to be fed. They would have to wait until after breakfast when she carried the leftovers and slops out. In the woodlot, the birds sang louder than they ever had in town, as loud as though it were the first day of creation. Except they didn't sound sweet but savage, like wild things that would peck out her eyes if she gave them half a chance.

She went into the pantry to see what she could cook for breakfast. There on the shelf, between the soup cans and boxes of oatmeal and Cream of Wheat, were at least twenty packets of Dr. Nod's Sleeping Powder. Enough to kill a horse, Penny thought. She grabbed an open box of Cream of Wheat from the shelf and returned to the kitchen.

When she carried the breakfast tray up to the bedroom, the Maagdenbergh woman's face was pale, her lips colorless, her eyes swollen with bruised-looking circles beneath them. Penny stepped forward, about to say that she had to change the baby's diaper and her napkin. But in the Maagdenbergh woman's silence, she found it hard to speak. Although she didn't seem to have the strength to lift her head from the pillow, the woman's eyes were sharp and full of fire.

"Who are you?" The way she framed the question, it sounded as though she were asking her for far more than her name.

"Penny Niebeck." But even this information Penny offered indecisively. The Maagdenbergh woman's scrutiny left her reeling, uncertain who she really was. "You saw me at Renfew's yesterday morning," she added, but the woman regarded her blankly, appearing to have forgotten the incident.

"Who sent you here? There was a doctor yesterday, as I seem to recall." She spoke harshly. "Did he put you up to it?"

"You were looking for a hired girl."

For a second she looked as if she were going to laugh. "You came for my ad?"

"I'm not staying. I'll be gone as soon as you're on your feet again." It seemed best to be honest about it.

She nodded. "You're too young for this." Then her voice trailed off, her face going white as the bedclothes. "Is there tea?" She sounded feeble as she glanced at the tray on the bedside table.

Penny poured her a cup, but when she tried to give it to her, the Maagdenbergh woman's hands were so unsteady, she feared she would spill it all over herself. So Penny pulled her up a little, leaned her against the bedstead, and held the cup to her mouth, tilting it so she could drink. The woman's eyes were downcast. Penny sensed her pride, her rage at her own helplessness, at this terrible intimacy neither of them had bargained for. She drank four cups of tea before allowing Penny to start spooning the Cream of Wheat into her mouth. In the silence following breakfast, Penny gave the baby her bottle and changed her diaper. Even though she had done it a few times already, it still terrified her, trying to fasten the fresh diaper around those twitching legs, making sure the safety pin was pointed away from the baby's flesh so it wouldn't poke into her belly if it accidentally came undone.

Now came the most embarrassing part. Penny picked up the box of Kotex napkins Dr. Lovell had left on the dresser. "Excuse me, ma'am, I have to . . ."

"I'll do it myself. Just help me to the bathroom." Grabbing the bedpost, she pulled herself upright and planted her bare feet on the floor. Penny put an arm around her and walked her to the bathroom across the hall. She thought about the stitches she had down there. Even walking must hurt.

"Thank you," the Maagdenbergh woman muttered, taking the box of Kotex and shutting the door.

On the second day, when Penny carried up the breakfast tray, she found the Maagdenbergh woman nursing the baby at her breast. The woman pulled up the sheet, blocking Penny's view. Penny set the warm sterilized bottle of cow's milk on the bedside table, but the Maagdenbergh woman ignored it. Although it seemed to sap the life out of her, she kept on nursing, even managed to burp the baby before sinking back into the bedclothes.

"She's been eating and drinking," Penny told Dr. Lovell when he arrived a few hours later. "She still seems pretty weak, though."

"Needs her iron." He handed Penny a bundle wrapped in gray butcher's paper. "Put that in the icebox. That's calf liver. Now let me go up and have a look at her." After he had washed his hands, Penny led him up the stairs.

"Who is it?" Pushing herself upright, the Maagdenbergh woman glared at the doctor.

"This is Dr. Lovell, ma'am. He's here to —"

"Thank you, Penny," he cut in. "I won't be needing you just now. Why don't you go down to the kitchen and start frying that liver for Mrs. Egan's lunch?"

"She will stay right where she is." The Maagdenbergh woman turned to Penny. "As long as he's here, I want you here, too." She grabbed Penny's wrist, her fingers sinking into her.

Dr. Lovell proceeded with the examination. Each time he touched her, she flinched and squeezed Penny's wrist. "Will you hurry that up?"

"I'll have to come back in a few days to remove your stitches," he said thinly. "Now, if you would be so kind as to provide the information I need to fill out your daughter's birth certificate, Mrs. Egan."

"My name is Cora Viney."

Dr. Lovell cast an exasperated look at Penny. "Have you chosen a name for your daughter?" He got his fountain pen and a form out of his bag. From where she stood, Penny could make out the heading: CERTIFICATE OF LIVE BIRTH.

"Phoebe Helena." Her voice was less grating now. "Phoebe Helena Viney."

Penny had never heard the name Phoebe before. It sounded

pretty, like some kind of songbird. Meanwhile Dr. Lovell filled out the form, using the marble-top dresser as a writing surface. The baby lay wriggling at her mother's side, her mouth opening in a silent cry. Releasing Penny's wrist, the Maagdenbergh woman picked up the baby, rocking her gently.

"I need the mother's full name and date of birth," said Dr. Lovell.

"Cora Elizabeth Viney," she said. "May 11, 1898."

"Birthplace?"

"Puerto Natales, Chile."

"Ma'am, I have no time for —"

"Puerto Natales, Chile," she said again. "It's written on my birth certificate if you don't believe me. Do I have to spell it for you?" Impatiently she rattled off the letters.

Penny glanced at her sideways. So she had been born in Chile, not Argentina, as Mr. Renfew had believed. It was still all the way at the bottom of the world. Maybe her foreign birth accounted for some things and explained her strangeness.

"Do you have any other children that are now living?" the doctor asked.

"None."

"Any fetal deaths? A fetal death would be, for example, a miscarriage . . ."

"You don't have to tell me what fetal deaths are." She spoke in a tone of quiet rage that left a chill on Penny. "Yes. One." Her eyes seemed to sink all the way back in their sockets.

Dr. Lovell was silent for a moment. Then he glanced up and cleared his throat. "Ma'am, I'll need the father's full name, age, and date of birth."

"Unknown," she said with a ghastly smile.

"Surely you don't take me for an ignoramus," he said. "I think you know that lying about a child's paternity is a crime."

"That certificate isn't worth anything until I sign it." She wrapped her arms around the baby. "You'll never get a signature from me unless you write *unknown*."

The baby opened her mouth to suck, rooting against her

mother's chest. As she started to cry, the front of the Maagden-bergh woman's nightgown — *my* nightgown that she's wearing, Penny thought — darkened as her breasts began to flow.

"Get him out of the room." Although she addressed Penny, her eyes were on the doctor, glowering at him until he walked out the door.

"There aren't very many educated city women who do it that way anymore," he whispered when Penny followed him out into the hallway. "But it figures, doesn't it? She has to be so contrary."

After she finished nursing, Dr. Lovell showed her the filled-out birth certificate. She inspected it for what seemed to Penny to be an absurd length of time.

"How can you purport that my daughter was born at three forty-six P.M. if you weren't even there?"

Dr. Lovell pursed his lips. "It's an estimation, ma'am. Do you have any objection to that?"

Peeking over her shoulder, Penny saw that he had followed the Maagdenbergh woman's instructions — after *Father's Name*, he had written *unknown*. Finally she took his fountain pen and signed her maiden name at the bottom.

When Dr. Lovell left, Penny prepared the Maagdenbergh woman's lunch of fried liver and creamed spinach, and served it to her with a glass of fresh milk.

The Maagdenbergh woman's argument with the doctor still rang in Penny's head as she fished the dirty diapers out of the soaking pail and plunged them into the bubbling wash kettle on the stove. Sweat poured down her face as she put the diapers through the wringer, then hung them up to dry. The sheets soiled from the Maagdenbergh woman's labor took a good boiling and a bottle of bleach before they looked decent again. She washed the tea towels that the Maagdenbergh woman had used when she burped the baby. By the time she took the laundry down from the line and folded it, she had to start preparing the evening meal.

Penny regarded the pile of clean diapers and then her raw

wrinkled fingers. It hardly seemed worth the effort, considering that by the next day the diapers would all be filthy again.

After serving the Maagdenbergh woman's supper of fried liver and mashed potatoes, Penny threw the leftovers in the slop pail and dragged it out to the chicken coop. She poured half the mess in their feed dish. When the roosting hens bustled over to eat, Penny stole their eggs, still warm from their feathered bellies, and tucked them inside her apron pockets. She fed the rest of the slops to the geese, who didn't attack her anymore. When she walked down to the barn to put the cow in for the night, they followed her, but kept a respectful distance.

At the end of the day, Penny concluded that her work here was harder than anything she had ever done at the Hamiltons'. When the Maagdenbergh woman and the baby went to sleep, Penny bathed in cool water and decided to turn in early. It felt a little funny to be sleeping in Roy Hanson's bed, though. She kept picturing him with his elaborately pomaded hair and his strutting walk. Her mother used to say he reminded her of a bantam rooster. He'd certainly left his mark behind on the room — there was a cigarette burn in the rug and an old almanac with his name in it. When she drew back the sheets, she noticed something sticking out between the mattress and springs. Tugging on the end, she pulled out a slim booklet with a blazing red cover and curlicue letters spelling *The Gallery of Love*. She snorted. Since when did men like Roy Hanson read romance stories? When she opened it, she found no stories at all, just pictures of naked ladies. Some of them were plump with monstrously large bosoms. Others were so slender, it looked as though a person could break them as easily as snapping a twig. Their lips were painted, their cheeks darkly rouged. Some of them had long loose hair tumbling down their backs. Some had bobbed hair; others had elaborate coiffures. They posed on velvet sofas and bentwood chairs, their lacy underthings falling off them like petals from a flower. The pictures made her giggle, her hand clapped to her mouth.

Then she turned to a picture that made everything stand still. She didn't hear the kitchen clock ticking, didn't hear the cicadas outside. If Phoebe had started screaming, she wouldn't have heard that either. On a satin-covered bed, a man embraced a woman. This time the man's body was revealed. He was beautiful and young with his long muscled legs, his smooth chest, his slim hard hips. His penis rose from the hair of his crotch. Penny tittered, nervous and uncertain, the blood rushing to her face as her eyes traveled up his body to his arms, his hands that cradled the woman's face. She was pretty. Delicate and blond, not as heavily made up as the other ladies in the booklet. Her eyes were locked with his. The way they looked at each other, that gaze that was as tender and fierce as the way the Maagdenbergh woman looked at her baby, but different. Of course it was different. The man's face was so gentle, the way his dark hair fell over his brow. Penny felt as though she was in the same room as them, not looking at a book of dirty pictures. She studied the way the man's eyes drank in the woman with such longing.

Penny's hand shook when she finally turned the page to a picture of a naked lady riding a rocking horse. Were there any more pictures of that man? Stuck between the pages of the booklet were loose pictures of more naked bodies. Flipping through them, she came to a picture of two ladies kissing and fondling each other. The sight was so preposterous that she quickly flipped to the next loose picture, which made her nervous laughter die. On a bearskin rug, a woman cowered on her hands and knees. She was gagged, her eyes bulging in pain. A hairy man came at her from behind and mounted her like a dog. In one hand he held a horsewhip. It was so ugly and hurtful, yet for half a minute or more she couldn't look away. Her throat clamped shut as she nearly choked on her own saliva.

She remembered the way Roy used to visit the Hamiltons' kitchen and mooch coffee off her mother, the way he used to gawk at her mother's behind. Did he think about her mother when he ogled these pictures? Something hard struck her in the belly. Did her mother let Mr. H. do such hateful things to her? Penny told herself she was sick for even looking at such pictures. She burned *The Gallery of Love* in the kitchen stove, but as the flames consumed the photographs she felt a flicker of regret that she was burning the picture of the beautiful man along with all the others.

Taking her suitcase, she marched upstairs in search of another bed. The house was silent, the Maagdenbergh woman's door shut. Penny pushed the other doors open to see what lay behind them. With a flick of the electric light switch, the rooms revealed themselves. The bathroom, a room that looked as if it had once been a sewing room, then a second bedroom where lilies bloomed on chintz curtains. There was a secretary desk and shelves of books. Penny sat gingerly on the lace-covered bed. This room was at least as nice as Irene Hamilton's. True, it didn't have a window seat, but look at the silver-backed brush on the dresser. Look at that lamp with the fringed satin shade. She pulled the switch and was bathed in a circle of light. Her bare feet touched the edge of an Oriental rug, and then her mind was made up. For her few remaining days at the house, she would sleep here. Her place as hired girl was in the room off the kitchen, but after all she had been through, would the Maagdenbergh woman hold it against her for wanting to stay in a nice room? It made it easier to change the baby's diapers in the middle of the night. If the Maagdenbergh woman needed her, she'd be right across the hall.

She went to the bookcase and pulled a thick book off the shelf, puzzling over the words in a language she couldn't read. It was probably Dutch. Old man Van den Maagdenbergh had come from Holland when he was young, or so she had heard. At first glance, the foreign words were incomprehensible, then she realized it was the Bible. Irene thought she was so important because she was learning French in high school. Had she ever even looked at a Dutch book?

Another book had its spine sticking out from the others. Someone must have been reading it recently. *Self-Reliance and Other Essays* by Ralph Waldo Emerson. The closely set paragraphs looked tedious until she found a marked page and an underlined sentence: "If solitude is proud, so is society vulgar."

Vulgar. Roy's awful book of pictures paraded through her mind. *Solitude.* She considered her lonely trips to Renfew's to buy bleach, the loneliness that was eating away at her like the laundry soap that ate into her hands when she washed that endless stream of diapers. *Solitude.* She conjured up another picture, this time seeing it as something beautiful — standing at the edge of a pristine lake, toes in the calm water.

Flipping through the book, she came to the inner leaf. In the top right-hand corner was the Maagdenbergh woman's name, her married name, written in beautiful handwriting. *Mrs. Cora Egan.* She had brought this book along when she ran away from her husband, carried it all the way from Evanston, Illinois. Penny reckoned it was probably one of the few things she had kept from her old life.

6

SHE DREAMT OF a long tunnel of trees, sunlight turning the transparent leaves into a kaleidoscope. The Hamiltons kept a kaleidoscope in their parlor. When you looked inside, you saw church windows that kept shattering and changing colors. Windows and tunnels, dancing light.

Her eyes flickered and her fingertips touched the edge of something delicate. The lacy coverlet brushed the edge of her throat. So this was what it felt like to wake up under lace. Milky gray light shone on the lily wallpaper as she sat up slowly, taking in the bookcase and the walnut-framed mirror that threw her bewildered face back at her. Where was she? Her bare feet found her shoes. Yesterday's dress lay crumpled over the back of a chair. When she pushed open the curtains, the light turned golden as the full force of morning poured into the room. The sun had already risen over the woodlot, where the birds sang and sang. It was late. How could she not have heard the cow? There was no noise at all, apart from the birds.

The baby. She hadn't heard her cry all night. Throwing on her dress, she stepped out into the hallway. The Maagdenbergh woman's door was wide open, her unmade bed empty. Penny rushed down to the kitchen, which was swimming in light. How the sunlight transformed everything. How it made the dusty cupboards and icebox gleam. You had to look hard to see past its radiant spell. The sunlight seemed inseparable from the aroma of freshly roasted coffee beans.

The Maagdenbergh woman stood at the stove, heating up a pan of milk. She was wearing overalls, work boots, and a man's shirt. The sun caught her chestnut hair in a fiery blaze. The gold bathed her face. Penny had to look carefully to see how pale she still was, the gray circles etched under her eyes.

"Morning," she said, her eyes glued to the stove.

"Morning," Penny replied. "You must be feeling better." Her eyes dropped down to the Maagdenbergh woman's work boots, dark and wet from the dew. So she had milked the cow herself while Penny was sleeping.

"I feel fine." The Maagdenbergh woman couldn't look her in the eye. She seemed embarrassed, as though she didn't want to remember how Penny had found her when she was bleeding and helpless. Penny herself was embarrassed when she remembered. Turning away, she glanced at the table where the baby slept, tucked into a large basket lined with a quilt.

"Do you want some coffee? I brewed some. I always take my coffee with hot milk."

Penny looked past her to the pan, in which she had roasted the beans, and the wooden coffee mill, in which she had ground them. The smell was heavenly, but she didn't like coffee. On the back burner there was a pot of bubbling oatmeal. The Maagdenbergh woman had made breakfast, which should have been Penny's job. She should still be in bed. Penny watched her pour two cups: first the strong coffee, then the hot milk. She took the pot of oatmeal off the burner and ladled it into two bowls.

"We're nearly out of coffee," she told Penny, handing her the cup. "I need to make a run into town to get some groceries, but first I should go out and have a look around the farm."

"Dr. Lovell said you had to stay in bed for another week." Penny set her cup on the table. It seemed too late to tell her she didn't like coffee and that she thought that hot milk was what you drank when you were sick.

"I've been in bed a whole week. Another week of doing nothing would kill me. Dr. Lovell doesn't have a farm to run, does he? With all this heat, harvest might be early this year. Would you mind watching the baby for me while I go around the fields?" Sitting at the table, she spooned brown sugar on her oatmeal.

"Ma'am, I can't." Penny went to the screen door and looked out at the geese promenading across the lawn. "I can't stay here anymore."

"Call me Cora, please. And come and eat your breakfast." She spoke quickly, as if to hide her shaky authority. "You really helped me out. The doctor said you might have saved my life. I want to give you something for your trouble."

Penny stared out at the back lawn, littered with white goose feathers. If her mother were here, she would make her gather those feathers in an old flour sack. When they had enough, they would wash them clean, dry them, and sew them into a pillow. Her mother never liked to see anything go to waste. Pressing her hand against the screen door, Penny felt her heartbeat quicken. Did she miss her mother already? A memory intruded before she could push it away. She was a little kid curled in her mother's lap, gazing up at her and stroking her long black hair, telling her how pretty she was. *Sweetie*, her mother had said. *You're such a sweetie.*

"I don't want money," she heard herself tell Cora. "I don't want to take money just for helping you." She spoke so decisively that she startled herself. "But I'm going home today. The doctor said I could go as soon as you were better." Her eyes lingered on the geese as they cropped grass and preened their feathers. "My mother wants me to come home," she lied. This time her voice didn't sound nearly as strong.

"Is Penny your real name or your nickname?"

She let out a long breath. "My real name's Penelope, but nobody ever calls me that."

"That's a lovely name." Cora paused. If you didn't look at her but just listened to her talk, she sounded like any other woman. Right now her voice was as gentle as Mrs. Hamilton's had been in the old days. "Penny, why don't you finish your breakfast before it gets cold?"

She joined Cora at the table, taking her place across from her. The baby in her basket was in the middle of the table, blocking Penny's view of Cora. When Cora spoke to her, Penny's eyes rested on the sleeping infant.

44

"Put some sugar in the coffee," Cora told her. "It tastes better that way." She moved the sugar bowl across the table toward Penny, her hand snaking around the baby's basket. "You can see that I need a hired girl," she said.

Penny raised the cup to her lips and took her first sip of the sweet milky coffee that was completely unlike the bitter black stuff her mother made. "You said you were looking for someone older."

"How old are you?"

"Fifteen."

"You should be in school."

"I'm finished with school." The words shot out of her mouth.

After a moment's silence, Cora said, "I left school early, too."

Penny wondered how old she was when she married Dr. Egan. Cora had been born in 1898, which made her twenty-five — ten years older than she was. When she tried to imagine where she herself would be in ten years, she saw only scrub buckets, worn-down shoes. A life just like her mother's.

"If you could at least stay until after the harvest is in. You can name your own wages. My grandfather left me some money. That's the way those old Dutch farmers are. They hoard every nickel."

Penny sprinkled sugar on her oatmeal and took a spoonful, allowing its thick warmth to fill her mouth. Cora made good oatmeal.

"I know I must have shouted at you. I can't even remember what I said. Maybe something awful. I was delirious. I think every woman gets a little delirious when she goes through labor."

Penny wondered how she could get up from her chair and say goodbye without being rude. She should never have come here — it was all just too much.

"I used to work in a maternity clinic," Cora went on. "I never knew a woman who didn't curse and swear and say the most terrible things when she was giving birth."

The baby began to cry. Bending over the basket, Cora stroked her daughter's cheek, cooing to her. When Penny saw

Cora's face suddenly go soft, she had to look away. It seemed so private, the look she was giving her baby.

"I have to go." Penny stood up and pushed her chair back under the table as her mother had taught her. She carried her cup of coffee and her bowl of barely touched oatmeal to the sink before heading toward the back door. "Your offer is nice," she said, "but I promised my mother I'd come home." Her hand on the doorknob, she imagined the reception her mother would give her. A cold guffaw. She could already hear her. *I told you that Maagdenbergh woman is as strange as they come.* Sometimes she wished she was a kid again, back when loving her mother had been easy. She missed the days when they used to go to the lake together or when they went to get ice cream after church. Back when Mr. H. was just their boss and not her mother's dirty secret.

"Penny," Cora called after her. "At least finish your breakfast. If you can wait an hour or two, I'll drive you into town. We can put your bicycle in the back of the pickup."

The bicycle was where Penny had left it, propped against the porch, its handlebars glinting in the sun. She considered the long dusty stretch of road. She imagined her mother bent over the stove making soup broth, her fist clutching the wooden spoon like a club. Would she hit her again? For taking the bicycle and disappearing like that?

"Penny?"

Slowly she turned.

Cora was rocking the baby when she met her eye. "There aren't many people I trust. But I trust you."

The back of Penny's knees went soft. Then Cora went red in the face, and they both looked away.

"Can you hold her for a second?" Cora handed her the baby, then set Penny's coffee and oatmeal back on the table. Penny marveled how sweet and trusting the baby was, as peaceful as she had been in her mother's arms. Well, she knows who I am, Penny thought. She had given the baby her first bath. She had been the first person to put diapers on her. When Cora took Phoebe again, Penny sat down and finished her breakfast.

7

THE MORNING AFTER her daughter ran sobbing from the house, Barbara took her statue of Saint Barbara from its hiding place. Her mother had given it to her as a confirmation present when she was eleven — the year before her parents had taken her out of school. She had always kept the statue secret from her daughter, taking it out only when things were so bad she wanted to throw herself down and never get up again. She didn't pray to the saint so much as silently pour out her grief. Saint Barbara had more mercy for her than anyone else, more than God or Jesus. Saint Barbara knew exactly what her namesake had suffered. Her face was stern but compassionate, and in her outstretched hand she held a miniature tower with three windows. The saint's heathen father had locked her in that tower. When she converted to Christianity, he tried to beat it out of her, then turned her over to a judge who had her tortured. Finally her father took her to a lonely mountaintop and beheaded her. On his way home, he was killed by fire that rained down from heaven.

Whenever people asked Barbara about her family, she'd say they all died in a blaze when their barn, full of hay, was struck by lightning. Of course, the truth was that her parents lived on unpunished, but the story gave her comfort. Sometimes she wondered why they had named her Barbara. Had they done it on purpose, knowing what would happen?

Barbara had named her own daughter Penelope because she liked the sound of it, because she didn't have any relatives with that name, and because it wasn't a saint's name or a name from the

Bible. To her knowledge, there was no story of martyrdom attached to it. Yet still she had managed to make her daughter run away.

"Bring her back." She fingered the saint's head, the smooth sweep of her black hair. Penny was all she had, the only person she loved.

Before going down to make breakfast, she washed her face and put a witch hazel compress on her eyes so Mr. H. wouldn't notice she had been crying. As it turned out, she could have spared herself the trouble. When she handed him his plate of bacon and eggs, he didn't meet her eyes or touch her fingers. It seemed he was afraid that Penny would burst into the kitchen at any moment. How long would it take him to figure it out? Men confounded her sometimes, the way they failed to notice simple things. But it was better this way. He wouldn't demand an explanation. And maybe Penny would be back soon. Maybe after one night away she'd want to come home.

After he left for work, she washed the dishes and swept the kitchen floor. The broom fell from her hands when she heard someone coming up the porch steps. "Penny?" She wrenched the door open to see Dr. Lovell holding his hat to his chest. The contrite expression on his face made her cry out. Something had happened to her daughter.

"Mrs. Niebeck, I came by to thank you."

Dazed, she shook her head.

"It was very good of you," he said, "to send your daughter over to check on the Maagdenbergh woman."

The Maagdenbergh woman. Barbara felt herself shrink, air escaping her lungs.

"I asked Penny to stay and take care of her for two weeks. If you don't mind, of course. It was a difficult birth. She lost a lot of blood. That woman was as ill-mannered and contrary as contrary can be, but Penny kept her head on straight. I don't know how I could have managed without her."

Barbara could not even begin to take the pieces of what he had told her and put them together.

"I know a lot of people don't care for that Maagdenbergh woman," he said, "and she doesn't exactly welcome help and friendship, but Penny stepped right in there and did her Christian duty. A true Samaritan. You must be very proud of her."

"I tried to raise her right." Barbara became aware that her legs were shaking. Dr. Lovell slipped past her into the kitchen and pulled out a chair for her. "Penny wanted to go over there," she told him as she sat down. "It was her idea." She clasped her hands in her lap and stared at the linoleum.

After the doctor left, her belly filled with a pain strong enough to make her double over. She hoped Mr. H. wouldn't come home in the middle of the day and surprise her. Even in this heat, she made herself a hot-water bottle to press against her cramping uterus. The clots that came out were as thick as gooseberries. She soaked the soiled rags in a bucket of cold water and vinegar. If he came to her, she would tell him she was feeling poorly — wasn't that the truth? If she saw him coming through the back gate, she might even creep out the front door and pretend to go to Renfew's. She could hardly imagine telling him to his face that she had the curse.

A week after Penny's departure, the Maagdenbergh woman was seen in town again, driving her pickup, dressed in her overalls and work boots. But Penny did not return. Gradually the word went around. Dr. Lovell told his friends, including Mr. H., with whom he played chess once a week. Even the deliveryman who brought the ice for Cora's icebox had a hand in spreading the news that Penny had gone to live at the Van den Maagdenbergh farm. When Penny didn't come home after Cora recovered, people really started talking. That's when her staying ceased to be Christian charity and became a choice.

"She's doing it for the money," said Mrs. La Plant, sitting at the counter at Renfew's. Her fork hovered a few inches above her half-eaten piece of plum coffeecake. "I'm sure the Maagdenbergh woman had to bribe her to get her to stay."

Mr. Renfew looked thoughtful. "It stands to reason that she'd want to earn her own money. I'm sure every cent she made at the Hamiltons' she had to hand over to her mother."

"I think she's just too young and foolish to know what she's getting herself into," said Mrs. Deal. "Alone on that farm with that woman and her gun."

Mrs. La Plant threw her friend a despairing glance. "Oh, Edna."

Mr. Renfew wiped the counter. "Well, I'm hoping that everything works out for the best. Maybe having that girl around will make the woman a little more agreeable. People develop strange habits when they live alone."

"Still, I'm surprised her mother let her go there." Mrs. Deal swirled the broken ice in her glass of Hamilton's orange pop. "What kind of mother would let her daughter live with such an odd woman?"

Barbara feared her daughter's defection and the gossip it raised might get her fired. If everyone in Minerva was talking about Penny, then they would also talk about her, and about Mr. H., too. Everyone knew his daughters were off at camp. Penny's unexpected leave-taking drew attention to the fact that she and Mr. H. were alone in the house. People might begin to surmise. Although she avoided the subject with him for as long as she could, one morning before breakfast he asked her why Penny had left.

"You sent your girls away," she reminded him. Cutting a loaf of bread, she concentrated on making the slices even. "I decided it would be best for Penny to try her own wings for the rest of the summer." She wouldn't allow him, of all people, to paint her over as a failed mother.

"You sent her to the Maagdenbergh woman." The disapproval in his voice was plain. Although she tried not to let him intimidate her, she felt a prickle of fear. In the bedroom she might be his master, but here in the kitchen she was just his cleaning woman. His eyes were so sharply inquisitive that she made herself focus on the red mark where his tight collar chafed against his neck. "Why did you let her go there?"

"She's fifteen." In spite of herself, Barbara felt her face go miserable and hot. "She has to learn for herself. Make her own way in life."

"But the Maagdenbergh woman . . ."

"She might be an oddball." Barbara tried to squeeze past him in order to carry the breadbasket to the table. He stood firmly planted, not letting her by. "But she's harmless," she said, addressing the tight knot of his brown tie. "And she pays well. Besides," she said, using the same excuse she had given to Dr. Lovell, "it was Penny's idea." What goddamn business did he have asking her these questions? Since he wouldn't let her pass, she laid her hand on his arm and felt the heat rising through the thin fabric of his shirtsleeve. This was a bold gesture, and one she had never before wagered outside their hours in the back bedroom. "It's for the best." Staring into his eyes, she watched his expression turn from sober to bashful — no longer that of an employer but of a guilty lover.

"If you say so, Mrs. Niebeck." He drew away from her touch. "You're her mother." Abruptly he turned, heading past the breakfast table and up the back stairway. He only went up the back stairway for one reason.

Fists clenched, she went up after him. Tears pricked at the back of her eyes. She couldn't make herself walk slowly this time, couldn't force him to wait. She was at his heels, shutting the door as soon as he had stepped into her room, yanking his ridiculous tie loose before he could reach her bed. She went after him in a fury, extracting her pleasure from him until she cried out, over and over, her neck jerking back, her head thrashing, her hair falling in her face. She was not going to let him dismiss her and leave her no choice but to go back to the Commercial Hotel and clean up after the traveling salesmen who thought they could feel her up for free.

She would not let him cast her off like that. Finally she collapsed on top of him, her body covering his. His heart beat hard against her breast as their sweat welded their bodies together. Tentatively at first, his arms wrapped around her. She felt his hand stroking her hair, his breath in her ear as he whispered, "Barbara."

He had never called her by her first name before, and she had never called him by his, even to herself in her private thoughts. He had always been Mr. H., her employer, Hazel Hamilton's husband. She tried to make her face a mask, as stern and otherworldly as her statue of Saint Barbara. A woman as pure as a frozen waterfall. Yet her hand trembled as she smoothed back his hair and traced his eyebrows and the line of his jaw.

"Laurence," she said. Her voice astonished her. It was soft, not hard. Sweet as water falling.

Two hours later Barbara went to buy groceries at Renfew's. She never stepped out the door in her housedress and worn-down mules, the way some women did, but always put on a fresh dress, her good shoes, and white gloves before slinging her shopping basket over her elbow and heading down the alley. Before Penny had taken off on her bicycle, Barbara had cycled to the store, but now she was obliged to walk in her two-inch heels, which threw her hips into a swing she could not avoid. Walking to the store took twice as long as cycling and gave the men driving down Main Street a better chance to eyeball her. Well, let them stare, she thought.

When she reached Renfew's, a bunch of women were jabbering away.

"Sadie Ostertag from over near the railroad yard," Mrs. Fisk was saying. "She lived in that little house with all the potted geraniums."

"I don't believe it," Mrs. La Plant said.

"Her house," said Mrs. Fisk, "was always so clean."

"It's right here in the paper," Mrs. Mader said. "Read the paper if you don't believe me."

"How could she do that to her own children?" Mrs. La Plant began to cry. "She must be a *monster.*"

Barbara froze, a sick weight in her stomach. "What are you talking about?"

Everyone looked at her. She saw the corners of their mouths crimping, their faces suddenly aloof. At the counter stood Miss Ellison, Irene's piano teacher, that forty-year-old spinster who had her sights on Mr. H. She seemed to claw at Barbara with her eyes. It was almost as if Miss Ellison could smell the perfume of lovemaking rising from Barbara's skin. The thought made Barbara smile. *He'll never marry you*, she wanted to shout. *Not even if his wife drops dead tomorrow.* Then she heard Mrs. Mader speak in a voice as dry as sawdust.

"Sadie Ostertag took an ax to her children. All four of them. Then she tried to hang herself, but she couldn't finish the job."

Mrs. La Plant wiped her eyes. "Only a monster would raise a hand to hurt her own babies."

"An ax murderess," Mrs. Deal said. "Who'd have thought we'd have our own ax murderess?"

Barbara had seen Sadie Ostertag every Sunday in church. Her thin, silent husband was a railroad mechanic. Sadie had appeared all fluttery in her ruffled dresses, her hair frizzed from the crimping iron. She'd made matching sailor outfits for her children, who had marched behind her into church like ducklings. "Maybe there were things going on that we didn't know about," Barbara said.

Miss Ellison gave her a cold, appraising look. Barbara held her head a little higher. She wasn't tall, but her heels gave her an extra two inches, so she could look down on Miss Ellison.

"She was such a kindhearted girl," old Mrs. Lansky said. "Never talked too loud. Her children were so nice."

"Will they hang her now?" Mrs. Deal asked. "Or put her in the electric chair?"

Everyone was silent. Even Barbara bowed her head until Miss Ellison finally spoke.

"Don't be ridiculous. They send people like that to the asylum." Though she spoke about Sadie Ostertag, her eyes rested on Barbara. Something about the calculated way Miss Ellison pronounced the word *asylum* made Barbara shiver.

At church on Sunday, Barbara sat on the hard oak pew and stared at the empty place where the Ostertag family used to sit. Sadie's sin, of course, was the subject of Father Bughola's homily, but Barbara could hardly concentrate on his words. Instead she scanned the church for Penny. Surely the Maagdenbergh woman would at least be decent enough to drive Penny into town for Sunday Mass, but three Sundays had come and gone with no sign of her daughter. Barbara decided that she would have to beg one of her fellow parishioners to drive her out to the Van den Maagdenbergh farm. The logical person to ask would be Mr. Wysock, who was dozing across the aisle from her. When she glanced at him, his wife, Lucy, stuck out her wattled turkey neck and glared. Barbara looked away. No, she wouldn't ask the Wysocks.

Who else could she ask? No one but the Wysocks lived out the Maagdenbergh woman's way. It was too far for anyone to drive her unless they really wanted to help her. Supposing she walked all those miles, getting herself dirty and disheveled, and arrived at the door looking like some tramp? Supposing Penny didn't want to see her? She would just end up humiliating herself for nothing.

Mrs. Wysock was still staring at her sideways. Barbara tried to sit up straighter. It was hard to breathe, wearing her new black crêpe de Chine dress in this heat. The jet bead choker squeezed her throat. Mrs. Wysock smiled smugly as if she knew Barbara Niebeck's secrets — that under her good clothes, she was nothing. Inside her there was something rotten and wrecked beyond all mending.

When she came home from church the house was empty. Creeping into the parlor, Barbara slipped her fingers into the porcelain vase containing the key that unlocked Mrs. Hamilton's old roll-top writing desk. Keeping the desk locked had been Irene's idea. That girl acted as if her sick mother were a saint and her possessions holy relics. Barbara turned the key in the lock, then pushed up the top. Tucked in the cherrywood pigeonholes were envelopes and writing paper. She found a gold-nib fountain pen and a bottle of rose-scented ink. In her head, she had already composed her letter. *Dear Penny, I'm so sorry. Come home. I miss you. You don't have to live at that woman's house. I want you back. Love, your mother.* But since she wasn't used to writing with a fountain pen, the ink smeared all over the fancy paper. Crumpling up that sheet, she took out a pencil and a fresh leaf. *Deer Penny, I am so sory.* Her letters were awkward, misshapen, like the scribbling of a child. She recalled the grocery lists she used to write. "Your mother's stupid," she had once heard Irene tell her daughter. "She can't even *write*." Penny used to snatch the lists away and write them over again, correcting Barbara's mistakes.

Barbara tore up the letter, hiding the fragments in her apron pocket, and locked the desk. If she sent her daughter a letter, Penny would either just laugh at it or else be ashamed of her. Retreating to the kitchen, Barbara heated up the iron on the stove. She had a whole basket of Mr. H.'s shirts to iron. She pondered the look he had given her when she touched his arm the other day. What lay behind that fleeting glimpse of vulnerability? He's lonesome, she told herself as she sprinkled water on his shirt, then guided the iron over his sleeve. Lonesome, just like she was.

That night Barbara jerked awake and sat up, her chest heaving. There were footsteps coming down the hall, stopping outside her room. She held her breath, staring at the golden ribbon of light under her door. "Barbara?" The voice was barely louder than a whisper. Had she been a deep, peaceful sleeper, she never would have heard it.

She called out, her mouth dry, the darkness rushing past her face in a dizzying blur, and then the door opened. The light from the hallway streamed around his body. He was still dressed, must have just come home from the Fisks' dinner party.

In his stocking feet, he entered the room and knelt beside her bed. With clumsy hands he touched her face, then tugged at her hair. In a second, the sheet was off her and his hands were under her nightgown. This wasn't the way it was supposed to be. In her shock, she forgot she had to push him away, run to the bathroom, and insert her diaphragm. How could such a thing be possible, his seizing her in the dark like some demon lover? I must be good, she thought as the bed began to buckle and creak. Good as some high-class whore. Gave him back his manhood. Wasn't that why he'd been paying her so much? When he finally grunted out her name, he was trembling. His wet face rubbed against hers until she tasted his tears. As he kept kissing her, she could almost taste his grief.

"Shh." Stroking his back, she tried to comfort him, though she scarcely knew where to begin. His sadness was a ghost that stalked him wherever he went. It followed him when he came to her bed. The best solace she could offer was flimsy and over too soon. He hadn't asked for any of this. Before his wife had fallen ill, he had been a faithful husband, hadn't even looked in Barbara's direction. He and Hazel used to go cycling together, used to sing duets while Hazel played the piano. Once Barbara had come up the stairs with a stack of clean folded linens and found them kissing on the landing like two lovesick kids.

He hadn't asked to be locked in this cage of secrets any more than she had. Silently she began to cry with him.

Night after night, he stole into her bed. It became necessary to insert her diaphragm before turning in. He was gone before she awoke, but he always left behind a crisp ten-dollar bill on the dresser. Barbara hid the money under her bed in an old cigar box. As the stack of bills grew thicker, she bound them with rubber bands.

.   .   .

Laurence Hamilton spent most of the day away — at the pop factory, the Rotary Club, rehearsing with the Presbyterian church choir. Barbara passed her solitary hours scrubbing floors, washing windows, doing his laundry. Sometimes the silence was too much. She carried on imaginary conversations with Penny. In her daydreams, she could refashion herself into a storybook mother. She put her arm around her daughter, smoothed back her hair, and announced they were leaving Minerva forever.

While dusting the parlor, Barbara regarded the souvenir plate from Santa Barbara, where the Hamiltons had gone on their honeymoon. She could only laugh at the name, but the scene painted on the plate was so tempting. A city with lovely white bell towers that rose against a backdrop of purple mountains and a deep blue sky. Once she got to California, she would find a job as a waitress or coat-check girl in some respectable establishment where she could meet a man who would woo her by daylight, no more hiding and sneaking around. Turn me into an honest woman, she thought, her mouth twisting into a smirk as she dusted the Hamiltons' wedding portrait. Mrs. H.'s long veil swirled around her bridegroom's feet like a sticky web.

One evening when Mr. H. was at his Rotary Club meeting, Barbara slipped inside Hazel Hamilton's old dressing room, where her clothes still hung from padded hangers, neatly arranged, as though she would return any day. She traced a silk sleeve, drawing a faint film of dust onto her finger. Mr. H. kept all his things in a separate, lesser closet. The only one who went here anymore was Irene. Like the writing desk she kept locked, this was another shrine she kept for her mother. With any luck Irene would grow out of this nonsense soon.

Barbara shook the dust out of a fragile gown of blue voile. Then, hesitating only a moment, she shrugged off her housedress and put it on. How soft the voile was, how gracefully it draped over her shoulders and hips. It was five years out of fashion, but it wouldn't take too much work to redo the dress in the modern style. Positioning herself in front of the dressing room mirror, she hitched the skirt up to her knees. Her hand reached out and fingered the sleeve of a hunter-green traveling suit, which would be perfect for Penny. The color would set off her daughter's hair and eyes, her dark freckles. When she left town, Barbara intended to take a few of these items with her. Hadn't she earned them?

8

CORA'S FARM was so cut off from Minerva, Penny began to think of it as an island. Standing at the mailbox, she looked out over the fields. The wind skimmed the wheat, a tawny ocean stretching to meet a horizon unbroken by silos or rooftops. Last summer she'd read *Robinson Crusoe*. On a remote island, a person could create a whole new world, become someone they could never be if they stayed on the mainland.

An electric current ran up her arm when she opened the mailbox and found the *Chicago Tribune*, which still came, even though Cora talked about canceling her grandfather's subscription. After years of reading only the *Minerva Gazette*, it was exciting to peruse a big-city newspaper. Penny glanced over the headlines: SOUTH SIDE SHOOTOUT KILLS SIX. ROSA PONSELLE TO SING AT CHICAGO OPERA. MAYOR DECLARES MEATPACKER STRIKE ILLEGAL. DR. COUÉ'S AUTOSUGGESTION TAKES NATION BY STORM.

Tucking the *Tribune* under her arm, she reached inside the mailbox to check if there was anything else. Her fingers landed on an envelope of nearly transparent thinness, emblazoned with foreign stamps. It was from a Mr. Jacob Viney of Arles, France. Who on earth was he? Penny studied the blue envelope. Then she remembered — the brother. At Renfew's they had said something about Cora having a brother. And the name Cora had cried out after her daughter's birth: *Jacob, don't let him take the baby away.*

"Sweetie," she whispered when she returned to the shady spot at the edge of the driveway where she had left the baby carriage.

"You got a letter from your uncle." Phoebe slept on, her little fists curled to her chest. Careful not to wake her, Penny placed the newspaper and letter at the foot of the buggy, then started pushing it back down the long driveway. The trees arched above her, throwing lacy shadows across her path.

It was up to Penny to decide what they would have for their midday meal. Cora wasn't picky about food — there just had to be a lot of it. Although Cora had grown lean in the three weeks following her daughter's birth, she ate more than any woman Penny had ever met. After a quick look around the pantry, she decided to make shoestring potatoes and frankfurters, a salad of garden greens, and a dessert of canned peaches and whipped cream. According to the paper, canned food was nutritionally superior and far more hygienic than the vegetables she pulled out of the garden and washed by hand. She moved through the pantry, taking the things off the shelf without glancing at the stockpile of Dr. Nod's Sleeping Powder that Cora had shoved into the far corner, out of harm's way. She had explained to Penny once that her grandfather had suffered terrible insomnia.

Phoebe slept on, giving Penny a chance to spread out the *Tribune* on the counter and read while she peeled potatoes. Perusing the article on autosuggestion, she nearly cut her finger in her enthusiasm. Dr. Emile Coué was a Frenchman touring America to spread the word about his revolutionary new technique. Changing your life, he declared, was a matter of willpower. All a person had to do was sincerely believe the change was taking place. He said his technique tapped into the amazing power of the unconscious mind, a notion Penny had a hard time grasping. When you sleep and have dreams, she thought, maybe that was when the changes happened. Although it sounded like hocus-pocus, Dr. Coué insisted that autosuggestion was pure science, verified by painstaking research. To harness the power of autosuggestion, all you had to do was recite the following sentence twenty times a day: *Day by day, in every way, I am getting better and better.* He recommended taking a length of cord and tying twenty knots in it to keep track of how many times you repeated the sentence. For something scientific, it sounded an awful lot like counting off rosary beads, but she was willing to give it a try. While the potatoes were frying, she cut a length of household string and tied twenty knots. When she ran out to the garden to pull up a head of lettuce, plucking the slugs off the outer leaves, she chanted her new sentence over and over like an incantation. When Phoebe soiled herself, she went on chanting feverishly, mesmerizing the baby as she scraped away the shit and plunged the diaper into the soaking pail. *Day by day. Better and better.*

Phoebe didn't stay mesmerized for long. By the time the food was ready, she was screaming. Sweat dripping from her hair, Cora staggered in the door and washed her hands at the kitchen sink. She had been cutting hay all morning. Taking the baby from Penny's arms, she went upstairs to nurse. It transpired without her saying a word, too immersed in her task to make eye contact with Penny, who hovered over the stove, keeping the food warm until Cora came down to eat.

"Here, let me take her," Penny said when Cora and Phoebe returned. Holding Phoebe, she watched Cora eat with grave concentration, just like any other farmer, too weary to talk. Phoebe fussed in Penny's arms, no doubt wanting her mother to hold her again, so Penny got up and paced the kitchen with her. Ignoring her own hunger, she tried to distract the baby by dangling a ring of keys. "Your mama has to eat," she whispered.

As she watched Cora stuffing a forkful of shoestring potatoes into her mouth, it was impossible to believe she had ever been a society lady or a surgeon's wife. Her legs were splayed without care, as though she had never worn a skirt in all her life. A streak of dirt marked the side of her neck. Penny decided that Cora was living, breathing proof that it was possible for someone to leave her past behind and become wholly different.

"That was good, Penny." Cora spoke only after she had finished her second bowl of peaches and cream. Then she dragged herself up from the chair, went to kiss her daughter before heading toward the door.

"You got a letter today," Penny said before Cora could go. She had nearly forgotten to tell her. "It's over there on the windowsill. Looks like it's from overseas." She didn't say anything about its being from her brother — it would be too much to confess that she had scrutinized the letter so carefully.

When Cora looked at the envelope, something in her face changed. "I'll read it later," she said.

Phoebe was screaming again, her face nearly purple. When Penny picked her up, the baby rooted against her flat and milkless chest, then screwed up her face in rage. Cora had nursed her only an hour ago — how could she be hungry again so soon? Penny reckoned she could bring Phoebe to her mother in the hayfield in less time than it would take to sterilize the bottle and heat up cow's milk, so she took off with the baby in her arms. Phoebe's bawling made Penny's feet fly faster. Skirting the pasture, she reached the field where the cut timothy grass lay flat and glossy on the ground. Halfway down the meadow she spotted Cora working her way across the swath of long waving grass with her grandfather's scythe. In the heat, Cora had taken off her work shirt and wore only an undershirt beneath her overalls. Her bare arms flashed in the sun, her muscles flexing as she swung. She looked strong enough to throw a horse into the air.

When she heard her daughter crying, she threw down the scythe. Wiping her hands on her thighs, she snatched Phoebe from Penny. Before she could unsnap the bib of her overalls, it went dark with gushing milk. Penny could not look away fast enough as Cora freed her pink breast. Penny stumbled off, her face burning when she heard the loud smacking noises Phoebe made while she sucked. Why did the sight of it make the blood rush to her face? What disturbed her most was how the pieces of Cora just didn't fit together. Men's clothing, a man's posture, swinging the heavy scythe, and then the exposed breast. What did it mean if Cora thought she could be a man and a woman at the same time? Who was she trying to fool? She was a woman, and not even Dr. Coué's method could undo that. There was simply no escaping the body that bound her to her daughter and kept unraveling her disguise. Penny knelt down and sifted her hands through the new hay until Cora called her to come and take the baby again.

"Next time you take her out, make sure her skin is covered." Cora had draped her work shirt over Phoebe. "Her head needs to be protected from the sun. There's that little hat I bought her." The front of Cora's overalls was still sodden, but it would dry fast in the heat. The smell of milk mingled with the mown hay. "A baby's skin can burn easily."

Penny nodded as she took Phoebe and watched Cora pick up the scythe and resume her work. She observed how Cora threw her weight behind each swing of the blade, how she stood with her legs apart, bent slightly at the knee. Her work boots were lost under the cut hay as though she had roots sinking into the earth. She looked as if she had sprung up in that field, like the grass she was cutting.

That night at supper, Cora didn't talk much more than she had at lunch. She turned in early, carrying the still unopened foreign envelope to her room. When Penny went upstairs an hour later, she saw a strip of light under Cora's door and imagined her reading her brother's letter. Penny settled in bed with the Chicago newspaper, which Cora never looked at. Turning to the society page, she glanced over the pictures of debutantes and socialites. Once Cora's picture had been here among those beautiful smiling ladies. If she combed through the whole paper and looked hard enough, would she find anything that mentioned Dr. Egan? She didn't even know his first name. No wonder Cora never opened the paper.

Penny longed to ask her all kinds of questions about her girlhood in Chile, about her life in Chicago and Evanston before she had come to Minerva, but Cora never talked about herself. She did not invite questions, didn't invite much in the way of casual conversation. It was beginning to get on Penny's nerves. She remembered the way Cora had fixed her with that stare after Phoebe's birth and asked *Who are you?* Now she wanted to ask Cora the same question. They lived in the same house, but Cora was still a stranger, as much a puzzle as the day Penny had first seen her at Renfew's. The biggest gossips in Minerva didn't really know anything about her — they hadn't even gotten the country of her birth right. They had no clue what she was hiding under her disguise.

But Penny could find out if she tried. It was a sneaky thought, but one that filled her with excitement. It was only a matter of patience and time. Hired girls had a way of uncovering secrets no one else could. Often it didn't involve that much snooping — most people left an amazing number of private things in plain view. Hadn't she read Irene Hamilton's diary twice, learning about her crush on Ned Fisk? She had certainly found out more than she wanted to about Mr. H. and her mother. Now she would unravel Cora.

Sweeping Cora's room the next morning, Penny found no trace of the letter, but there was an old photo album under the bed that hadn't been there the last time she cleaned. The cover was worn brown leather, the surface fingered shiny. Penny knelt on the floor and held it in her lap. Phoebe was sleeping in her basket downstairs, Cora off baling the hay she had cut the day before. For a moment Penny hesitated, but then, before she could stop herself, the album fell open in her lap, revealing a photograph of a child on a pinto pony. A girl with a braid like hers, a flushed and exhilarated face. It looked as though she had just reined in after a wild ride. That girl was Cora, unmistakably. Penny recognized the stubborn chin, the challenge in those eyes. Even as a kid she had worn pants, her legs hugging the shaggy flanks. There was no saddle, just a bridle on the pony. One hand reached out to stroke the pony's neck. Behind her, jagged mountains reared into the sky. Written underneath the photograph in pencil was *My birthday, 1907.*

There was another photograph of the same trousered girl fishing in a stream. Her parents stood on either side of her, everyone laughing at the camera. Her father was a handsome man with a turtleneck sweater and a clean-shaven face. Her mother had a nest of wildly curling hair. Like her husband, she wore dungarees and waders. In a different picture, the mother posed with a rifle. Stretched out at her feet was a dead wildcat. Standing over her trophy, she grinned as any sportsman would. In the next picture, she and her husband held hands. Although the date said 1909, they looked like young newlyweds, not a couple that already had half-grown children. There was a photograph of a boy with large eyes and a full, almost puffy mouth. Half a head taller than Cora, he stood beside her on a front porch under a big sign that read HOSPEDAJE PARAÍSO. *Jacob and I, 1910.* Their Sunday clothes appeared rumpled, as though they had been climbing trees in them. Cora's hair was messy, her face tilted to gaze at him while he stared straight at the camera. Her eyes were filled with the unmasked adoration of a girl who worshiped her big brother. Her face seemed to shine. Here was a shot of the whole family riding on horseback. Jacob looked less comfortable in his saddle than his sister did in hers. Then came pages of photographs with no people in them at all — only valleys, lakes, and steep mountains plunging into the ocean.

After the space of one empty page, Penny found a black-edged card glued into the album. The card was marked with a black cross, and printed beside the cross were two names:

Christopher E. Viney 1870–1911
Theodora Van den Maagdenbergh Viney 1876–1911

Following the gap of another blank page was a picture postcard showing the Chicago skyline and then a series of photographs of Jacob. His sober suits couldn't conceal the fact that he was growing into a striking young man. In each photograph his boyish face grew more angled, firmer. But his eyes remained large in his face and there was something thoughtful about his mouth. He looked sensitive and intelligent, the kind of boy who, despite his quiet nature, had many friends. In one photograph, Cora sat beside her brother on a velvet sofa, her long hair flowing over her pale frock. That photograph made Cora look so vulnerable. Penny turned the page to pictures of Cora dressed in the tiered and gusseted gowns of a debutante.

Finally there was a picture in which she looked like the Cora Penny knew — her chin raised with a touch of bravado. She wore the uniform of a Red Cross nurse. *On my way to France, 1917.* On the opposite page there was a picture of her brother in an officer's uniform. So she had followed her brother to war. There were more pictures of her in uniform, one of them a group portrait with other nurses and doctors. One corner of the photograph — the back row, where the men stood — had been cut away. Something about that missing piece made Penny uneasy. Who would take scissors to a picture like that? There was another picture of Cora and her brother, sitting at an outdoor table with a jug and three glasses. *Mykonos, Greece, 1919.* Again, part of the photograph had been cut away. The next one, dated 1920, showed Cora in a delicate blouse with pearls at her throat. It appeared that someone stood beside her, but the photograph had been cut in half, rendering her companion invisible.

Penny felt a jolt when she figured it out. The missing piece must have been Cora's husband. The next page was blank. When she turned the page again, she came to the ragged edges where all the other pages had been ripped from the album.

The investigation continued, between frying potatoes and mopping the kitchen floor. In the parlor, Penny found a big leather-bound volume called *Patagonia: The Star of the South.* When she paged through it, she saw watercolor illustrations of glaciers and fjords, which, along with the photographs, helped her put together a picture of the landscape in which Cora had been born and raised. In the lull between chores, when Phoebe was asleep, she stole time to read about Patagonia.

The first Spanish explorers, she learned, had named the southernmost point of land Tierra del Fuego, the land of fire, because of the great bonfires the Yahgan Indians built up and down the shoreline, which could be seen from miles away at sea. Despite the cold, wet climate, the Yahgan people wore no clothing. They had their fires to warm them, even in their bark canoes when they paddled the icy waters. The book said that most of the Yahgans were dead now, killed off over the centuries by diseases the white men brought, such as measles and influenza. As Penny boiled diapers in the copper wash kettle on the stove, she thought about those vanished people and their blazing fires.

One afternoon she finished her chores more quickly than expected. Phoebe slept quietly, allowing her to steal out to the orchard to read in the hammock. Only twenty minutes, she told herself, only five pages. But the longer she rocked herself and read, the harder it was to drag herself back to the kitchen. The wind moving through the apple branches swallowed the noise of Cora's approaching footsteps. When Penny heard Cora call her name, she was so startled that she gave a little scream and leapt up from the hammock. The book fell from her hands and landed in the grass. Before Penny could do anything, Cora picked it up and smoothed her hand over the front cover.

"This was my grandfather's. My mother gave it to him." In Cora's tone, Penny understood that this book had been one of her grandfather's most cherished possessions, a memento of both her departed grandfather and her dead mother. Penny began to squirm when she considered that she, the hired girl, had taken it from its place of honor in the parlor without asking permission. Swallowing hard, she braced herself for a good bawling out.

"I'm sorry. The baby was sleeping. I —"

Cora cut her off. "I've noticed you like to read."

Penny closed her eyes and wondered if Cora had also noticed she'd been looking through her photo album.

"You don't have to sneak around behind my back. As long as you don't neglect Phoebe, you can read all you like. Next time," she said, handing the book back to Penny, "bring Phoebe out with you. I think she likes the hammock."

The following day Penny read for a whole hour with Phoebe in the hammock beside her. The baby's soft breath mingled with the wind in the apple trees, the whisper of turning pages, the scratch of her pencil as she jotted down unfamiliar words so that she would remember them. If she couldn't go to high school, then she would learn about things in other ways. Educate herself. In the paper, she had read about the Self-Made Man. *Guanaco*, she wrote. *Refugio, rhea, estancia, archipelago, milodon*. The guanaco, she found out, was a wild antelope, the milodon a giant ground sloth that had died out long ago. She was so entranced, she nearly forgot it was Cora she was supposed to be investigating. Once she started, she couldn't stop reading on and on about the Patagonian wilderness until those strange creatures became as real to her as the cow in her pasture and the geese on the lawn. When she had finished the chapter, she reached up and grasped one of the low-hanging green apples and tried to gauge the size it would ripen into come September. A fat red apple, too plump and ripe to fit in her hand.

The first time Cora offered to drive her into town on Sunday, so that she could visit her mother and go to church, Penny begged off by saying she wasn't feeling well. It was a sweltering, humid day, and she did have a stomachache. Her alibi appeared to give Cora no cause for doubt. But when the next Sunday morning came and Penny again turned down the offer to take her into town, Cora wouldn't let it rest. "Your mother hasn't seen or heard from you in three weeks. I thought you said before that she wanted you to come home."

They sat at the kitchen table and ate their breakfast. Avoiding Cora's eyes, Penny gulped her coffee, swallowed wrong, and choked, spewing over her plate of fried eggs and bacon. When she tried to breathe, she could only gasp.

"Put your head down and breathe through your nose," Cora told her.

Her eyes watering, Penny obeyed, breathing with her head in her lap until the choking subsided. Cora brought a napkin and a glass of water.

"Your poor mother's probably wondering why she hasn't heard from you in so long," she said as Penny wiped her face.

To put an end to the questions, Penny got up from the table and scraped her ruined breakfast into the slop pail. She silently recited her list of new vocabulary. *Puma, cormorant, rookery.* Meanwhile Phoebe started to fuss. Cora scooped her out of her basket and started talking sweet to her. Penny was about to steal off with the slop pail to feed the geese when Cora called out to her.

"Do you like to swim?"

When their eyes met, Penny had to struggle not to start crying. It was plain that Cora understood that something had gone wrong between her and her mother. And that Cora wanted to make her happy. That she wanted her life to be more than washing diapers, cooking, and cleaning.

"Pack some sandwiches, and bring your swimming suit and a towel. Bring a book, too. I'll drive you to Lake Griffin."

Everyone went to Lind Lake on the outskirts of Minerva. On hot Sundays, the beach was carpeted with children flinging sand into each other's eyes and parents yelling at them. Well-to-do families like the Hamiltons owned cabins on the more remote stretches of Lind Lake, but Lake Griffin was something else altogether, tucked away in a state park.

On the eight-mile drive out there, Penny held Phoebe in her lap and teased her hands with the end of her long braid. The baby gazed up at her, her eyes focusing for the first time, locking into Penny's with such an intensity that she felt her middle go soft. When Cora noticed the look that was passing between them, she pulled over to the side of the road and laughed. "Watch out, or she'll think that you're her mother." She sounded jealous.

Penny gently traced the baby's forehead and the tip of her nose. Which one of them *did* Phoebe think of as her mama, she wondered. Even though Cora nursed her, Penny spent the most time with her. Cora started driving again, her rough hands on the wheel, her eyes fixed on the road.

"I've never been to Lake Griffin before," Penny told her. "I heard there's a forest in that park. They must have planted a lot of trees."

"The trees were always there. Didn't you know this part of the state used to be covered in woodland?"

Penny shook her head. "No, you're wrong. This land was prairie. Everybody knows that."

"I'm sure that's what most people believe," Cora said, "but it's not true. Once there was a forest that stretched all the way up to Saint Cloud. It was called the Big Woods. Full of deciduous trees." She paused, guiding the pickup over a rut. "Oak, maple, elm. They grew to be over a hundred feet tall."

Penny still didn't believe her. "Then what happened to them?"

"The settlers came and chopped them down to clear the land for their fields. They could have farmed on the real prairie and saved themselves the trouble, but most of them came from countries in Europe that were covered in forest. When they saw the prairie, they didn't believe it could be fertile."

Penny held on to Phoebe, cradling her head as they drove over another bump.

"So they settled in the Big Woods and made most of the old trees disappear. They were farmers, not lumbermen. They didn't even use most of the wood. My grandfather came over as a very young man. He used to own all this land we're driving over now. Lake Griffin was on his property. He decided he'd keep his own little piece of the woods. Sometimes he went there just to walk and think. Later he sold the lake to the state. I'm the only one besides the ranger who has the key to the entrance on this end."

When they came to the gate, Cora climbed out and unlocked it. Then she drove through, parked, and locked the gate again. "You go on ahead," she said. "I'll catch up with you later. Just keep following the path. In about half a mile you'll come to the lake."

The trees were as tall as Cora had said they would be. Walking beneath them, Penny felt tiny, as though she could melt into the green like a deer and never be seen again. The path was a narrow ribbon through the underbrush. Penny picked her way carefully around the clumps of poison ivy. A blue jay fluttered overhead, the sun lighting its bright wings. She wondered if this was how Cora had grown up, walking through the wilderness with her parents.

As she drew closer to the lake, the trees dwindled to scattered birches and willows. The path led to an old wooden dock that jutted through the cattails and over the reeds. She spotted a heron, then a leaping bullfrog. Walking to the end of the dock, she came to the open water. There was no beach here, no chance of wading or testing the water. She would have to dive right in.

The midday sun reflecting off the lake nearly blinded her. A blazing sapphire, she thought. That phrase sounded as if it had come from one of Cora's books. About two hundred feet from where she stood, a small wooded island rose from the water. Hesitating only a moment, she tugged the hand-me-down dress over her head and threw it on the dock. Underneath she was wearing Irene's hideous castoff swimsuit with the faded stripes and the ridiculous bloomers. But even that ugly swimsuit wasn't going to spoil this. With a wild yelp she launched herself into the water. Her body hit the lake with a hard splash before she broke into a crawl, kicking up waterweed.

When she was eight years old, Mrs. Hamilton had taught her to swim, taking her to Lind Lake with her own daughters. From Mrs. H. she had learned the crawl, the butterfly, the breaststroke. Irene had been so jealous that Penny was the better swimmer.

A fish brushed her ankle. Rolling over on her back, she kicked up a cascade that showered down on her belly and chest. For a while, she floated and stared at the cloudless sky until the sun hurt her eyes. Flopping over on her belly again, she swam at a brisk clip, her arms and legs slicing the cloudy brown water, which smelled faintly of fish. She pushed herself farther and farther from the shore until the lake bottom dropped away and the water turned cold and clear. She swam until she reached the island and pulled herself up on a flat granite boulder, where she lay in the sun and caught her breath until the mosquitoes drove her back into the water. *My island*, she thought as she headed back.

There was a stretch of shoreline with big smooth boulders where she saw Cora waving to her. "Well, look at you," she said when Penny hauled her dripping body out of the water. "You're a real selkie."

Penny felt her cheeks grow hot, aware of how dumb she must look in Irene's old swimsuit. Cora busied herself with the picnic hamper. "Here, have a sandwich."

After wrapping herself in a towel, Penny sat down and ate. Cora rolled up her overall legs and waded into the shallows with Phoebe, gently dipping her feet in the lake until the baby shrieked in delight. "They say babies are born knowing how to swim," Cora said. Then she lifted Phoebe in the air above her head. "Now you're flying, aren't you? My flying baby." Penny watched how Phoebe arched in the air, held carefully aloft in her mother's hands. Cora turned to her again, her face flushed, the happiest Penny had ever seen her.

"What's a selkie?" Penny asked.

"A kind of water witch. A seal woman, really."

Penny thought of the barking circus seals she had seen in the movies.

"She can take the form of a seal in the water and a woman on land. A shape-shifter."

Penny looked at the dark mark the water left on Cora's rolled-up overalls. She could tell Cora was aching for a real swim.

"I'll watch Phoebe if you want to go for a dip."

Cora shook her head. "I don't have a swimming suit."

"It's all right," Penny heard herself say. "Go on and swim. I won't look." She held out her hands to take the baby, then turned her back on the lake and stared into the shifting green forest. She heard a splash, then the sound of Cora swimming steadily away from the shore. It was probably her first swim since she'd come to live on the farm the previous November. By the time it got warm enough to swim, she would have been too pregnant. And maybe afraid to come here alone. In the grass beside the picnic hamper, Penny picked out the long slender shape of Cora's Winchester rifle. When the noise of splashing grew faint, she turned to the lake again. Cora was a long way out. All Penny could see of her was her dark head bobbing, her arms and legs cresting. Her men's clothes lay on the shore like shed skin.

Shape-shifter. Selkie. She would add those words to her list.

The morning Penny turned the pages of the calendar from July to August, she realized she had been living at Cora's for an entire month. Except for Dr. Lovell and the ice deliveryman, no one from Minerva had seen her in all that time. It was as if she had disappeared, hopped a freight train to British Columbia.

Sometimes when she watched Cora and Phoebe together, she couldn't avoid thinking of her mother. There were moments when she wondered if she hadn't been too harsh. Surely after a month's absence her mother would have calmed down, have a new respect for her. One Sunday, instead of going out to Lake Griffin, she would ask Cora to take her into town so she could see her mother again. But the memory of the slap kept intruding on this fantasy, along with the recollections of that stinking lily-of-the-valley toilet water. Besides, she argued to herself, her mother had sent no word to her in all this time, either. *It takes two.* Maybe her mother didn't want to see her. Her greatest fear was that her mother would tear her down to size, make Cora out to be someone pathetic. And her mother would turn her reading, her vocabulary lists, her Sunday swims into a joke. She would keep cutting her down until she was nothing but a burden again, the unwanted bastard she had fished out of the rain barrel.

When she finally did go into town again after her weeks of seclusion, Minerva seemed like an alien place. She stared out the dusty pickup's window at the clapboard houses and the stone angel in front of the funeral parlor as if seeing these things for the first time.

"I've got some business at the bank," Cora told her. "Could

you get the groceries?" They were parked in front of Renfew's. "Here's the shopping list and here's some money." She handed Penny a five-dollar bill. "I'll pick you up in front of the store in an hour."

When Cora drove away to the bank, Penny settled Phoebe's weight in her arms and mounted the creaking wooden steps of Renfew's porch. The instant she stepped inside, everyone looked up. She glanced around at their unbelieving faces: Mr. Renfew, Mrs. Deal, Mrs. La Plant, and some man she didn't recognize.

What was the matter with these people, she wondered. She didn't look any different from before. She was still Penny Niebeck, wearing one of Irene's castoff dresses, her long braid hanging down her back. Except now she was the Maagdenbergh woman's hired girl, holding Cora's baby as proudly as any aunt would. As she approached the counter, it struck her that she had a different way of walking. Maybe it was only the baby's weight in her arms, but her feet seemed to touch the ground more resolutely than they ever had.

"Penny," Mr. Renfew said, his face turning pink. He had acted awkwardly enough around Cora, but she was an outsider. City people were expected to be a little odd. He didn't seem to understand why a local girl like her could suddenly do something so unexpected and turn herself into a stranger. "I hear you're living out there at the Maagdenbergh farm. Is that, um, permanent?"

She laughed. "I guess."

"How *are* you?" he asked, searching her face. Was he trying to see if living with Cora had left some mark on her?

"I'm just fine." Penny held up the baby so he could get a good look at her. She was turning into a pretty thing with her big eyes and tufts of strawberry-blond hair. "Her name's Phoebe."

Mr. Renfew's face eased into a smile. Penny smiled, too. Then she freed her hand to fish Cora's shopping list out of her pocket and give it to him. As Mr. Renfew turned to take the items down from the shelves, she felt an uncomfortable prickle. Slowly she turned around. Mrs. Deal and Mrs. La Plant smiled self-consciously before dropping their gaze back into their glasses of pop. But the strange man in the back of the store kept staring at her and the baby. He was about forty, she guessed, with a swank haircut and a white seersucker suit. His face was deeply tanned, but she guessed it hadn't come from farm work. His blue eyes seemed to leap right out of his face. She twitched uncomfortably. Why was he looking at her like that? She felt herself go red and wondered if he could see right through the thin fabric of her dress.

"There you go, Penny." Mr. Renfew packed the groceries into an apple crate. "Is she parked outside? Do you want me to carry it to the pickup?"

"She's coming to meet me around eleven. Could you hold on to the groceries until then?" She was about to ask him who that man was when Phoebe started to fret.

"How's everything on the farm?" Mr. Renfew pitched his voice above the baby's squalling.

"Fine." She jostled Phoebe in her arms.

"Let me hold her a second." Mrs. La Plant appeared at her elbow and took Phoebe from Penny's arms before she could stop her. "I know all about lil' babies," she crooned. Although she had been married for six years, Mrs. La Plant didn't have any children of her own.

"How on earth is she going to manage the wheat harvest?" Mr. Renfew asked.

Penny looked helplessly at Mrs. La Plant, who was jiggling the baby and singing "Ain't We Got Fun."

"Penny?" Mr. Renfew's voice drew her back to the question she hadn't answered. Mrs. Deal leaned forward on her stool. The man in the white suit stood poised beside a pyramid of Washington State apples, one shiny fruit balanced on his palm. Penny knew that whatever she said would be all over town before she and Cora sat down to supper that night.

Harvest was the time of year when no farmer could afford to stand alone. No matter how much you might dislike your neighbors, you wouldn't survive without them. How could Cora expect to get her threshing done without people pitching in?

"We're getting help," Penny said.

"That same bunch of Mexicans her grandfather had over?" Mr. Renfew asked.

She shrugged. Cora hadn't really discussed it with her.

"Listen, Penny." Mr. Renfew lowered his voice. "There's been trouble going around."

"Trouble?" She shook her head.

He sighed. "Gang of roughnecks set fire to the Pearsons' barn. They only just managed to get the fire truck out in time."

"Was it the Nelson gang?" Penny thought of the story of how Cora had shot through the Nelsons' windshield.

"The police couldn't say for sure. The Nelson brothers came up with an alibi. Nowadays any bunch of hooligans who get their hands on an automobile can ride around and make trouble." He lowered his eyes and cleared his throat. "There was a second incident. With the Stadler girl. Lived alone on the farm with her old dad. Whoever it was went by their place and messed her up pretty bad."

Penny winced. Why was he telling her this? She turned to look at Mrs. La Plant, who was still bouncing Phoebe up and down.

"Penny, if you were my daughter," Mr. Renfew said, "I wouldn't want you living out on that farm. It was good of you to help her, but it would be a lot safer if you came back and lived with your mother again."

Mrs. La Plant was heading toward the strange man, who now ignored Penny and directed his attention to the baby. A rising sense of panic blotted out everything Mr. Renfew was telling her. Dashing over, she snatched Phoebe back.

"I better take her outside."

"Why, I never!" Mrs. La Plant sputtered. "Look what you've done! She's really crying now. Let me take her again. I know all about babies . . ."

"I'll be back for the groceries at eleven!" Penny yelled over her shoulder as she ran out the door with the screaming baby.

How could she have let Mrs. La Plant — or anyone — take the baby away from her like that? And who was that man? She kept looking back, but there were just the Minervans she had known for as long as she could remember. It was hard to ignore their staring faces. Even the old Norwegians in front of the feed store could not take their eyes off her. She held her head high, trying to copy Cora's proud indifference. At least now she was somebody. They couldn't ignore her anymore.

The rhythm of her moving body eased Phoebe off to sleep. The baby's mouth went slack, and a puddle of drool blossomed on the front of Penny's dress. Turning on Maple Street, she found herself retracing her old way home from the store. Wouldn't her mother be surprised to see her? She would melt when she saw how adorable Phoebe was. Suddenly it seemed so simple and clear. Why hold a grudge forever? All she had to do was say hello. She didn't even have to step inside the Hamiltons' house.

She walked slowly, but steadily, by way of Minerva High School. The red brick school with its new gymnasium was the town's pride, but she gazed instead at the statue of the goddess Minerva on the school lawn. She would never tell anyone how much she loved that pink-veined marble goddess with her helmet, spear, and olive bough cradled beneath her breast. The figure was sweet-faced and pretty, a girl her age with rivulets of hair cascading down her slender back. Balancing Phoebe's weight, she freed one hand to trace the letters of the word WISDOM engraved on the marble tablet at the goddess's sandaled feet. The statue was so delicately chiseled, she could run her fingertip over the edge of each marble toenail. After giving the smooth marble one last stroke, she continued on her way.

Her heart rattled in her chest as she walked down Elm Street. She wasn't a child anymore; she lived at Cora's, earned her own keep. Her mother would have to respect her now. Maybe they could be friends. Yes, they could be friends. If only she didn't think too much about what her mother was doing with Mr. H.

She nearly stumbled on the uneven sidewalk when she saw him on his English bicycle, his face all flushed. Home from the pop factory in the middle of the day. Well, she knew exactly what he had just been up to. As he cycled along, his trouser legs were rolled up, revealing the red and green argyle socks his wife had knit and that her mother kept darning for him. When his eyes met hers, Penny gave him such a look that his face went purple. He swerved, nearly hitting a lamppost. Penny felt her face turn stony. I'm a witch, she exulted. A witch who had the power to make him fall off his bicycle and bleed. She glared at his back as he pedaled away. Then she let out a long breath and retraced her steps to Renfew's. She could have visited her mother. There was still time to have a quick chat before going to meet Cora. She could have at least knocked and said something through the screen door. But she didn't. Not after seeing him.

9

Barbara niebeck stirred the simmering pot in which a chicken carcass bobbed and slowly disintegrated. It was late afternoon. Mr. H. was home from work early, pacing the kitchen floor in a way that set her nerves on edge.

"This morning I saw your daughter," he said.

It took her a few seconds to digest those words. She held the wooden spoon aloft. Droplets of chicken broth dripped down the handle, glazing her rough red fingers.

"She was coming down Elm Street," he began, his voice shaky. "With that woman's baby. She . . . she looked at me," he said, giving Barbara an agonized stare before turning abruptly away. "She knows everything."

You idiot, Barbara thought. Of course she knows. "Afraid she'll talk?" she asked him tartly. "Well, she won't. That wouldn't be like her."

His anxious pacing made her want to fly at him with the wooden spoon. But she forced herself to remain rigid and cool. She made herself imagine a snow-covered field. In the steamy kitchen, she invoked the dry chill of deep winter. She clung to that notion of cold reserve while he studied the calendar on the wall. She saw his finger rise to trace the date of August 27, circled in red ink, when his daughters were due back from camp — only three weeks away. When he faced her again, she read in his eyes what was coming. He had his daughters to think of, their reputation. His daughters' return from summer camp would signal the end of their affair if not her outright dismissal. He would probably give her an envelope of money and send her on her way.

"You shouldn't have left the factory so early," she said frostily. "Someone might notice you're not keeping regular hours."

"Barbara, don't be like that."

"What way do you want me to be?" She stirred her broth, then tossed in a pinch of salt. The essence of that dead bird filled the kitchen. Curls of steam fanned upward, dampening her face and darkening her cheeks.

Standing only inches away from her, he was poised to speak, his mouth curving into an O. Then he must have thought better of it. Whatever he had intended to say, he kept to himself. Barbara closed her eyes as he walked noiselessly out the door. His voice echoed inside her. *I saw your daughter. She knows everything.*

Left alone in the kitchen beside that simmering carcass, she shuddered as sobs ripped through her. So Penny had been in town. Mr. H. had seen her, but she hadn't. Her daughter was avoiding her. She had discarded her as thoroughly as Mr. H. soon would. Each time Barbara went to the grocery store, Mr. Renfew asked her how Penny was doing. And each time she invented some pleasant-sounding lie to tell. "Oh, I had a long chat with her the other Sunday. She's awfully devoted to that baby. I guess it's good practice for when she has one of her own."

Once Penny had been small enough to swing in her arms. When she was little, Penny used to light up like a Christmas tree when Barbara finished her shift at the Commercial Hotel and went to get her from old Mrs. Novak at the end of the day. Once she had thought that child loved her more than anyone else ever could. She remembered when four-year-old Penny solemnly informed the other hotel maids that her mama was the prettiest lady in the world. Now twenty-one miles away from her, Penny was a boat drifting farther and farther downstream. One day she would slip away completely. As Barbara wept over the pot of chicken broth, the knowledge of her daughter's desertion hit her like a brutal blow. She had lost her. Penny would not be coming back.

10

PENNY WAS IRONING in the sweltering kitchen when she heard the automobile. Looking out the screen door, she watched a battered Model T come to a stop in a blaze of dust. Something clutched her throat. The Nelson gang drove around in a Model T. She remembered Mr. Renfew's warning about how they had roughed up the Stadler girl. *Rough up, mess up* — all the words that people used because they couldn't say the real word. A sense of helpless fury settled on her as her eyes moved toward Phoebe in her basket. She was about to scream for Cora when she saw the men spill out of the car. There were seven of them, dark and foreign-looking. She noticed the luggage strapped to their car roof.

Cora stepped into view, approached them with confident strides, and held out her hand for the men to shake. They fell into a half-circle as Cora spoke to them, pointing to the shed where her grandfather's old thresher was housed. She swept her hand toward the fields. The men nodded.

Penny let out a long breath. She had panicked for nothing. Those were the Mexicans, come to help with the harvest. She had to stop spooking herself over every piece of gossip she heard, otherwise she'd shriek and faint the next time the ice deliveryman knocked on the door. After setting the iron back on the stove, she took Phoebe from her basket and stepped out on the porch. Cora waved, gesturing her to come and join them.

She and the men were speaking in a flood of incomprehensible words. It took Penny a moment to figure out it must be Spanish, the language of Cora's childhood. Cora's face was flushed and animated. "Penny, I'd like you to meet the Ramirez brothers. This is Antonio." Cora took the baby so Penny could shake his hand.

"Pleased to meet you, miss." He spoke with a heavy accent. He was the oldest of the brothers, she guessed around thirty. He flashed her a smile before turning his attention back to Cora, who introduced her to the others. The youngest was a solemn, smooth-faced boy called Javier. Penny decided he couldn't be much older than she was.

Cora explained that the Ramirez brothers had been coming to her grandfather's farm for the past five years. "I told them about Grandfather passing away," she whispered.

Nothing in the men's faces betrayed any alarm at Cora's appearance. Perhaps in deference to her recent loss, they seemed to regard it as understandable that she had to wear men's clothes and do men's work in order to provide for herself and her daughter. Cora held up Phoebe so everyone could get a good look at her.

"Bonita," Antonio murmured, gently touching the baby's cheek. Penny threw a bewildered look at Cora, wondering how she could let a strange man touch her daughter, but Cora just smiled at him. She hadn't cut her hair since Phoebe's birth. Now it was growing out, softening the contours of her face. The change had come too gradually for Penny to notice until that moment when she saw Cora and Antonio looking at each other.

Antonio and his brothers slept in the hayloft in the clean bedding Penny dug out of the linen chest. Everyone ate together, packed around the kitchen table. Penny had never worked so hard, feeding nine people at every meal. The first night she used every burner on the stove, cooking up fried chicken, mashed potatoes, string beans, and dumplings. Flies buzzed around her in the ninety-degree heat until she tacked up more flypaper.

The following morning she cooked a breakfast of pancakes, bacon, eggs, and hash browns. She had hardly finished washing the dishes when she had to start preparing lunch. It took three loaves of bread to make the sandwiches. She baked four dozen cookies and made two canisters of lemonade, then loaded everything in a wheelbarrow and delivered it to the field.

In preparation for supper, she took the hatchet from the woodshed and marched to the chicken coop. She grabbed a fat capon by his feet, severed his head in one clean stroke. Then she brought down a second one. She didn't flinch or feel particularly sorry to see them dash around headless, leaving behind a bright trail of blood. Taking them by the feet, she dunked them into a bucket of scalding water to help loosen the feathers. Plucking the birds was tedious but routine. Gutting them was the foul part.

"Oh, *ish*," she muttered, slicing into the birds' bellies. She worked quickly, using a sharp knife. The blood sprayed her apron. Then she held her breath and reached inside the warm cavity to yank out the intestines. She had been doing this since she was twelve. The Hamiltons used to keep chickens in their back yard. Her mother had laughed at how squeamish she was in the beginning. "If you like to eat them, you shouldn't be so prissy."

After cutting the disemboweled birds into pieces, she washed them with soap and warm water, another trick she had learned from her mother. You had to think of all the dirt and droppings at the bottom of the chicken coop. When Penny served freshly butchered meat, she made sure it was clean.

While the capons roasted in the oven, she went into the woodlot to pick raspberries for the pies she planned to serve after supper. She dragged Phoebe along, mosquito netting draped over the top of the baby carriage. The mosquitoes bit Penny instead — the blood on her apron seemed to draw them. Slapping her arms and legs, she tried to fill the berry pail in a hurry.

A movement in the bushes caught her eye. As the mosquitoes whined around her, she stood absolutely still. There it was again — a rustling in the underbrush. Someone or something was backing clumsily away.

"Who is it?" she called out. "Who's there?"

Only silence welled up, along with the sense of staring eyes concealed behind the tangle of leaves. The inside of her mouth turned sour with fear. Dropping the berry pail, she grabbed the baby carriage and bolted for the house. Only when she reached the back yard did she stop and look back at the woodlot. Shaking all over, she breathed hard, but the trees were as placid as ever. She heard a redwing blackbird, then a mourning dove.

Wiping her sweaty hands on her apron, she decided it had probably just been a raccoon. Or one of Antonio's brothers answering the call of nature in the bushes, something she'd been doing herself that day. The single bathroom in the house and the outhouse in the yard were not enough for nine people. Yet as she trudged back into the woodlot to retrieve her abandoned berry pail, she couldn't escape the notion of hidden eyes watching her. She thought about the stranger in the white suit at Renfew's, the way he had gawked at her and Phoebe. But what would a well-dressed man like that be doing in their woodlot? The thought was so foolish, she had to laugh at herself.

The rest of the afternoon she spent in the kitchen, rolling out pie dough, peeling carrots and potatoes. She made a pot of gravy and a pot of string beans with pearl onions; shucked and boiled corn; made a salad with wilted lettuce and fresh mint leaves. Every farm wife prided herself on her harvest spread, and if any woman dared to present anything less than a feast, people would grumble behind her back, call her a stingy shrew. The farmer got all the glory; the farmer's wife got all the work. If the harvest went well, even the people who didn't like Cora would nod to her in approval when she brought in her wheat to be weighed and sold at the grain elevator. Everyone would say she had proved herself, even if she was a bit strange.

Penny doubted that anyone would ever mention this meal she was cooking. The moment it was finished, her work would be devoured and forgotten. That's the way it was with women's work. It kept getting undone — the clean dishes dirtied, the laundered diapers soiled. No glory in it at all. No wonder Cora had chosen the role of the man. Penny imagined cutting off her braid, putting on a pair of overalls, and never having to cook another harvest dinner.

In the heat of the kitchen, she raced the clock, hoping to have everything ready by the time the men returned from the field. Banished to Cora's bedroom, Phoebe howled and whined. Penny gritted her teeth and went on working.

While Penny dished out the supper, Cora laughed and spoke with the men in rapid Spanish that seemed to transform her tired face. Even in her grandfather's overalls and work shirt, she did not look like a man but a woman, a vivacious woman whose laughter made the teacups tremble on their hooks. Penny didn't know what Cora had told the men about her circumstances or Phoebe's father, but she read in the men's eyes that they did not see Cora as an outcast or a madwoman. Everyone fussed over Phoebe, passing her from lap to lap. If the baby cried, the brothers crooned and sang. Especially Antonio seemed to worship her. *Bonita, bonita.*

Once or twice, Cora glanced in Penny's direction and translated something one of the brothers said. "Pablo loves your chicken." But for the most part, Penny felt as though she wasn't there. She was invisible, the silent faceless hired girl who had cooked this meal and would stay up late washing dishes.

After the meal was finished and the men stumbled off to the barn to sleep, Cora told her they had clothes that needed washing. "Would you mind doing their laundry tomorrow?"

Her head bent over the sink, Penny nodded, stifling an irritated sigh.

"They'll thank you for that," Cora said. "Living on the road, it's hard to get their clothes decently washed." She helped with the dishes until Phoebe began to cry a few minutes later. "Oh, she's hungry again," she murmured, disappearing upstairs. Penny finished the dishes alone.

The next morning, to the accompaniment of Phoebe's wails, Penny washed seven pairs of overalls, stiff with dirt; seven shirts, pungent with sweat; seven pairs of socks and underwear that had been through more than she cared to think about. As the geese paraded across the lawn, she hung up the sopping clothes to dry. Her back and shoulders ached and her fingers were raw. For supper she would have to butcher another two capons. But the geese seemed confident in their knowledge that they were too big and intimidating for her to take on. With their glittering black eyes, they seemed to be sizing her up.

Phoebe was asleep upstairs when Penny heard the knock. The screen door framed the slim form of a young man she had never seen before. He looked about nineteen and had light brown hair and tawny eyes that locked into hers when she opened the door.

"Hello, miss. Name's Gilbert. Come to see if you need any help getting the harvest in. I saw the smoke from the thresher when I was coming up the road." The sweat that glistened on his cheeks told her that he had walked from town.

"I'm the hired girl," she told him. "You need to talk to the woman who owns the farm. She's already got seven men helping her." It seemed an awful pity that he had come all this way for nothing.

"What's your name, miss?" His eyes on her face made her want to run to the mirror and comb her hair.

"Penny," she flustered. "Penny Niebeck."

"Penny, my family used to have a farm over by Mankato, but you know how hard it's been. Lost my big brother in the war. My old man died of the Spanish flu. With him gone, we couldn't make our payments to the bank, so we lost our land. I'll be real plain with you, miss. I just want to earn a dollar or two to send home to my mother." He ran a hand through his hair and smiled at her sheepishly. "Your boss must have some kind of work for me to do."

The smell of roasting capon filled the hot kitchen. For a moment she was dizzy. She read the hunger on his face. If his eyes, darting past her into the house, seemed a little too inquisitive, she told herself it was simply his predicament. "Stay for supper." She led him in, pulled out a kitchen chair, poured him a glass of cold lemonade. "When my boss comes in for supper, you can talk to her yourself."

"So what's it like working here?" he asked between swallows of lemonade.

"Not too bad." Reluctantly she turned back to the sink and the colander full of potatoes she had to peel. "But cooking for the harvest hands is sure a lot of work."

"And now there's one more mouth to feed. Here, let me help you." He got up from his chair and took a potato from the colander.

"There's only one potato peeler," she said.

"Then I can peel potatoes while you do something else. Want to see something?" He took the peeler from her hand and moved the blade over the skin in one deft movement, producing an unbroken spiral of potato peel.

She looked at him in amazement. "I could never do that."

He dangled the piece from his fingers. "Didn't girls used to use potato peels for fortunetelling?"

"Fortunetelling?" She laughed in disbelief.

"They threw the peel back over their left shoulder. When it landed on the floor, it spelled out the first letter of the name of the boy they'd marry."

"You're pulling my leg." It was impossible not to return his smile.

"Ancient secret of the Gypsies. Go on, Penny. Give it a try." He handed her the peel.

"Here goes!" She tossed it, not backward over her shoulder but neatly into the slop pail.

"Aw, Penny, why did you do that?"

"I'm not in any hurry to get married." She went over to the pile of string beans she had to clean.

"So you're independent. A modern gal, eh?"

She smiled to herself as she snapped off the ends of the beans. "I'm not going to be a hired girl forever. One day I'm going to school to be a nurse." In her excitement, she snapped a bean in half. She realized she had just made a confession both to herself and to a stranger. The ambition, planted over two months ago by Dr. Lovell, unfolded and fell like a flower into her out-stretched palm.

"A nurse," he said. "You'll go live in a city."

"That's right. One day I'll go to Chicago. What about you?"

"Oh, I don't want to talk about myself." He cocked his head. "So how old are you, Penny? You look kind of young to be cooking the harvest dinner."

She tried not to act offended. "Fifteen."

"You must be going to high school in the fall then. Does your boss drive you into town?"

"I don't go to high school."

"Don't go to school!" He nearly sang those words. "Well, how are you going to be a nurse if you don't even go to high school?"

Penny snapped the beans briskly. "I'll go a little later. When the baby's older." That was the danger of speaking dreams aloud. People could just tear them down.

"Baby?" Now she had his full attention. "What baby?"

Penny looked at him for a moment, then burst out laughing when she realized the assumption he must have made. "My *boss's* baby."

"Your boss has a baby? So you take care of a baby on top of all your other work. Well, that's a heap of responsibility."

She smiled shyly at him. His honey-colored eyes seemed to bathe her in light. With his sleeves rolled up, she could see the muscles of his arms moving as he peeled the potatoes. When he caught her staring, he grinned.

"You're awfully pretty to be stuck out here on this farm. You like your boss? Is she nice to you?"

"She's all right."

"Does she pay well?"

Penny nodded.

"Well, I should hope so." He stepped a little closer. "This place is so far away from anywhere. Do you ever get to have any fun? Go to the picture show? You like going to the pictures?" His eyes moved over her face.

"I love Houdini." She blushed a little when she said the word *love*. "If I was a man, I'd want to be like him."

Gilbert laughed. "Oh, go on! You don't want to be a man. You said you wanted to be a nurse."

Before Penny could answer, the screen door opened and closed.

"Who is this?" Cora demanded, looking from Gilbert to Penny. "Who is he and what's he doing in the house?"

"Name's Gilbert, ma'am. Come to see if you need any help with the harvest." He didn't seem nearly as startled by the sight of Cora in her grimy overalls as Penny had suspected he might.

"Penny, where's the baby?" She spoke sharply. "Upstairs?"

Penny nodded.

Cora pressed her mouth into a hard line. "Come with me."

Penny threw a helpless look back at Gilbert before following Cora to her bedroom, where Phoebe lay asleep in her basket.

"Her nap's not over yet," Penny whispered, but Cora picked up the baby and started pacing the room with her. Woken too early, Phoebe began to cry. The bedroom curtains were drawn against the heat. In the corner, an electric fan whirled, stirring Cora's hair. Even in the dim room, Penny could see the strain in her face as she rocked her daughter and kissed the top of her head.

"Don't *ever* do that again." Cora spoke with a vehemence that made Penny tremble. "Don't ever let a stranger in the house without telling me first. Promise me."

Penny's throat was so dry and tight it was hard to speak. "His family lost their farm. He just wants to work to send a dollar home to his mother."

"Penny —"

"You don't know what it's like." This time she spoke defiantly.

Cora let out a breath. "I don't know what *what's* like?"

"To have nothing." Penny couldn't look at her. "Some people have nothing."

Phoebe stopped crying and fell back to sleep in her mother's arms. The fan lifted the curtains, making them stir and flutter like angel's wings. Apart from the grind of the fan, it was absolutely quiet.

"Penny, you have to promise me." There was something in Cora's face she had never seen before. A glimmer of fear that made her blink.

"I promise," she said. And that look vanished.

Cora stepped forward and handed her the baby. "You hold her. I'll go down and talk to that fellow."

Though she remained in the bedroom, Penny could hear their voices clearly. Had Gilbert also been able to hear Cora and her talking about him? She listened to Cora softening as Gilbert told the story of his family losing their farm. If it weren't for her grandfather's ten thousand dollars in the bank, Cora also stood to lose her land if grain prices continued to fall. "I suppose we could always use an extra set of hands," she said at last. "But I can't keep you on after the harvest is finished."

At supper Gilbert sat beside Penny, while Cora took her place at the far end of the table. She and the Mexicans chattered in their rapid-fire Spanish.

"You know what they're saying?" Gilbert asked.

Penny shook her head. "It's all gibberish to me."

"Sure must be funny," he said. "Listen to them laugh." Cora was too caught up in her conversation to notice the way he stared at her. "She seems awfully friendly with those fellows, don't she?"

He turned to Penny again. Sitting up a little straighter in her chair, she smiled and was about to ask him how he liked the food when he cut her off.

"You ever seen her in a dress?"

"Cora? No." A trickle of sweat moved down her ribcage, making her squirm on her chair.

"You're kidding!" He laughed. "Are you trying to tell me she wears those overalls and boots every single day?"

"Yeah." Boredom crept into her voice.

"She have any suitors? You think she would, a young widow with a big farm."

Penny sighed. "Why are you asking? You want to marry her?" She stared past him to the strip of yellow flypaper coated in wriggling bodies.

"You'd think she'd want a man around."

"You better eat your supper before it gets cold."

But he wasn't listening anymore. Penny grimly gnawed her drumstick. Gilbert had just been fooling with her. Cora was the beautiful one. It was obvious in this room full of men. Even her overalls couldn't hide that.

Gilbert didn't offer to help Penny in the kitchen anymore but followed Cora around everywhere he could. Although she seemed to tolerate him, Cora didn't encourage him. Penny had to give her that. Cora didn't pay any special attention to Gilbert at all.

The day they finished the cutting and threshing, Penny left the chicken in the oven too long. It came out stringy and tough, but no one seemed to notice. Cora built a bonfire in the back yard. Antonio got out his guitar and started to sing a ballad that sounded as if he were weeping and then laughing. His brothers joined in, every voice in harmony. Gilbert hung around the edge of the bonfire circle while Penny went back in to wash the dishes. Cora disappeared down the outside cellar door, then came into the kitchen with six dusty bottles. When Penny figured out what was inside them, she dropped her dishrag, which landed in a wet heap on her shoes.

"My grandfather was a Dutch Calvinist," Cora said, laughing at Penny's shock, "but look at what that old devil had hiding away." Six bottles of California wine.

"That's against the law."

Cora grinned. "When you're finished, come and join us. A little wine never hurt a person."

Rubbing the gray dishrag over the plates, Penny listened to the music. Part of her longed to join the circle around the fire, but the other part of her refused to sit cheek by jowl with all those men, who would just ignore her and gaze moon-faced at Cora. And Cora herself had turned into a stranger who served liquor.

After she had finished the dishes, she sat by the window with the baby in her lap. Her untouched glass of wine rested on the sideboard. Rocking Phoebe, she listened to a new song, one high clear voice rising above the rest. Cora's voice, the first time she had ever heard her sing. The Spanish words fell from her tongue like sparks. Something rose in Cora's voice, something filled with yearning, as she wove a melody that was tragic and joyous at once. The word *ave* came again and again like waves lapping the beach.

Cora trusted those Mexicans enough to show them a side of herself she'd never shown to her. An ache welled up inside Penny, a loneliness that sank into her bones until her shoulders heaved. She was sobbing. She wished she had *someone* special. A best friend, a sweetheart. A memory enveloped her, of her mother braiding her hair. They had been laughing together over something. How long had it been since she last heard her mother laugh like that? *Ave, ave, ave.* The song tapered off.

When Cora finally came in, she was still singing under her breath, too flushed with wine and laughter to notice Penny's swollen eyes. "Why did you stay in here? You could have joined us, you know." Her winy breath touched Penny's cheek as she leaned forward to take the baby from her arms. Penny said nothing.

"Good night," said Cora, shrugging at her silence. She turned to carry Phoebe upstairs.

"Cora."

She swung around again, her eyes widening a little.

"That song you were singing." Penny swallowed. "Was it about the Virgin Mary?" Immediately she cursed herself for asking such a stupid question.

"What song?"

"The song with *ave* in it." Penny felt her face grow hot. "Like 'Ave Maria.' "

Cora laughed softly, her hand cupping the back of Phoebe's

head. "*Ave* means bird in Spanish. The song was about migrating birds." She retraced her steps to Penny's chair. "Reach in my left pocket."

Penny looked at her in confusion.

"Go on." Cora smiled. "Reach in. I don't have a free hand."

Mystified, Penny stuck her hand into Cora's pocket and pulled out a little wooden bird with outstretched wings.

"How do you like it? Javier carved it for Phoebe. Wasn't that sweet of him?"

Penny traced the wooden wings with her fingertip.

"You're tired." Cora looked at her with the kind of expansive, indulgent smile she usually reserved for her daughter. "You should get some sleep." She carried Phoebe upstairs.

Lying in bed, Penny studied the pattern the moonlight cast on the wallpaper as it sieved through the lace curtains. Everything was quiet, yet the melody of the *ave* song played itself over and over in her head. There was a word for what she had witnessed that night, looking out the kitchen window toward the bonfire, listening to Cora's voice traveling on the cool night air. What was that word? Happiness.

"Ave, ave, ave," she whispered, rubbing her face against the pillow. The wooden bird rested on her bedside table, its wings stretched in eternal flight. When she finally fell asleep, she dreamt of Canadian geese soaring overhead, their dun bodies like the undersides of clouds.

11

THE NEXT MORNING, after an early breakfast, Cora left for town, hoping to be one of the first farmers to get her wheat weighed in at the elevator. She drove the pickup, dragging her load behind her in the big trailer she had borrowed from the co-op. The Mexicans followed, waving goodbye to Penny, who stood in the back yard with Phoebe in her arms. Gilbert had tramped off on foot right after breakfast. He hadn't even said goodbye.

The farm seemed so lifeless and empty with everyone gone. She spent the morning washing the linens the harvest hands had slept in. By noon the sheets were flapping on the clotheslines, but Cora hadn't come back. Penny knew she had to get the grain weighed and sold. She had to go to the bank to deposit the money, return the trailer to the co-op. And they were so low on provisions, she would probably stop at Renfew's to buy groceries. The afternoon dragged on. Penny took the sheets down from the line, ironed them, and put them away. But still Cora did not return.

The baby was cranky, refusing her bottle. Penny took her to the hammock and tried to amuse her with the little bird, waving it aloft and singing, but Phoebe kept on crying. When she was like this only Cora could soothe her. She writhed in Penny's grip and screamed until Penny was ready to scream herself.

Pacing the orchard with Phoebe, she thought of Antonio, how his face had lit up when he smiled at Cora. How Cora had laughed with him. How they had sung in harmony, their voices braiding together. She thought of the way the men had looked at her, how she had become lovely with her hair growing back, her face glowing when she spoke all those foreign words. Those green eyes of hers could pin anyone to the wall. The curve of her mouth when she smiled. Deep down, Cora was a woman like any other. Did every woman have it in her, have that kind of weakness for a man that would cloud her eyes and make her do idiotic things?

For one horrible moment, she wondered if Cora had gone away with Antonio and his brothers. The ghost of Cora's laughter burned in her ears as Phoebe went on shrieking like an abandoned child. She imagined Cora shedding her men's clothes as she had at the lake. Shedding her overalls and becoming a woman again.

What if she *had* run off? Penny held Phoebe close, crying as she cried. She smoothed her hand over the pale red-gold fuzz on her head. The baby howled in hunger. Why wouldn't she take the bottle? Once Penny had heard that if a childless woman was left alone with a baby she loved enough, milk might spring from her breasts. Hazel Hamilton had told her that, back when Penny had seen her nursing little Ina. Seven years old, she had just gawked, not knowing any better. Mrs. H. had been the one to answer her questions about mothers and babies.

Penny picked up the bottle again and held Phoebe against her chest as if she were Cora nursing her. As if she, not Cora, were her mother. Gently she guided the rubber nipple to the baby's mouth. As Phoebe began to nurse, Penny let herself relax, surrendering to the weight of the baby in her arms, the sway of the hammock that held her. She felt drowsy now, languid. "You're safe," she whispered fiercely. "I won't let anything happen to you." Phoebe grew heavier in her arms until the nipple fell from her mouth. Penny burped her before letting her drift off to sleep. She thought she herself would drift off, but she heard the grating of tires on gravel, Cora's pickup pulling in the drive. A cold weight settled in her stomach. Who was she trying to kid? She wasn't Phoebe's mother or her salvation, only the hired girl, the one everyone ignored. And now Phoebe's real mother had finally decided to come home.

. . .

Penny reached the kitchen before Cora did. When she looked out the window, she saw Cora getting something out of the front seat, taking her time. Penny eased Phoebe into her quilt-lined basket without waking her, then grabbed the last bread loaf in the pantry, the last can of tomato soup. Dumping the soup in a pan, she slapped it on the burner. When she heard Cora come in, she didn't turn around, just whipped out the bread knife.

"I thought you weren't coming home. I thought you'd run off with your *friends*."

"I stopped in Sandborn."

Hearing her mother's voice, Phoebe awoke and started crying. Penny had spent hours trying to calm her, but it took Cora only a few seconds.

"There's my baby," she cooed.

"I don't give a damn where you stopped off," Penny muttered, thinking Cora wouldn't hear. That she wasn't even listening.

She froze when she felt Cora's hand on her shoulder, her touch like her mother's had been the moment before she let loose and smacked her. Still clutching the bread knife, Penny spun around and steeled herself. Cora held out a large box of sky-blue cardboard.

"This is for you," she said quietly. "I drove to Sandborn to get it. To thank you for all the work you did this week."

The bread knife fell from her hand and clattered to the floor as Cora handed her the box. Then Cora picked up Phoebe and walked out the screen door.

Littleton's Apparel. The name of the most expensive shop in Sandborn was written in fancy script on the blue box. The Hamiltons bought their clothes there. Sinking into the rocking chair, Penny made herself count to twenty before she opened it. Parting the tissue paper, her hands brushed against softness. Kitten fur, she thought. Goose down. She pulled out an angora cardigan, silvergray, like a cloud. Folded in the box beneath it was a pleated skirt of dove-gray lamb's wool lined in ivory satin. She fingered each perfect tuck and seam. Rocking herself, she stroked the angora. Then she thought of the hurt and bewilderment on Cora's face when she had handed her the box. Her mother's words burned in her head: *Little shit.* While Penny sat there trembling, the tomato soup boiled over.

After cleaning up the mess, Penny made a pot of coffee and heated up a pan of milk to make café con leche, the way Cora liked it. She took the leftover chicken out of the icebox and fixed up a plate of chicken sandwiches, then put everything on a tray and carried it to the back-porch swing, where Cora sat staring into the orchard. Phoebe curled in her mother's arms, gurgling and content. Setting the tray at Cora's feet, Penny knelt to pour her coffee.

"I'm sorry," she said as she handed her the cup.

Cora's fingers were icy, but her voice was even colder. "So you thought I ran off. Did you think I was going to abandon Phoebe?"

Ducking away, Penny found an orange crate on the other end of the porch. She hauled it over to where Cora was sitting, upended it, and placed the tray on it. "I'm really sorry." There was a throbbing behind her ears, a feverish heat in her face. "Thank you for the nice clothes, but you shouldn't have. They're too fancy for me." If she ever had the nerve to wear them to town, people would surely laugh at her. She headed for the back door, the shelter of the house, her room upstairs. But it's not even your room, she reminded herself.

"You're not going to eat with me?" Cora called out.

"I'm not hungry."

"Come back here and sit down!"

Penny dragged herself to the porch swing and took her seat beside Cora, who handed her one of the chicken sandwiches. "My daughter," she said tersely, "is the dearest thing in the world to me. Why do you think I live like this?"

Penny shook her head.

"I left him the day I knew I was pregnant. He knocked me around, but nobody knew. He was a *doctor*, so he knew how to do it without leaving any marks on me. No one would believe me, not even my best friend."

"That's awful." Penny's throat was so dry, she couldn't swallow.

"She was a charity nurse, just like I used to be. When I broke down and told her what he was doing, she put her hand on my arm and asked me if I knew what a *real* battered woman looked like. Said she'd seen plenty of them in the South Side slums and that I should know better than to say such things. She couldn't believe a doctor could do that."

Penny thought about Cora's pictures in the photo album. It was true, she decided, that no one seeing her from the outside could comprehend the secrets she was hiding on the inside.

"In the beginning, even *I* couldn't believe what was happening." Cora spoke in a brittle voice. "I kept praying he would change. But it only got worse. I was afraid I'd lose the baby if I stayed. There was one before that I lost." Her eyes glittered like cold green glass. "Why do you think I cut off my hair and turned myself into a laughingstock?"

Her eyes were so intensely green, Penny had to look away. "I don't know."

"He used to drag me around by the hair. That's why."

Penny flinched. Cora's face was incandescent with anger. The wind kept blowing her hair into her eyes, the hair that now covered her brow, her thick hair the color of Ceylon tea. Penny saw up close the beauty Cora had worked so hard to obscure.

"What about your brother?" she asked in a small voice. Another letter from him had arrived. "Did you tell him?"

For a moment Cora looked lost. "He's in *France*," she said. "What could he do? I didn't tell him about it until after I left. I could hardly think of the words. It's one thing to tell someone face to face, but to write it in a letter . . ." She rubbed her forehead with the heel of her hand. "Of course, my husband wrote to him first and told him I had lost my mind."

Suddenly the look on Cora's face was unbearable. Penny wanted to squeeze her hand. She wished she could think of something wise and comforting to say, but she just changed the subject, hoping to ease Cora's sadness.

"Boy, it sure is quiet here now with the Mexicans gone."

To her relief, the color returned to Cora's face. She sipped coffee and looked like her old self again. "I still can't believe you thought I was going to run off with them." She smiled wryly at Penny. "All those brothers except the two youngest are married. They have wives and children back in Mexico they send money to. You know, they loved my grandfather. They thought he was a very good man. I wanted to be as friendly as he always was so they wouldn't think badly of me." She sighed.

"When I worked as a charity nurse, they had me treating the Mexican patients, seeing as I spoke Spanish. A lot of Mexicans come up to Chicago to work in the stockyards. At first I thought I wouldn't have any trouble communicating, but it turned out that the Spanish we spoke down in Chile is completely different from their Spanish. I almost had to learn a whole new language. When Antonio and his brothers were here, it all came back to me."

She let out a long breath. Then, without warning, she looked right into Penny's eyes. "So tell me. What happened between you and your mother? Why won't you see her?"

"Because she hit me good and hard." Penny kept her voice level even as her vision blurred and she struggled not to cry. "She threw me out. She never wanted me anyway. Maybe you heard the rumors — she was never married. I don't know who my father is." She held her shoulders rigid, not letting them buckle or bow. Cora had shed no tears when talking about her husband. Penny willed herself to be just as strong.

"She's fooling around with Mr. Hamilton . . . our boss. She was always sending me off to the store so she and him could . . ." There, she'd done it. Spat out her mother's secret, which she had been dragging around like a sack of filth. Before Cora could start feeling sorry for her, she faced her squarely. "I'm never going back there," she told Cora in her harshest voice. "You're never going back to your husband. Well, I'm never going back to her." Only after she had spoken did she realize she had addressed Cora not in the manner of a hired girl or a headstrong brat but as her equal. Someone who had a say in what went on.

Cora's face was pale. *She* was the one who looked all shaken up. Something filled her eyes — it wasn't pity but something else.

"You're right." She spoke gravely. "You never have to go back there if you don't want to. You can stay here as long as you like." Now Penny thought she really would start to cry. What Cora had done was promise her a home. Cora touched her wrist. "Aren't you going to try on your new clothes?"

Her hands shook as she put on those perfect garments, the first clothes she had ever owned that were brand-new. The satin-lined skirt was smooth as cream against her skin. The angora sweater hugged the curves of her body. For the first time, it was plain to see she had breasts. She was filling out, looking more womanly. No longer a gawky girl resigned to a life of wearing Irene Hamilton's hand-me-downs. In the mirror, she saw a young lady who could put Irene to shame. Spinning in a circle, she watched the pleated skirt unfurl.

When she came down to the kitchen, Cora was making a fresh pot of coffee. "Well, look at you. You'll have to go into town and show off."

Penny flushed in delight. Yet she had to wonder why Cora had given her the sort of clothes that she herself had renounced. All at once she felt self-conscious under Cora's gaze, but instead of dashing upstairs and changing back into her old clothes, she got the book on Patagonia from the parlor, brought it into the kitchen, set it on the table. "What was it like growing up down there?"

Cora poured them each a cup of strong milky coffee. "When I was a girl, my parents ran a guesthouse in a little town called Puerto Natales." She opened the book and pointed to a dot on the map. "It wasn't a fancy place, but clean and decent. Most of our guests were cattlemen and prospectors who weren't expecting luxury. We called it the Hospedaje Paraíso — Paradise Lodge." She smiled, lowering her eyes. "My parents were very idealistic. They weren't the stay-at-home-and-sit-in-the-parlor type. They loved the outdoors more than anything. Whenever business was slow, we'd leave the housekeeper in charge and go off camping and fishing." Her face softened, as though remembering something she hadn't allowed herself to think about for a long time.

"We'd load up the pack mules and go off into the Torres del Paine. The Torres are mountains." She showed Penny a picture in the book of jagged peaks. "They look like needles pointing into the sky. The weather in the mountains was always unstable, even in summer. I remember helping put up a tent in the pouring rain. Do you have any idea how heavy wet canvas is?"

Penny shook her head.

"I loved being out in the wilderness. In the grasslands, we had guanacos. Those are wild antelope."

"I saw the pictures of them in the book." Penny grinned.

"I used to sneak up downwind of them, get as close to them as they would let me. I loved being around wild things. My big brother didn't know what to do with me — he was always trying to drag me back. He was afraid they'd kick me, I guess. But I was always sneaking off and doing whatever I wanted. They tell me I was a handful."

She spoke slowly. "Once I saw these white things in the grass. I thought they would be rocks, but they were bones. The vertebrae of some small animal."

"Vertebrae," Penny said. "That's the spine. The parts of the spine." There was an old anatomy textbook in Cora's room upstairs. Penny had paged through it a few times. If she was going to be a nurse, she would have to learn the names of such things.

"That's right. They were only about this big." Cora made a circle with her thumb and forefinger. "I wanted to take one vertebra home with me as a souvenir. I liked to collect things like feathers and bird nests, but I didn't have any bones yet. So I put the vertebra in my saddlebag and took it home. My brother told me I was the oddest child — who ever heard of a little girl collecting bones?" She was silent for a moment, sipping her coffee.

"I want to be a nurse," Penny said shyly. The talk of vertebrae triggered her confession, forcing it from her lips. "Dr. Lovell said I'd make a good nurse."

"I could have told you the same thing." Cora smiled. "Then I imagine you'll be going to high school this fall. Are you registered?"

Penny remembered Gilbert's words. She'd have to go to school every day, return to the world she thought she had left behind.

"Don't look so worried," said Cora. "We'll find a way . . . somehow. I'll drive you to town. Maybe I'll have to get another girl to help watch Phoebe while you're in school, but we'll manage."

"But it's so far." Penny chose her words carefully. "If you drove me there in the morning and picked me up after school, you'll be driving over eighty miles a day." How could she tell her it was learning she wanted, not Minerva High School. Penny had no desire to return to Irene's realm of gossip and cliques. If she showed her face in high school, Irene would find a way to ruin it for her. She was perfectly happy with her life of solitude, here with Cora and Phoebe, in a place where Irene couldn't touch her. "Do I *have* to go to high school to get my diploma?" She threw Cora a quizzical look. "Can't I just read books on my own?"

"Maybe there's another way." Cora took another sip of coffee. "They must bend the rules for families on remote farms. I could talk to Evelyn Haselstrom."

"The English teacher?" Miss Haselstrom lived only a few houses down from the Hamiltons.

"She was my mother's best friend," Cora said. "They used to write each other every month. Maybe she can do something."

Penny's dream took shape, rising before her. Sometimes she thought of her future as a thing she could nourish like a baby in her womb. It would grow and grow until it was too big to fit inside her anymore.

Her dream became manifest in the stack of textbooks, frayed by many hands, that Cora brought back from town one day. Instead of the customary groceries, she laid out the books on the kitchen table. *Great Expectations, English and American Literature, Finch's Algebra, Introduction to Biology, A History of Art, The Story of Our Nation, The Odyssey.*

"How do you like them?" Cora asked as Penny picked up each book in turn. She leafed through the algebra equations in awe and fear, then looked wildly at Cora.

"I don't know. This looks so hard."

"I'll help you." Cora smoothed her hand over the biology book. "That's how Jacob and I got our schooling down in Chile. At the kitchen table. Our parents were the teachers. My father loved algebra."

"Did you go talk to Miss Haselstrom?" Her head was ringing. The floor seemed to give way beneath her feet.

"I explained your situation. She drew up a study plan, gave me the books, and told me you'll be expected to mail in your homework and assignments. You'll have to do essays and work-sheets. A few times a year, she wants you to come in and take exams. She says if you work hard and get good grades, you'll graduate and get your diploma when you're seventeen, just like the other students."

Penny looked at Cora, at how casually she stood there in her corduroy trousers and pressed white shirt. She tried to picture her going into the high school like that, talking to Miss Haselstrom on her behalf. Penny's hand reached out over the books, randomly choosing one. *The Odyssey.*

"You have to start reading that one today," Cora said. "You can learn about the original Penelope. Think carefully about her story. She was a lot smarter than anyone gave her credit for. A true heroine."

Penny opened the book and began to read, the strange words snaring her in a jeweled net.

Tell me, Muse, of the man of many ways, who was driven far journeys, after he had sacked Troy's sacred citadel.

"It's best if you read it as an adventure story instead of a long poem," Cora told her. "Just read it and let it sink into you."

The Odyssey was so thick, she thought she might never finish it, but just go on reading forever about Odysseus's adventures and Penelope at her loom. She and Cora took turns reading passages aloud, Cora correcting her pronunciation as she stumbled over the unfamiliar names.

> *She set up a great loom in her palace, and set to weaving*
> *a web of threads long and fine. Then she said to us:*
> *"Young men, my suitors, now that the great Odysseus has perished,*
> *wait, though you are eager to marry me, until I finish*
> *this web, so that my weaving will not be useless and wasted.*

She had to think hard to make sense of the story. Some of the events were so strange. If Troy was so sacred, then why had they sacked it? And why kill an entire group of men just to punish them for stealing cattle? She kept telling herself there was a reason people still read this saga, even though it was almost three thousand years old. There was a reason why she should try to put herself in Odysseus's shoes. Why she should care about his struggle to get home to Ithaca. Why she should learn the unpronounceable names of vanished heroes, monsters, and gods. And about cities like Troy that didn't exist anymore.

It was a mystery to Penny why Cora wanted her to pay special attention to Penelope, whom she considered dull and maddeningly weak. She hated Penelope for letting the suitors barge into her house, eat all her food, and force their attentions on her. She especially hated the way Penelope let her own son boss her around. Even Athena put Penelope to sleep when she wanted to get her out of the way.

Sometimes the gods struck Penny as unsympathetic, too, the way they meddled in people's affairs; helping them, then hurting them; separating them, then bringing them back together. The gods were fickle and could do anything they wanted. Sometimes they disguised themselves as humans and lived for a time among them. Athena usually disguised herself as a man. Who could blame her when being a woman meant being weak and silly like Penelope?

Cora taught her about the ancient world and the Greek pantheon. "Athena's the same goddess as the Roman Minerva."

"I know *that*," Penny replied, a bit annoyed that Cora could assume her ignorance of how her town got its name. "There's a statue of her in front of the high school."

When she confessed that she had never tasted an olive, Cora bought a small jar of green California olives from Renfew's. One night after putting Phoebe to bed, they ate them, licking the brine from their fingers.

"Olive trees grow everywhere in the Mediterranean," Cora told her. "They're as important for the people there as wheat is here. They put olive oil into everything they cook."

"Have you ever been over there?" Penny asked. "To Greece?" The words *wine-dark sea* trilled in her head. The taste of olives was still in her mouth. She recalled the photograph labeled *Mykonos, Greece, 1919*. Cora and her brother sitting at the outdoor table with the jug and the three glasses. The missing corner of the picture where her husband had been before she cut him out. But maybe he hadn't been her husband yet in that picture. He had probably been her suitor then.

"I went overseas as a nurse during the war," Cora said.

Penny nodded, hoping the eagerness on her face didn't reveal what she already knew.

"Then, after the war, my brother and I went to Greece. When we were young, we promised each other we would go one day." Her fingers traced the rim of the glass dish where the olive pits lay in their pool of brine. "We celebrated my twenty-first birthday there."

The table and the three glasses. The man cut out of the picture. Penny reckoned that Cora must have married him not long after that photograph was taken. According to everything she had heard, Cora had returned to Evanston in late 1919 as Dr. Egan's wife. Why had she married right away, Penny wondered, when she could have stayed single, at least for a while? And why had she married him, of all people? She thought of Penelope's suitors in *The Odyssey*, how menacing they were. But Cora hadn't lived in ancient Greece. She had wealthy grandparents, an education, a real profession. Penny considered the pictures she'd seen of Cora as a nurse. The group portrait with the other nurses and the doctors. She could have done so many things.

"What's your brother like?" she asked.

"We were very close when we were growing up. Best friends. After we lost our parents, Jacob was all I had. I don't know how I would have endured it without him." Cora pushed her hair back from her forehead. "In the beginning, I hated Chicago. Our parents had let us run wild, but my grandparents expected me to behave like a proper young lady. Oh, I'm sure they meant well, but it wasn't easy. I wanted to run away. Jacob promised me that if I held on until I was eighteen, we would go somewhere beautiful and wild together. He would paint and play the piano. He was the artistic one. I would do something outdoorsy like raise horses or fly airplanes." She met Penny's eyes and laughed. "When I was a girl, I had big dreams. But then I got practical and decided to become a nurse.

"Well, Jacob kept his promise to me, in a manner of speaking. He volunteered for the war. Went over as an artillery officer. Thought he could serve his country and see the world. And I went with him. My grandparents couldn't do anything to stop me." She smiled sadly. "After the war, of course, my grandparents expected Jacob to come back to Chicago and take his place running their meatpacking firm. That's how my Viney grandparents made their money. But Jacob wasn't cut out for that kind of life. Instead he bought an old cottage near Arles, among the vineyards and lavender fields. He invited me to stay on with him there, the life we always dreamed of." Cora rested her hands on the edge of the table.

"He was always such a romantic. Through everything, he

stayed true to his dreams. I was the one who ended up coming back to Chicago, but he's still there in his little stone house. He teaches English at a boys' school. During the school holidays, he teaches French and art to English boys who come over for the summer. He has a fiancée, too. I think his life is simple but happy."

"You miss him," Penny said.

Cora nodded. "In his last letter, he said he was asking his school for a sabbatical. I hope he can visit me and see his niece."

Upstairs Phoebe whimpered in her sleep. Cora looked up at the ceiling. When her daughter fell silent again, she folded her hands and gazed down at the oilcloth. Everything, Penny thought, boiled down to a handful of choices. She tried to imagine the shape Cora's life would have taken if she had stayed with her brother in France.

"Did you meet your husband over there?" she asked softly.

"He saved my brother's life." Cora spoke with her head bowed, not meeting Penny's eyes. "Jacob was hit by a shell. At the very least, we thought he would lose his leg. But he . . . he worked all night without sleep to save him. Jacob still has a limp and some terrible scars, but it's a miracle he's still alive and can walk." Her voice sounded hollow. "He was a brilliant surgeon. No matter how awful it was, he never lost his courage. Even when we ran out of morphine and had nothing to give our patients for the pain."

Cora was white in the face. She couldn't bring herself to call her husband by his name, Penny realized.

"After he saved my brother, I thought he was the most noble, heroic man ever. He and Jacob became good friends. I fancied him, of course, but tried to hide it. I thought he would never return my affection. When he did, I couldn't believe my luck. By then, I'd seen too much death. He made me feel so alive. I couldn't believe how happy I was. Then he proposed."

Cora got up and carried the dish of olive pits to the sink.

The next day when Cora was out, Penny went to her room and opened the wardrobe door. Lifting a pair of rubber boots and then a folded blanket, she uncovered the photo album. She sat on the bed and returned to the pictures of Greece. Here were buildings she now recognized as temples. Pillars carved in the shape of women bore the weight of the roofs. She found a picture of Jacob sitting under a tree. Was it an olive tree, she wondered. He looked so different than he had in the earlier Chicago photographs, his face full of sad wisdom. This was a picture of someone who had crossed over into the land of death, she thought. But then Dr. Egan had rescued him and carried him back into the land of the living. She wished Cora had left at least one of her husband's pictures intact. One day Phoebe might want to see his photograph.

On their next trip into town, Cora took care of the grocery shopping while Penny walked to the library to get some books for her schoolwork. She was wearing her brand-new clothes. Her arms swung freely at her sides as she cut through the Minerva Civic Park, where the Junior Jaycees were having their annual picnic. She strolled past the girls with their hair molded into waves and ringlets, past the boys with their slicked-back cowlicks and their ears that stuck out like jug handles. They couldn't unglue their eyes from her. The sight of her in beautiful clothes seemed to shock them as much as seeing Cora dressed like a man. She drank in the way their heads turned, the way their unbelieving eyes rested on her. Inside she glowed. Everyone who looked at her had to see she was lit up from within like a lamp.

Even Ned Fisk, the boy Irene Hamilton was sweet on, stared at her so intensely it was hard not to burst out laughing. Then, with an electric jolt, she recognized that stare — that was how men looked at her mother. She kept her head up, her pace steady as she walked away from him.

Sometimes, if she was honest with herself, she had to admit she had envied her mother's beauty, wondering if she would ever match up. And sometimes she wished she could tell her mother that she could do better than sneaking around with Mr. H. With her looks, she could have a real suitor who would bring her flowers, take her out to dances. Part of Penny still dreamt of running home, having her mother fuss over her the way she used to, before the business with Mr. H. had started. But it was too late to go back now. It hurt like a wound that wouldn't close, but Penny couldn't cross that divide anymore.

The best she could do was learn from it all. It seemed that a girl had only one chance in life, and she better make the right choice or else spend the rest of her days paying the consequences. She promised herself that she wouldn't get in trouble the way her mother had, wouldn't marry the wrong man the way Cora had. And she wasn't going to be like those girls she passed in the park, either, prancing around with their little boyfriends. Silly crushes and flirtations weren't for her. What a fool she'd made of herself, gushing all over Gilbert, and for nothing! She would hold herself firm and upright as Athena's spear, remain pure and apart until she met the boy she was destined to love. And when she met her true love, she would know at once. It would strike her like lightning, and then she would be capable of any act of passion. Just like Cora's mother, eloping with her love to the bottom of the world.

That was for the future, however, which seemed as distant and ethereal as a star in the sky. She felt so rooted on the Maagdenbergh farm. Even with the diapers to wash, even on the days when Phoebe fussed and screamed, that was her home. At night after she put the baby to bed, she sat up at the kitchen table with her books and struggled with her algebra problems until she mastered them. Sometimes Cora sat down and helped her with an equation. But even algebra was easier to grasp than the idea of the passing of time or the passing of her youth. She told herself that she belonged here with Phoebe and Cora. There were days she believed that this happiness and this dreaming over books would go on forever.

12

BARBARA WALKED down Main Street, passing the Bijou Motion Picture Theater. They were showing *The Sheik*, starring Rudolph Valentino. A group of farm girls gathered around the marquee poster of the limpid-eyed hero bending over his lady like a lover in a dream. In church last Sunday, Father Bughola had condemned the movie, proclaiming it scandalous and lewd. Any of his parishioners who saw it would have to reckon with penance. Those farm girls would have to content themselves with Valentino's picture. Barbara nearly sniggered aloud at the sight of them smoldering over a movie poster. They put their heads together and tittered, as if they longed to be seduced and swept off their feet, surrendering to an imaginary lover who could spirit them away to a magical world where priests did not exist.

Poor cows. They better have some dream to help them through their lives. Barbara cast her eyes over their patched-together shoes and drooping stockings, their crooked hems and clumsy braids. She was willing to bet good money that they would all be married by the age of eighteen — at least half of them with a baby already in their belly. From their wedding onward, it would be a downhill journey into drudgery, a new baby every year, a husband with dirty fingernails who barked at them if they didn't have supper on the table at exactly five-thirty every night. Sigh over your movie star while you still can, she wanted to tell them. There will come a day when your dreams will dry up and turn to dust.

As if reading her mind, one of those hayseed girls spun

around and threw Barbara a hard look. Barbara started at the sight of her freckled face, her wide-open eyes, the brown braid pinned around her head. Penny? Then the leap in her stomach subsided in a cold wash of disappointment. That wasn't her girl. Ducking her head, she walked on, her cheeks smarting. Of course it wasn't. Penny wasn't silly enough to stand around gawking at some movie poster. She was too sensible for that.

Barbara was about to walk into Renfew's when she stopped just short of the threshold.

". . . the Maagdenbergh woman," someone inside was saying. A loud, braying voice. Peering through the screen door, she saw it was Mrs. Fisk with her yellow horse teeth. "Which goes to show," she said, "that maybe we misjudged her. That girl's getting an education now. They're letting her study for her high school diploma out at the farm."

"Well, they'd have to," Mr. Renfew replied. "That farm is too far away for her to come in to school."

"They never bent the rules before," someone else said. "The Maagdenbergh woman talked them into it."

"I saw the girl in town the other week," another voice said. "She's turning into a pretty young thing. Who'd have thought?"

"You have to admit," Mrs. Fisk said, "the Maagdenbergh woman is doing more for that girl than her own mother ever did."

Barbara walked away as fast as she could without breaking into a run. Her tears spilled right out in the open. By the time she reached the Hamiltons' back door, her legs were so weak that she had to sit down.

That Maagdenbergh woman came from money. What did she know about raising a girl on four dollars a week? What did anyone know about that? She had kept her daughter fed and clothed, decent and healthy, given her the best life she could afford. Hadn't she? She wasn't a monster like Sadie Ostertag. Most kids around here never saw high school anyway. Those farm girls she had seen in front of the movie marquee had probably not finished eighth grade. Penny already had a lot more education than anyone in her family ever had.

Not sending her daughter to high school was the choice any other woman like herself would have made. Why have her waste three years sweating over books when she could be earning wages? Unlike the Hamilton girls, Penny would have to make her own way in the world. She didn't have a daddy to send her off to college.

But Penny was smarter than the Hamilton girls, Barbara told herself fiercely. She should have been the one to tell her how smart she was and send her to high school. *You've got a brain in your head and that will help you rise above this life.* It should have been her, not the Maagdenbergh woman. Barbara held her head in her hands. Was it really too late to try to patch things up?

Every Sunday after church she had planned to ask Mr. Wysock for a lift to the Van den Maagdenbergh farm. And every Sunday, cowed by Mrs. Wysock's tight-lipped glare, she had lost her nerve. If she asked Mr. H. to drive her out there, he would refuse. She knew he would — if they were seen driving together, people would really start to talk. There was only one thing left to do. Only one chance, and she had to take it this Sunday, before the Hamilton girls returned from summer camp. She had to take her chance or lose it forever.

On Sunday, instead of going to Mass, Barbara unlocked the garden shed where the Hamiltons' bicycles were kept. Since Penny had disappeared with her own bike, Irene's imported English bicycle was the only one that would do. Mr. H.'s was too big for her, Ina's and Isobel's too small. As she wheeled it out of the shed, she told herself that no one would ever have to know she had borrowed it. Mr. H. had already left for church and would be going straight on to visit his wife in the Sandborn Nursing Home. He had a dinner invitation, wouldn't be back until late. After locking the shed again, she pedaled off through streets that were empty, since everyone was in church. The warm morning air rushed past her, lifting the hem of her apple-green skirt. The wind streamed over her face as she left Minerva behind in a blur. Soon she was pedaling down that long dirt road with shorn cornfields on either side. In a few weeks' time the farmers would plow the stubble under and plant the winter wheat. But at this moment it lay fallow and empty.

Only when she had cycled halfway out in the rising heat did she realize how long twenty-one miles could be. She kept pedaling, wiping the sweat off her face with a handkerchief that soon turned a dirty gray. About five miles from the Van den Maagdenbergh farm, an old Model T came up at her rear, nearly knocking her into the ditch as it barreled past. Three half-baked boys hung out the back windows, hooting and yelling how sweet her ass looked on that bicycle seat. Panic washed over her when she recognized them as the Nelson gang. Their speeding tires threw gravel in her face and left her coated in dust. Nearly losing her grip on the handlebars, she pulled to the side of the road, trembling and terrified. Only when their trail of dust disappeared over the horizon could she breathe again.

Hate welled up in her throat. She thought of the latest gossip going around about what had happened to poor Ellie Stadler. The girl hadn't been seen in town since it happened. Barbara reckoned she was too humiliated. Of course, no one could prove the Nelson gang had done it. According to the story going around, even the girl couldn't say for sure — it had been dark and the culprits had thrown a blanket over her head. So those boys were still roaming free, acting as if no one would dare to stand in their way.

Well, the Maagdenbergh woman sure had. Grimly Barbara climbed back on the bicycle, straddling the seat with her raw thighs. The Maagdenbergh woman had shot up their windshield, which must have cost them a pretty penny to fix. At least she had proved she was too much trouble to take on. Scum like that preferred easy victims, girls too young and scared to fight back. Barbara hoped the Maagdenbergh woman had taught the Nelson gang to leave her alone. Still, it made her ache to think of Penny out on that farm with nothing but that woman's rifle and temper to protect her if anything went wrong.

Finally she reached the farm and saw the sign: ALL TRESPASSERS WILL BE SHOT. For all she knew, the Maagdenbergh woman might take aim at her. As she made her way down the driveway, she almost felt like ducking and hiding behind the trees. But when she reached the farmyard, it was quiet. White geese dozed on the lawn. Before going up to the door, she went to the pump, working the noisy handle until water gushed forth. First she drank in long greedy gulps, slaking her dry throat. Then she rinsed out her handkerchief and wiped the dust from her face, neck, hands, and arms. She straightened her stockings and shook the wrinkles out of her skirt. Smoothing her hair, she made herself as neat as she could without a comb or mirror. She took a handful of grass and cleaned her shoes. By the time she looked at the house again, she saw the Maagdenbergh woman in the doorway. She was holding the baby, not the rifle.

"Who are you?" she called out.

Summoning all the dignity she could muster, Barbara marched past the geese and up to the back door. "I'm here to see my daughter." She drew back her shoulders in an attempt to hide her trepidation in addressing this monstrosity, this man-woman Penny had chosen over her. From the look of it, the Maagdenbergh woman had just finished nursing. Slung over her shoulder was an old tea towel the baby had spit up on.

"You mean Penny?" She shifted the baby's weight in her arms. "She's at Lake Griffin."

"Lake Griffin?" This Barbara could not grasp. "How did she get out there?"

"She drove the pickup."

Barbara shook her head impatiently. "That girl can't drive."

"She can now," the Maagdenbergh woman said. "It's not very difficult on the back roads."

That was no good at all. What if Penny ran into the Nelson gang somewhere on the road? What would she do then? "You let her swim alone?" she asked, not hiding her anger and fear. "Everyone knows that's not safe."

The Maagdenbergh woman looked at her for a moment before speaking. "She's a good swimmer. I was going to go with her, but the baby was feeling poorly."

"What time do you expect her back?" Barbara felt ridiculous, having to ask her.

"On Sundays she keeps her own hours, but usually she's back around sunset. Maybe a little later."

Sunset. Barbara thought of her wasted journey. Even if they gave her a lift back to town, how could she spend any time with Penny and still return the bicycle to the shed before Mr. H. came home? "I noticed you haven't been bringing her to church," she said.

"Church? Penelope's going on sixteen. It's her business whether she goes to church."

I don't need you to tell me how old my daughter is, Barbara wanted to shout. And what nerve she had, calling her Penelope. Nobody but Barbara had ever called her that. She felt betrayed that her daughter had told the Maagdenbergh woman her true name.

"Did you cycle out here?" The Maagdenbergh woman glanced across the lawn at Irene's bicycle, coated in dust. Then her eyes returned to Barbara. "We haven't even introduced ourselves. I'm Cora Viney. And you're Barbara Niebeck, aren't you?" She looked as though she was about to extend her hand for Barbara to shake, but then the baby started fussing and she had to rock her back and forth.

"Is it colic?" The question shot out before Barbara could stop it. "Try weak fennel tea and honey for that. And if you're nursing, don't eat any spicy food until the baby's weaned."

The Maagdenbergh woman looked thoughtful. "Was Penny colicky when she was a baby?"

Barbara looked away.

"You work at the Hamiltons', I hear."

When the Maagdenbergh woman gazed at her, Barbara felt

herself shrink. Those eyes. She didn't just look at her but *into* her. She could open her up like a box and see everything inside. Barbara could read the knowledge in her eyes. Penny must have told her about Mr. H. About how her own mother had hit her and chased her out of the house. But those eyes seemed to know even more. Barbara had to fight to keep from breaking down and crying. What else had Penny been saying about her? What other secrets that were none of anyone's concern?

"She's a good kid," said the Maagdenbergh woman. "You must be proud of her."

"Oh, yes," Barbara managed, even though her throat felt as if it would collapse on itself. "I'm very proud."

"If you like, you can come in and wait for her. You must be thirsty. Can I offer you some lemonade?" Balancing the baby in one arm, she held the screen door open, inviting Barbara into the farmhouse kitchen. Barbara ached for a tall glass of lemonade. If anything more potent had been on hand, she would have downed that, too, the law be damned. But she could not step over the threshold, now that this woman knew so much about her. The Maagdenbergh woman's sympathy was too much to bear.

Barbara found it grotesque and just plain wrong that Penny lived here, that Penny had stumbled into this house and seen the Maagdenbergh woman sprawled in the aftermath of labor. The pervasive smell of mother's milk coming off of her brought back memories of her own childbirth, her painfully swollen breasts, and the baby that wouldn't stop crying. Barbara thought she would be sick.

"Mrs. Niebeck? Are you all right?" The baby turned in her mother's arm and regarded Barbara with eyes that were the same shade of blue as the delphiniums that grew in Mrs. Hamilton's perennial bed. "If you like, you can wait for her on the porch." Her voice was gentle. "It's nice and cool out here. I'll bring you some lemonade and sandwiches. Why don't you sit down on the porch swing?" She touched Barbara's arm.

"*No.*" Barbara backed away. "Just tell her I came by." But before she made her escape, she braced herself one last time and held the Maagdenbergh woman's gaze. "Is she happy?"

"I think so." She paused. "She seems happy. I hope that if she wasn't happy, she'd say something."

"You fixed it so she can get her high school diploma." Barbara couldn't look at her anymore. "Well, that's good." She swallowed. "She's smart. She should get an education." Then she walked away. If the Maagdenbergh woman said anything more, Barbara didn't hear it for the rushing of blood in her head. She climbed back on the bicycle and pedaled off, unable to put into words how frightened she was of that unspeakable woman who had made her daughter flower.

Cycling down the road, it struck her that she didn't know Penny anymore. She had lost all claim on her. She'd chased her away, and Penny had forsaken her. It was only a matter of days before the Hamilton girls returned home and Mr. H. cast her off, too. She had no one. Eight miles from town, her front tire hit a sharp stone and punctured. Skidding, she lost her balance and tumbled with Irene's bicycle into the ditch.

Penny swam in the lake, clothed in nothing but pure water. This time, since she was alone, she had left Irene's hideous swimsuit on the shore. She splashed up liquid diamonds, then rolled over to float on her back. Her hair had come out of its braid and fanned around her head. Strands lay plastered on her chest. Closing her eyes, she let the sun baste her — a thing she would have to pay for that night when she returned home with the worst sunburn in her life. Cora would give her a bottle of calamine lotion. In the bathroom, her feet soaking in a pan of cold water, she would rub the cooling lotion into her fevered skin. But for now she let the sun burn into her like the eyes of a lover. She thought of the poster of Rudolph Valentino she'd seen on the theater marquee. Then she let that image fade and dreamt of the landscape of Cora's stories, the Patagonian mountains. She dreamt of Odysseus's sea voyage. Rolling over again and breaking into a gentle breaststroke, she dreamt of Circe the witch and of Calypso the nymph. She didn't dream about Penelope. If she had been Penelope, she wouldn't have waited twenty years for her husband's return. And she certainly wouldn't have wasted all those years just weaving and unraveling the same cloth. Swimming naked to her island, Penny thought of the lines she had memorized:

> *Helios, leaving behind the lovely standing waters, rose up*
> *into the brazen sky to shine upon the immortals.*

She took comfort in the grace of the words, in the strength of her arms and legs as she swam. She never felt safer than when held aloft in the water.

When she emerged from the lake and began to dry herself, a shiver of fear played at her. Girls weren't supposed to go swimming alone, especially not if they swam naked. But the forest rustled around her, the sun filtered through the dancing leaves, and she refused to let herself be afraid. I would die if I couldn't do this, she thought. Dressed again, she whistled as she made her way to the pickup truck.

It was dark by the time she got back. The farmhouse windows were lit up like jack-o'-lantern eyes, and the smell of Spanish beans and rice drifted out the screen door. On Sundays, Cora cooked supper. The way she made rice and beans, it didn't taste like poor people's food but like something rich and exotic. Coming in the door, Penny didn't feel her sunburn yet, just her hunger. At the table, between heaping forkfuls, she told Cora about her swim.

"I saw the geese flying south. The sky was full of them." She had cleaned her plate and was about to help herself to seconds when she noticed Cora was looking at her in a strange way. "What is it?"

"Your mother." Cora paused, letting those two words hang in the air like smoke. "She stopped by today."

Penny seized up in shock before she got a hold of herself. Taking a breath, she allowed the familiar resentment to ease back into place. "What did she want?" It was impossible to keep the sarcasm out of her voice.

"Not much. Just to tell you that she was here. She was all dressed up."

Penny said nothing.

"She made a special point of asking if you were happy."

Penny closed her eyes. "Did *he* drive her out here?" She imagined her mother stepping out of Mr. H's car.

"Nobody drove her. She came by bicycle."

"What bicycle?" Penny stopped short, remembering that she had taken her mother's old bike. Now it was in the woodshed collecting spider webs.

"She seemed pretty disappointed you weren't here," said Cora. "It was a long way for her to come."

Penny stared at the wall behind Cora's head.

"She misses you. I think she might be sorry."

A noise tore out of Penny's throat. She began to itch and throb. When she touched her forearm, she could feel the terrible heat rising from her skin.

Cora frowned. "You're awfully red. Did you get too much sun?"

Virgil and Lucy Wysock were driving slowly in the direction of Minerva when they came upon Barbara limping and pushing a bicycle down the road. Two spokes on the front wheel were broken, and the wheel itself was mangled.

"Looks like you got yourself into a little scrape." Mr. Wysock pulled up beside her and clambered out of his pickup. "I s'pose you need a lift back home."

Shielding her eyes from the declining sun, Barbara nodded.

"Why look here," he said, bending down to examine the bicycle. "You got one of them fancy foreign models." Barbara stiffened as his eyes moved up her legs, traveling over her torn stockings and dirt-streaked skirt, over her bosom to her face and ruined hat. He grinned at her. "Now my kid brother Gus has a French bicycle he brought back after the war. A racing bicycle, he calls it. So I ask him if he thinks those Frenchies know anything about bicycles that we don't. And he says back to me that French ladies sure know a thing or two that ladies over here don't!"

Barbara forced her lips into a smile as he chortled at his own joke. She certainly didn't believe he had a brother young enough to have served in the war. He was sixty and had hair growing out of his ears. She helped him lift the bicycle and put it into the back of the pickup.

"Looks like you got kinda dirty there, Barbara. Hey Lucy! You got any newspaper for Mrs. Niebeck to sit on?"

They found an old *Minerva Gazette* for her to tuck under her bottom so she wouldn't dirty their seat. Wrinkling her nose, Lucy Wysock shifted her bulk to make room for her.

"I never knew you had such a swell bicycle, Barbara," Mr. Wysock remarked as he drove into town. "In fact, that looks an awful lot like Irene Hamilton's bicycle. I've seen her riding it all over the place." He threw Barbara a sly grin. She just smiled blandly. Mrs. Wysock wouldn't even look at her.

"Thank you kindly," she said when Mr. Wysock dropped her off in the back alley behind the Hamilton house. "If we could keep this between us, Mr. Wysock" — she made herself gaze beseechingly into his eyes — "I would be very much obliged."

"I reckon you would, Barbara." He broke into a smile. "I reckon you would." Turning his back on his glowering wife, he tipped his hat.

Barbara returned Irene's bicycle to the shed and washed off the dirt. She would have to wait until morning to see what could be done about the broken wheel. Locking the shed, she ran into the house to clean herself up before Mr. H. got home. Her arms and legs were scratched and bruised from her fall into the ditch. At least she managed to salvage her clothing. If her stockings and hat were ruined beyond hope, diligent soakings and washings saved her dress and gloves. But her heart wouldn't stop its awful pounding. What was she going to do? The Hamilton girls were due back in two days.

When Mr. H. came to her that night, he kissed her water-wrinkled fingers and buried his face in her hair, still damp from her bath. Stroking her body, his fingers traced the angry red scratches.

"Barbara, what happened to you?" His voice was full of concern.

She heard herself laugh even as she blinked back tears. "Oh, that's nothing." She breathed in unsteadily. "I fell off the ladder when I was washing the outside windows. I landed in the rose bushes."

He held her close, tenderly stroking her wounds while she trembled in shame at how easily the lie had sprung to her lips.

"Well, promise me you won't bother about the outside windows anymore," he said. "Someone else can do them. I don't want you hurting yourself again."

Squeezing her eyes shut, she kissed him and wondered what would happen if she told him the truth — that she had fallen in a ditch on his daughter's bicycle. The way he held her, anyone would think he was falling in love with her. What sweet relief it would be to nestle in his arms and spill out her secrets. Look into his eyes and make her confession. *I only did it because I missed my daughter so much.* If he truly cared for her, he would try to understand.

But she was no fool. Men like Laurence Hamilton did not fall in love with women like her. He might act all besotted now, but how long could it last with his daughters due back? If she wanted to come out of this unscathed, she would have to keep her head. Twisting in his arms, she vowed to get the bicycle wheel fixed before he discovered the damage.

The next morning, Barbara set off for Timmerman's hardware store. One glance through the plate-glass window showed they had what she was looking for — two long rows of bicycle wheels hung from the ceiling. Her kid-gloved hands clutched her patent leather purse. She had the money to pay for it, whatever it cost.

The store was full of men who gathered around to gab. The place even smelled masculine, with the rubber of the bicycle tires competing with the metallic scent of screws and nails. Her high heels clicked on the dusty floor as she made her way to the counter. She smiled tightly, privately, careful to keep her eyes lowered, hidden beneath the brim of her hat. Stepping up to the cash register, she rested her gloved hands on the scarred wood and waited until Mr. Timmerman, blond and ruddy-faced, engrossed in a conversation about the price of yearling hogs, bothered to glance in her direction.

"I need a bicycle wheel," she told him when he finally sauntered over, laying his huge, oil-stained hands on the counter opposite hers.

He looked her over, his tongue curling over his bottom lip. "What model?"

"Thirty-three inches in diameter." She had made sure to take the measurement before coming to the store.

"That's the *size*, ma'am." He rubbed his greasy chin. "I asked you what *model* you was looking for. What particular make of bicycle?"

"Does it matter?" Her voice rose, then she shook her head and sighed. Why was he making it so complicated when any number of the wheels hanging from the ceiling would do the trick? "It's an Oxford Flyer."

He threw his thick neck back, one paw slapping the counter. "You ride around on an Oxford Flyer, Mrs. Niebeck?"

Behind her, she heard the men in the store laughing along. She bowed her head as she trembled in rage. Wysock, that old bastard, had been blabbing all over town.

"I don't see what difference it makes to you," she said.

"Oh, it sure makes a difference, sweetheart." His eyes moved over her face, down her front. "See, we don't got any foreign wheels in this shop. I'd have to order one from the Cities, and that'd take around three, four months."

She rolled her eyes. If he thought she was going to believe that . . . "You got plenty of wheels." She had to fight to keep her voice steady. "You got to have one somewhere that's thirty-three inches in diameter."

"It'd look funny." Timmerman leaned across the counter and breathed on her face. She took a step backward, bumping against someone who had edged up behind her. "An American wheel on an English bicycle . . . now that would stick out like a sore thumb." He licked his lips again before delivering his punch. "Miss Irene wouldn't be fooled."

It was really hard to keep herself from smashing the boxes of screws to the floor.

"But maybe," Timmerman went on, tilting his head to one side, "if you was to be extra sweet . . ." He moved his hands across the counter toward hers. She jerked them away. "I might be able to arrange a special order for you."

All the men in the store were howling by now.

She didn't let herself cry until she was back in her room, the door locked. She sat on the floor and hugged her knees to her chest. Sometimes she was so lonesome, she feared she would dry up like a toad trapped in a child's bucket. Back in her early days at the Commercial Hotel, she'd had a friend named Agnes who comforted her when she was like this. Who knelt beside her, rubbed her hair, let her drink from her secret bottle of hooch while baby Penny slept in a dresser drawer. In the summer of 1908, Agnes had wrapped her arms around Barbara and said, "Honey, a gal as pretty as you can play a man like a bugle. Make them dance to your tune. You need to learn to play them so they can't play you." A year later Agnes had married and gone away.

Barbara rested her throbbing forehead on her knees. From where she was sitting, she could look under the bed and see the cigar boxes full of money. If she was smart, she'd take it all and run before the girls came home and discovered the bicycle. But right now the thought of how she had earned that money made her half sick. She was so tired that her bones ached. Once she thought she could follow Agnes's advice, play men and be their master, but she couldn't do it anymore. She was all played out.

That night when she lay in his arms, Barbara thought that surely he must tell her they had to stop it now, before his girls came home. She waited for him to lay it out in the open. But he said nothing.

In the morning when she came down to the kitchen, she expected to find an envelope of money and a note of dismissal. A man like him would prefer a note to a messy confrontation. She steeled herself in expectation of this. But there was no word from him just yet. She wished he would have some mercy and get it over with. He was stringing her along, prolonging the miserable suspense.

"It's awful what she's doing with Mr. Hamilton," Penny told Cora over breakfast. It was the morning after her mother's visit. Her skin chafed and gave off an agonizing heat. Although she wore her loosest cotton dress, the weight of the fabric on her burnt skin was almost unbearable.

"Sleeping with him, you mean? Maybe she really cares for him."

"But he's her boss. And he's married."

"These things rarely follow logic, Penny. The head and the heart are two different things."

"He gives her money for it." Penny's voice came out in a strangled whisper.

But even this failed to shock Cora. "It doesn't sound like your mother had an easy life."

So now Cora was taking her mother's side. Penny let out a tense breath. "I don't even know who my father is."

Cora regarded her calmly. "Did you ever ask?"

"Once or twice. She got mad and told me it was none of my business."

"Maybe she has a good reason for not telling you." Cora paused. "At first I couldn't believe it when she said she was your mother. She's so young and pretty."

"She had me when she was fifteen."

"The poor girl." For a moment it looked as if Cora was going to cry. "Think about it. What kind of person would take advantage of such a young girl?"

Penny's sunburn seemed to eat all the way inside her. She felt like clawing off her skin. Had her father been someone her mother worked for? Someone like Mr. H., except even older? Someone ugly and cruel?

"She's so pretty," Cora said again. "You know, she got all dressed up to come out and see you. She was wearing a yellow-green dress. Usually that color wouldn't suit a person with her complexion, but your mother would look good in anything."

"Not like me, you mean." Penny twisted in her chair. "I don't look anything like her, do I?" She wondered if she took after her unspeakable, unnamable father.

"Sometimes it's not easy being a mother." Cora looked over at Phoebe, curled in her basket. The baby had been screaming with belly pains, but now she was finally resting. Cora's eyes were shadowed and bruised-looking from her sleepless night. "One day Phoebe will want to know about her father. And I won't know what to tell her."

Penny couldn't think of anything to say.

"What bothers you most?" Cora asked. "The thing about your father? Well, trust me — it wasn't her fault. She was just a kid — your age. You can't blame her for wanting to forget someone who used her like that." She took a sip of coffee. "Or is it that she's having an affair? Do you think sex itself is something shameful?"

Penny couldn't look at her. For a moment she couldn't think. Cora had said the word *sex* so calmly, as if it were something as

125

harmless as the weather report. "Sex." Penny managed to say the word aloud herself. She rubbed her burning arms. "What's it like?" She couldn't imagine Cora doing it with that man she had abandoned and threatened to shoot. Couldn't imagine Cora lying naked with him in an unmade bed, their legs tangled in the sheets. But Phoebe had come from somewhere. And if Cora thought she knew all about sex, then what was she doing here on this farm, alone with a baby and dressed in men's overalls?

"I want to be honest with you." The emotion drained from Cora's voice. "Most people aren't honest about sex. They can't even talk about it. But I'm a nurse and I . . . I suppose I should tell you that when you're in love with someone, it's the most beautiful thing there is. But I can't honestly say that. Not from my own experience." She lowered her eyes. "Well, I hope it's beautiful for some people.

"Before I got married, I used to think that it was the most primal thing, that it would completely transfix me and turn me into some kind of heroine." She looked away from Penny. "He said that if I married him, I could be a free spirit. I traveled with him and my brother to Greece and then to Sicily, where we were married." She paused, pushing her hair away from her face. "It was the winter after the war ended. I remember it as a winter of oranges. In the Mediterranean, they have orange trees lining the public streets."

Penny had never seen an orange tree, but it sounded so lovely.

"I always wondered what it would be like," Cora continued, "to pick one of those oranges off the tree and taste it. I thought it would taste different than an ordinary orange bought in the market. He . . . he told me that on our honeymoon he would pick me one of those oranges himself and feed it to me by hand." She rubbed her face, hiding her eyes. "But when he did and I finally got to taste it, it was bitter. A bitter orange." She met Penny's eyes. "There are bitter oranges and sweet oranges. Bitter oranges are for making marmalade and liqueur but not for eating on their own. I wanted to spit it out."

Penny held her glass of cold milk against her arm, letting it cool her burning skin. She couldn't think of anything to say. The words *free spirit* and *bitter orange* flitted through her head.

"Sometimes I like to imagine what it would be like with somebody who wasn't him." Cora's voice was distant.

Penny thought of Antonio, the way he and Cora had looked at each other. "What about love?" she asked suddenly.

"Love?" Cora laughed. "Don't believe any of that romantic gibberish you see in the picture shows. I only found out what real love is when I became a mother." Penny watched the color rise to her face at this admission.

The night before the Hamilton girls' homecoming, Barbara lay naked, the weight of Mr. H.'s body grinding her into the mattress. The noise of the creaking springs filled the silent empty house. Swallowing her own sweat, she thought she was drowning. Someone had taken her by the shoulders and dunked her under the surface of a lake. She fought for air. Then her skin fevered as she grew pliant and liquid in his arms. Over the course of the long summer, he had turned into a lover. A good lover who knew just what to do to render her aching and limp. She let him push her over the edge until she cried out his name. Biting his hand, she tasted his salty flesh. Cold tears spilled over her cheeks as she thrashed in his embrace. He held her down, pinned into place, and traced the wet marks her tears had left.

"Barbara." Unlike anyone else in Minerva, he distinctly pronounced all three syllables of her name. Bar-bar-a. He made her name sound lovely, like water flowing over rocks. He was from out east — someplace in New Hampshire that she couldn't even begin to picture — so he talked differently from everyone else in town, his speech completely devoid of the flat nasal drone of the Minervans. Before, she'd taken his way of talking for granted. But now she couldn't shut it out. His voice sounded noble and pure. She hated him for making her love his voice.

"Barbara, don't cry like that," he pleaded, cupping her face in his unsteady hands.

13

THE NEXT MORNING Barbara woke up early, but not early enough to catch him before he slipped from her bed. On her dresser she found a ten-dollar bill, neatly folded in half. After a breakfast of black coffee and dry toast, she went to work. She opened the windows in the Hamilton girls' rooms to let in fresh air. She swept and dusted, got linens from the cupboard to make up their beds, which had lain bare all summer. Housekeeping wasn't only a matter of sweeping the dust out of the way but also getting the little details right. She went out to the flowerbed to cut zinnias and asters to put in the crystal vases on their bedside tables. She dug Ina's and Isobel's dolls and teddy bears out of the closet and arranged them on their beds. She fluffed their pillows.

He had left a note for her in the kitchen, asking her to prepare a roast beef dinner and also angel cake and pink lemonade — the girls' favorite foods. She baked an angel food cake so light it would float off the fork. In the gloomy dining room with its blood-colored curtains, she laid the table with the lace cloth and the Sunday china. The room, she thought, was crying out for flowers.

Taking the kitchen shears, she went out to cut the dark red roses Mrs. Hamilton had planted the first year of her marriage. Her husband took good care of them, making sure they were pruned once a year. Three times during the growing season, a gardener came with a load of horse manure, the best rose food there was. The dark roses grew in lush profusion, rising taller than Barbara, the fist-sized blooms arching over her head. Their intoxicating fragrance mocked her and their thorns cut into her calf.

. . .

That evening when Mr. H. brought the girls home from the station, Barbara went to the door to greet them. Ina and Isobel were in high spirits, tugging on their father's arms and competing for his attention. "I rode more ponies than *she* did," Ina said, jumping up and down. "And Irene hardly rode at all. She didn't even *like* the ponies."

Irene stood apart, hunched behind the row of leather suitcases. Her sisters were tanned from their summer in Wyoming, their blond hair bleached nearly white from the sun. But Irene was pale as mushrooms that grow in the dark. She had always been a plump girl, well developed for her age, yet now she was thin and hollow-cheeked. As Barbara began to wonder if she had been sick, Irene caught her eye and gave her a blistering look that made the blood rush to her face. Barbara fled to the kitchen and waited for her hands to stop trembling. Irene had given her the same look Penny used to give her.

While the Hamiltons ate their roast beef dinner, Barbara sat in the kitchen and darned Mr. H.'s argyle socks. Drawing her cardigan tight, she braced herself against the chill of the first cool night that marked the end of summer. Mr. H. had lit a fire in the dining room hearth. From the kitchen, Barbara could hear the crackle of the flames eating the logs. She could follow snatches of their conversation. Irene's voice was particularly loud.

"Where's Penny?"

"She's gone to work for the Maagdenbergh woman," her father replied before addressing Ina. "Tell me about your favorite horse at camp."

"Ponies!" Ina cried. "I rode *ponies*."

"You had to ride ponies, because you're little," Isobel said haughtily. "I got to ride real horses."

"Father, I don't believe you!" Irene's voice was challenging and shrill. "Why would Penny do that? Even she isn't stupid enough to do something like that."

"Irene," her father said sharply, "please lower your voice."

. . .

After her first solitary night in weeks, Barbara woke up to cook the Hamilton family's favorite breakfast of oatmeal, bacon, eggs, and sausage. When she carried the tray into the dining room, Mr. H. glanced up at her, his face reddening when she set his plate in front of him. "Thank you," he said before looking away and resuming his conversation with his daughters.

Her own breakfast went untouched. The walls of her stomach were so raw, she couldn't imagine getting so much as a glass of water past her lips. As she went to the dining room to collect the dirty dishes, Mr. H. was telling jokes to Ina and Isobel. Barbara heard their giggles but couldn't concentrate on the words. Irene had already left the table.

Barbara had started scouring the burnt oatmeal at the bottom of the saucepan when a scream ripped the morning apart. The door of the garden shed slammed. Methodically Barbara continued scouring the pot with steel wool while Irene charged in through the back door and began railing at her father. "My bike! Someone wrecked my bike." Barbara heard drawn-out weeping. It was then she remembered that the English bicycle had once belonged to Irene's mother. Her shoulders went rigid as she listened to their approaching footsteps. They came right up to the sink, where she was up to her elbows in dirty water, the dish soap stinging the scratches on her arms. Irene's face was white, pinched, and teary. Her father's was tight with anger.

"Mrs. Niebeck, do you have any knowledge of what might have happened to my daughter's bicycle?"

Barbara struggled not to flinch as Irene threw her a look of pure hate. When she tried to speak, she found she couldn't. Nothing she said or did now would make any difference.

"Do you have anything to *say* about this, Mrs. Niebeck?"

Mrs. Niebeck! She wanted to spit in his face. Instead she grabbed the dishtowel and dried her hands. Then she looked right into his eyes. "I borrowed it to visit my daughter last Sunday."

"You *borrowed* Irene's bicycle?" His voice was incredulous. "You thought you could just borrow it without saying anything?"

Barbara yanked off her apron, folded it briskly in half, and laid it over the back of a chair. "I'm leaving." She stepped out of the kitchen and climbed the back stairs. Through the pounding in her head, she heard him coming after her, heard him yell at his daughter to stay back. Closing her bedroom door against the noise, she dragged her suitcase out from under the bed and started hurling her underwear and stockings into it.

He entered without knocking. "What do you think you were doing? Irene's bicycle?"

"There's money under the bed," she told him. "Take that and buy her a new one." Turning her back to him, she opened the closet and pulled out her four dresses. She took her statue of Saint Barbara from its hiding place.

"Look at me!" He tried to grab her arm, but she slapped his hand away. "How could you do that to my daughter?"

"Well, what about *my* daughter?" She swung to face him and raised her voice to a pitch that made the color drain from his face. "I have a daughter, too!" Snapping her suitcase shut, she dragged it to the door.

"Barbara!" He stepped between her and the door. When he laid his hands on her shoulders, she dropped the suitcase, which hit the bare floor with a bang. She beat her fists against his chest.

"Because of you, I lost my daughter." Before she could fight her way out the door, he pulled her against him, kissed her forehead. He held her as she sobbed and cursed him. He told her he was sorry, begged her not to leave.

In the kitchen below, Irene trod up and down, her footsteps ringing through the house.

14

PENNY WAS DEEP in the woodlot, her hands stained purple-black, sweet and slick with juice. She sucked her fingers, then picked more blackberries to fill the pail. Late afternoon in September, Cora had gone into town. Beneath the veil of mosquito netting, Phoebe dozed in her buggy, lulled by the rasping cottonwood leaves. White tufts of cottonwood fluff and milkweed drifted like snow in the slanting sunlight. The leaves were starting to turn, the wild grapevine twisting up the trunk of a dead oak like trembling blood-red hands. Going down a shallow ravine where the berries grew thick, Penny ate another handful, darkening her mouth. Then she started at the sound of tires tearing up the yard. It seemed curious that Cora was back so early. And since when did she drive so carelessly?

She pricked her ears to male voices. Their hooting and catcalls carried all the way into the trees that hid her. Rude, awful words, the kind that only roughnecks say to girls. *Pen-ny, oh Pen-ny!* They called out her name in menacing singsong. The geese were making a mighty racket. They could have driven off one person, but not a whole gang of boys. She wondered why Cora didn't have a big mean dog instead — some powerful mutt who would go straight for the throat. What good were a bunch of geese?

They kept singing out her name, their voices louder and louder. The woodlot echoed with the noise of snapping branches, big-booted feet smacking the ground. So this was it, what Mr. Renfew had warned her about. Why girls and women weren't supposed to live on remote farms without a man to protect them. At the bottom of the ravine, she crouched against the damp earth.

Although she summoned all her will, she could not stop shaking. If they found her, they would rape her just like that Stadler girl. Throw a filthy blanket over her head and rough her up, one of them after the other, until she was too brutalized and ashamed to hold up her head in public again. How could she keep Phoebe safe? She began to sob uncontrollably.

She could already imagine people in town yakking about her sorry fate. "Well, it's a pity, but what was that girl thinking of when she went out to live on that farm?" Pictures flitted through her head of the rifle in Cora's pickup, of Cora's work boots and trousered legs. Then she considered her own flimsy skirt, ankle socks, and bare knees pressed against last year's dead leaves. If she could, she would have hacked off her braid then and there, turned herself into a hard-bodied, loudmouthed, big-fisted boy whom no one would dare to meddle with.

Phoebe began to cry, her thin wail echoing through the woodlot.

"Hey," a voice said. "Did you hear that?"

"Hear what?"

The footsteps grew louder.

No. Without rising from her cowering huddle, Penny grabbed the buggy frame and rocked it. *Please be quiet, please.* Her sweaty palm could barely hold on, but she managed to keep rocking until Phoebe's cries tapered off.

She lost all sense of time. The boys' voices echoed louder, softer, louder again. She could no longer decide where they were, if they were coming closer or heading away. Jagged laughter rang out, a drunken howl. The back door of the house kept slamming. The noise of something being shattered sent a shudder up her spine.

Stiff and cold, she lay on her stomach. When she arched her neck, she could see the black sky and sharp sickle moon that shone starkly through a break in the leaves. Night sounds drowned out whatever was happening in the house and yard. Raccoons crashed through the bushes. Mosquitoes whined, their bites covering her skin like a rash. Twigs and dead leaves glued themselves to her bare shins. When Phoebe screamed in hunger, Penny eased her hand into the buggy and tried to soothe her by letting her suck on her berry-stained finger. Footsteps tore through the woodlot. A hoarse voice called out her name. Frozen to the earth, her legs were useless, all pins and needles. Phoebe spat Penny's finger from her mouth and howled.

Someone came stumbling down the ravine with a kerosene lantern. "Oh, my God."

Before Penny could say anything, Cora set down her lantern and rifle, then picked her up off the ground and hugged her so hard that Penny gasped. Cora was in tears.

"I saw the mess they made in the house, then I couldn't find you."

Penny clung to her, too shaken to speak. Cora touched her face, then let go of her and reached into the buggy for Phoebe.

"Are they gone now?" Penny found her voice again. "Are they gone?" Somehow or other, she found the words to tell Cora what happened.

They had made a mess of the kitchen, throwing crocks of flour and sugar to the floor, breaking dishes and jam pots. In the parlor, all the books had been knocked down from the shelves, one lamp broken. They'd ripped into the mattresses upstairs, looking for hidden money. They had pissed on Cora's bed. While Penny and Cora cleaned up the mess, Penny kept thinking it could have been worse. There could have been something else that lay broken on the floor if she and Phoebe hadn't been in the woodlot when they came. She helped drag the ruined mattress outside. Then they carried the mattress in the hired man's old room up to Cora's bedroom.

Penny discovered the phone was still in order. "Let's call the police."

Cora took the mouthpiece from her and placed it back on the hook. "I don't want the law out here."

"But Cora . . ."

"Penny, listen." There was an edge of pleading to her voice. "My husband's brother is a district court judge. If the authorities came out here, they might make more trouble for us than the Nelson brothers." She rubbed her face, then looked at Penny wearily. "The law hasn't been able to do anything about the Nelson brothers anyway. The bastards always find an alibi, don't they? Trust me on this. I can protect us better than the sheriff."

While Cora made up the bed with fresh sheets, Penny cooked supper. But she couldn't eat any of it.

"They came by once before," Cora said. "I thought I'd frightened them off for good. I swear, if they ever come back, that will be the last time."

A tremor of fear passed through Penny when she saw the firmness in Cora's jaw. She meant it. If she had to, she would really shoot the Nelson brothers dead. Penny stared at her plate of baked beans and mulled over the story of how Cora had nearly gunned down her husband in this very kitchen. Her rifle was still propped in the corner. She observed Cora's hands, imagined her finger pulling the trigger. The thought jarred her so much, she pushed her plate away and hauled herself out of her chair.

"What is it, Penny?" Cora got up and followed her. "You're still shaking." She took both of Penny's hands. "You're scared, aren't you? Listen to me, honey. Scared is the worst thing you can be."

Penny looked straight into Cora's eyes, green and clear as glass.

"If you're scared, that means you let them win. Get good and mad, for God's sake. Say a few swear words."

All Penny could manage was a feeble *shit*. Cora went to check the bolt on the door. "It's dark now, but tomorrow morning, bright and early, I'm taking you behind the barn and teaching you to shoot that rifle."

. . .

They stood ankle deep in the grass. On the other side of the barbed-wire fence, the cow lolled on her side and flicked away flies. Chickens scratched in the weeds. Phoebe babbled in her buggy a few feet behind them. Twenty feet in front of them was the old hitching post on which Cora had nailed a rusty coffee can.

"That's your target. And this is the rifle. First you should learn how to load it. Like this." Penny watched her feed bullet cartridges into the chamber. "Later I'll teach you how to clean and oil it, but now I want you to practice firing it. You have to hold the barrel at the right level." She demonstrated, the rifle butt against her shoulder, her hand holding the barrel steady. "Not too high, unless you're duck hunting, and not too low — you don't want to shoot your own foot. When you take aim, you look down the barrel. Now, this is the lever." She pointed to the long, flat oval lever behind the trigger. "You have to cock the lever downward and back up again between every shot. The lever releases the spent cartridge and chambers the new cartridge. Do you see, Penny? All right, now I've cocked the lever, and you can pull the trigger and fire at the target."

When Cora handed her the rifle, Penny's arms trembled under its weight. Stories raced through her head of deer hunters accidentally blowing their faces off. She recalled Mr. H.'s seldom-used rifle, which he kept locked in a glass cabinet in his study. He forbade his daughters to go anywhere near it. "Guns can go off, just like that," he had warned them. Besides, she thought, anyone seeing her with the rifle would notice how scared she was. They would grab it away and turn it against her.

"What's the matter?" Cora asked her.

"I can't."

When she tried to give the gun back, Cora refused to take it. "Supposing those louts come back. What are you going to do?" Impatience crept into her voice. For an instant, Penny thought she sounded exactly like her mother. "Hide on your belly at the bottom of the woodlot? This is how you hold it. The barrel should be this high. Brace the butt against your shoulder." She positioned

Penny's limp and unwilling hands. "Come on, you're no sissy. I've seen you go after chickens with a hatchet. You don't even flinch. Why are you so afraid of the rifle?"

The Winchester was alien, so metallic and hard. It felt wrong for her to even touch it. When she tried to explain that, Cora placed her hand on Penny's shoulder — a firm and steadying grip.

"Maybe you heard all kinds of stories about how girls aren't supposed to shoot guns. Penny, that's a load of bunk. My parents used to take me hunting. My mother taught me how to shoot. I swear she was a better shot than my father."

Penny thought of the photograph of the woman in dungarees posing in triumph over the wildcat she had brought down. She could not possibly imagine herself doing such a thing. "It's so heavy." She wielded her last excuse like a butter knife.

"You'll get used to it." Stepping behind her, Cora placed one hand on Penny's under the barrel, helping her support the weight. With her other hand, she reached around, her finger steadying Penny's on the trigger. "When we pull the trigger," she said, her voice in Penny's ear, "you'll feel the recoil. The rifle will push back against you. That can give you a fright if you aren't prepared. If you don't know how to brace yourself, it can throw you back a couple feet or even knock you over. But I'm right here behind you. We'll brace together." It didn't matter anymore that her hands were shaking and sweating. Cora held them in place.

"That coffee can is about the height of a man's chest. This is just for practice. I don't want you to aim to kill unless it's your last resort. But it's a powerful thing, knowing you could do it if you had to. Because once you know how, your opponent will see it in your eyes. Usually that's enough to make him back off. If you shoot over his head, then he'll hightail it. Now squeeze the trigger as gently as you can. If you pull too hard, the rifle will jerk and you'll lose control of your aim. You don't want that."

Before Penny could protest, Cora's hand helped her aim for the coffee can and her finger pressed Penny's on the trigger, pulling it back. The crack of the bullet's report exploded inside her

head. The recoil threw her back against Cora, who kept her upright and held her hands in place. The cow bolted to the other side
of the pasture. Phoebe shrieked. But for the first time, Cora ignored her cries.

"Look, Penny! Look at that hole you shot through the coffee can."

Only then did she see how the morning sky glimmered
through the bullet hole.

"Let's try it again. Brace yourself for the next shot. Bend your
knees a little. Remember, you won't always have me behind you.
Cock the lever like I showed you."

Penny moved the lever down and back up again, listening to
the click of the new cartridge settling into place.

"Good. Now stand steady and pull gently."

This time Penny braced, anticipating the hard push against
her shoulder and the ache that followed. She tried to close her
ears to the deafening racket. She cocked and squeezed the trigger
again, another bullet ripping through the coffee can. Phoebe's
cries were lost as they fired over and over. Cora's hands steadied
hers and corrected her aim until Penny couldn't say anymore who
was shooting. Then, without a word, Cora stepped away, leaving
her to hold the rifle's full weight. Bracing herself, knees supple,
Penny looked down the barrel at her target and fired. As the bullet
tore another hole in the coffee can, a blinding sense of elation
pierced her.

Cora picked up Phoebe. Penny thought she would take the
baby back to the house, but she stayed and watched. When Penny
missed the coffee can, Cora told her to sight her target again and
aim steady. Cora watched her progress until Phoebe got used to
the loud bangs and stopped crying.

Penny's arms ached and her shoulder felt bruised, but she
went on cocking the lever, squeezing the trigger. When she ran
out of bullets, Cora showed her how to reload. Prizing the old coffee can off the post, she nailed up a new one. As Penny started firing again, something new took possession of her. She contemplated

the force that had driven her mother's hand when she slapped her, how she had let her mother hit her without raising her hands to ward off the blow. Now the force behind her mother's hand was moving through her. She would never be defenseless again, never just stand there and take it. She kept firing until she ran out of the second round of bullets. When Cora finally took the rifle away, she looked at Penny in a way she never had before. A few seconds passed before Penny recognized the awe in her gaze.

"Well, well," said Cora. "You nearly had me fooled into thinking you were a timid little mouse. But look at how fast you got the hang of that. You're a natural, Penny. You have a natural talent for this."

A natural talent. The words engraved themselves in Penny's head. Every morning they practiced. Cora set more difficult targets, having Penny aim at an old tire that hung from a tree and swung in the wind. She made her shoot from farther away. She had her fire from a crouch, then from a kneeling position. The tender spot on Penny's right shoulder grew tough. Together they practiced until Penny was nearly as good a shot as Cora. As she read *The Odyssey*, she kept reminding herself that Athena was a warrior goddess, armed and ready to strike.

"When I fire and hit a target, it feels so good," she confessed after rifle practice one morning. Though she had never touched liquor, Penny imagined that the singing pleasure that rushed through her when she was shooting must be as intoxicating as wine. "Does that mean I'm crazy?" She said this jokingly, catching Cora's eye with a grin.

Cora didn't return her smile. "As long as you don't go around shooting people for the sake of it. Remember that these lessons are only for defending yourself."

Penny nodded, about to change the subject.

"Don't ever get tripped up by blood lust," Cora went on. There was something alien in her voice.

"Blood lust?" The expression made Penny laugh.

Cora remained sober. "It's just like any other kind of lust except it's hate that's behind it. Be careful what you hate. Especially now that you know how to shoot a rifle." She paused for breath. "What you hate will become your master as much as what you love."

Penny felt a blow. She considered the way she resented her mother and what she was doing with Mr. H. She told herself she didn't actually *hate* her. Hate was far too strong. She thought about her eleventh birthday, when her mother had taken her to the pictures to see Charlie Chaplin, squeezing her hand as they laughed together.

"Once I was too soft," Cora was saying. "I hated myself for being so weak. Each time he hit me, I felt like I . . . I hated myself even more. He fed off that. He . . ." Cora stopped short. A strand of hair had blown into her mouth, and she drew it out. When the wind blew, her hair was long enough to get into her eyes. It covered her ears and neck. "But then, when I was pregnant for the second time, I started hating him instead. I made a promise to myself that I would never let him touch me again. I hope you never feel as much hate in all your life as I did when he showed up at the farm that night."

"Is it true you almost shot him?" Penny searched Cora's eyes, but they slipped right past her. "That's what people in town say."

Cora pressed her lips together. "I hope you don't go around spreading rumors about me the way that hired man did."

Penny let out a breath. "I'd never say anything behind your back. I don't even *talk* to anyone." She looked away, miserably aware that she had just confessed to Cora that she had no friends apart from her.

"At least that rumor is true." Cora's voice was emotionless. "I came so close to killing him. But just imagine if I had. Would I be free of him then?"

Penny shrugged in confusion. "Well, he'd be dead, wouldn't he?"

"And I'd be in jail."

"Even if you shot him to defend yourself?" Penny's forehead began to throb.

"Maybe the jury would've had some sympathy for me. But then again, maybe not. Certain judges like to make examples of women like me. I have no evidence that he hit me. It would have been my husband's reputation against my word. He's a chief surgeon." Cora shoved her hair out of her face. "It wouldn't be like taking a shot at one of those scruffy boys. I'd have his family coming after me. His brother's a judge. They would want justice. Or their idea of it. And what would happen to Phoebe if I was in jail?"

"But what if he comes back?" When Penny saw Cora shrink and turn away, she regretted the question.

"When it comes to protecting Phoebe, I'll take any consequences." She raked her hair, pulling it back tightly, stretching the skin on her forehead. "If it comes down to that, I would really kill. But that's not hate anymore." She smiled brokenly. "That's love for my daughter."

"If he's ever stupid enough to come back, he'll have both of us to worry about." Penny touched her arm. "I'd never let anyone hurt you or Phoebe."

Cora pulled away from her. "Don't talk like that. He's my burden, not yours. I don't want you thinking those kinds of thoughts."

That night after supper, Penny sat in the rocking chair with Phoebe while Cora took a bath upstairs. Penny heard the faint splashing of water, then the sound of the water draining away and Cora padding back to her room.

"Look how strong you are," Penny whispered, holding out her forefinger to Phoebe, who grasped it in her fist. She looked into the baby's eyes and made faces until she smiled.

"Penny! Could you come up here, please?"

Penny swept up the baby and climbed the stairs.

Wrapped in her grandfather's old dressing gown, Cora sat in

141

front of the wardrobe mirror. She had combed the tangles out of her wet hair. Before Penny could say anything, she handed her the kitchen shears. From the shine on the blades, Penny could tell they had been sharpened that day.

"Could you cut my hair?" She took the baby and held her in her lap. "When I do it myself, it looks crooked."

Penny looked at the shears and then at Cora's face in the mirror. She looked so tired, so pale. "But why do you want to cut it? It looks nicer when it's a little longer. You have such pretty hair."

"Just cut it, Penny." Cora swallowed, then looked up at her. Her face softened. "Please."

So Penny reluctantly snipped at her chestnut locks, already starting to curl even though Cora had combed them out straight. She tried to cut as little as she could get away with.

"Shorter," Cora kept saying. "I want to get it off my neck and out of my eyes."

But that wasn't the real reason. A voice spoke inside Penny, as clear as the moonlight that shone through the opening in the curtains. Cora was afraid. Afraid that if she let her hair grow back, those hooligans would lose their fear of her. She was scared that if her hair got too long, it would make her vulnerable again, no different from any other woman. Penny kept cutting until Cora seemed satisfied. Though her hair wasn't quite as severely short as when Penny had first met her, she couldn't help noticing how exposed Cora's brow and cheekbones were. The tendons in her neck. And her face seemed new again, as naked as if she had just shed her skin.

One Saturday in September, they drove to Sandborn. "It's good for you," Cora said, "to see that there are other places in the world besides Minerva." She parked on Sandborn Main Street, which was twice as long as Main Street in Minerva. When Penny got out of the pickup and looked around, she swore that the buildings here were twice as high as anything she had seen before. There were more shops than she could count, at least four different banks, even restaurants and cafés. There was an opera house with Greek pillars and a fountain in which children tossed pennies. She couldn't resist peering into every shop window to ogle the things that weren't available in Minerva. The mannequins in Littleton's Apparel were dressed in scandalously short skirts that rose above the knee and bared the thigh. No one in Minerva would dare to wear something like that.

One store window was full of phonograph records. The tune "Charleston" blared out the open door. "Listen!" she called out to Cora. "That's that song they all talk about." She had read about the dance craze in the Chicago paper. The music made her want to sashay down the street. She could almost imagine she was in a big city where people danced all night. Then she moved on to a shop that sold radios. "Why don't we get one?" she asked breathlessly. It would be like bringing the city dance halls right into their house. "We could listen to music all day long." Washing diapers wouldn't be so bad if there was jazz in the background. The Hamiltons had a radio. Sometimes she used to listen to the serials and soap operas. Suddenly her time at the Hamiltons seemed so long ago. When she tried to remember certain things, like the wallpaper pattern in the back bedroom where she and her mother had slept, her memory grew fuzzy.

"Too much racket," Cora said. "Why do you want to spend your time listening to a box?" Then she looked thoughtful. "I think there might be an old gramophone somewhere in the attic. I can get it down if you like."

Penny had already moved on to the next shop window, belonging to E. J. Duvall, Fine Photographer. On display was an arrangement of his work: wedding portraits, high school graduation pictures, family reunion photographs. But what caught her eye were the baby pictures. "Cora!" She grabbed her sleeve and pointed. "Don't you want some pictures of Phoebe?"

"I suppose I might. This place looks too pricey, though. I'm surprised at these gewgaws on display. Small towns didn't used to be like this."

It was shocking to hear Cora refer to Sandborn as a small town. It had fifteen thousand people, five times as many as Minerva.

"My grandfather got to be well-off because he worked hard and never parted with a penny unless he had good reason. Now it seems they just want everybody to spend, spend, spend."

"Why are you so stingy about baby pictures?" Penny rolled her eyes.

On a street corner, a man played an accordion and sang in a language she couldn't understand. Cora gave him a dime. "French Canadian," she whispered to Penny.

Penny didn't see a soul she recognized. For the first time, she was among strangers who knew nothing about her or Cora. To them, we could be any two people, she thought, savoring the novelty of anonymity. Some of the boys eyed her legs in the brand-new silk stockings, but nobody gave her any funny looks. The most extraordinary thing was that no one gave Cora a second glance. Her hair had just been cut, and she had grown lean and muscled since Phoebe's birth. Since the weather was getting cooler, she wore a loose Chesterfield jacket over her freshly ironed white shirt. They must be worldly here, Penny decided. The sight of a woman in trousers seemed nothing out of the ordinary to them.

After strolling around the lake that skirted the center of town, they stopped in a corner shop to buy a bag of peanuts and two bottles of pop to tide them over on the way home. Penny took Phoebe when Cora went to the counter to pay. An old farmer asked Cora a few questions, which she answered cheerfully while waiting for the shopkeeper to bring her change. Balancing Phoebe in one arm, Penny leafed through the ladies' magazines and carefully memorized the pictures of the new bob hairstyles. Maybe one of these days she would pluck up the nerve to ask Cora to chop off her braid. She wouldn't want her hair as short as Cora's, just something fresh and sophisticated. And it would sure make washing it a lot simpler.

The old farmer ambled in her direction. "Say, that's a sweet baby you got there."

"She's our little sunshine, all right." She gazed proudly at Phoebe, who smiled for the old man.

"Penny, are you ready?"

Since Penny was carrying the baby, Cora held the door for her on their way out. Penny smiled back over her shoulder to the old farmer. When they were out on the sidewalk, she heard him talking to the shopkeeper. "That one looks awfully young to be a mother." At first she wondered what he was talking about. Cora was twenty-five. Then she stood reeling, hugging the baby for comfort.

"Penny!" Cora called out. She was already in the pickup. "Are you coming?"

He thought *she* was Phoebe's mother. That meant he probably thought that Cora was her husband. When Penny got into the pickup, she was too embarrassed to glance in her direction. Cora could pass, truly pass, as a man. That was why no one in Sandborn had looked at her peculiarly. She had everyone fooled. She was a shape-shifter, just like the selkie creature she once told her about. She could change herself from a woman to a man and back again.

"Are you all right?" Cora asked.

"I'm fine," she whispered.

"If you say so."

When Cora started driving down Sandborn Main Street, Penny looked out the fly-spattered windshield at the people who didn't know them. Something came loose inside her when she concluded those strangers would take one look at them and assume that she, Cora, and Phoebe were a family.

15

In the orchard, apples hung so heavy on the trees, they dragged the branches earthward. Setting Phoebe in the hammock, Penny plucked one. Heavy and fragrant, it was red with a tinge of green still on it. Holding it up to the light, she examined it for blemishes and wormholes, but the fruit was perfect. Her teeth pierced the skin, sinking into the tart white flesh, that winy crispness. She took one bite after the other until nothing but the core remained. Tossing it into the long grass, she imagined another tree growing from its seeds. Even with their load of fruit, the trees swayed in the wind like dancers.

Tomorrow they would pick the apples. Cora already had the wooden crates lined up on the porch. They would go up on ladders and try to get every last fruit, wrap each apple in newspaper, then tuck them in crates to store in the cellar. But today was Sunday and Cora had told her to wait in the orchard because she had a surprise. Nestling with Phoebe in the hammock, Penny turned her face to the sun. The almanac said this was supposed to be the last warm Sunday of the year.

She wondered what this surprise could be. Her birthday wasn't till January, and Christmas was still a long way off. Lying back in the hammock, she lifted Phoebe in the air above her and stared into her eyes. What color would they be when the baby blue faded? Green like Cora's? Or would she have her father's eyes? The wind-tossed branches blocked the sun for a moment, throwing a shadow over them both. What stamp had her father left on Phoebe? Even if she never met her father, he had helped make her — she contained his nature along with her mother's. Penny felt a dull ache when she considered her own unknown father. What was her secret inheritance from him?

With a bang of the screen door, she heard Cora coming out of the house. Lowering Phoebe to her chest, Penny pulled herself upright and sat on the edge of the hammock. Cora was whistling to herself, walking quickly with her long stride. Hanging on a strap around her neck was a Kodak camera.

"That's one of those new ones!" Penny had seen the small, handheld cameras advertised in the *Chicago Tribune*. "Where did you buy it?"

Cora ducked her eyes. "I brought it with me from Evanston."

"You had it all along! Why didn't you bring it out before?"

"I had to get film for it, didn't I? And I told you it would be a surprise. Now sit up straight. Knees together, shoulders back, chin up. Hold Phoebe so I can see her face."

Penny complied, too excited to ask any more questions. She'd never had her picture taken before, ever. Not even for her first communion. Her mother had never seemed to think about those things.

"Good!" Cora shouted. "Now smile!" She made silly noises until Phoebe smiled, too. "Let's do another one. This time look at Phoebe instead of the camera. That's right," she said as Penny held the baby close and locked eyes with her. "Put on that Madonna look you're always giving her."

Penny laughed, but when she stared into Phoebe's eyes, she felt her face go tender.

"Another one. Now look at the camera again."

When Penny smiled, she felt giddy, the taste of the apple still sweet in her mouth. After Cora had taken a few more shots, Penny offered to take one of her and Phoebe. She was itching to get her hands on the camera, but Cora shook her head.

"What's the point of having a photograph of myself? I already know what I look like."

"Well, maybe I want a picture of you." Penny tried to keep the disappointment out of her voice.

Cora just laughed. "Well, then you're out of luck. I'm camera shy."

What about that photo album upstairs, Penny wanted to ask her. What would Cora say if she knew she had been leafing through those pictures, those images of her with flowing hair, posing in those silky dresses? Cocking her head at Cora, she tried to imagine what her photograph would look like if she took it right now, freezing her face into a flat black-and-white square. A laughing woman with her shirt open at the collar, her head thrown back to expose her slender throat. Maybe that was why she didn't want her picture taken — she was afraid the photograph would show that she was still the same person who had posed in all those portraits. The society girl, the young wife in the picture with the other half cut out. That even with her rifle and shorn hair, she was still the same frightened young woman who had run away.

"Why are you looking at me like that?"

Flustered, Penny lowered her eyes. "I just wonder why . . ." She paused to find the words. "Why did you bring that camera all the way from Evanston if you're so camera shy?" *Evanston.* She had actually dared to say the word to her face.

Abruptly Cora's laughter died. "I was half afraid that if my grandfather wouldn't take me in, I'd need something to pawn." The wind picked up, knocking a few apples off their branches. They hit the ground with muffled thuds. "I brought some jewelry, too. That I did pawn, over in Sandborn. But I thought the camera might be nice to keep." Her face was so exposed, it frightened Penny. She had to look away. Silence stretched between them, then the moment passed.

Cora reached out and took Phoebe, shifting the camera on its strap so Phoebe couldn't play with it. "We better get up early tomorrow if we want to pick those apples."

Penny nodded, grateful to hear her voice sound ordinary and assured again. "The windfalls, too. Those are good for making applesauce. Babies like applesauce, don't they?"

Cora smiled at her daughter. "Pretty soon, you're going to be eating from a spoon, honey. How 'bout that? Penny's gonna make applesauce for you." As she spoke, Penny imagined Phoebe growing up, bit by bit. Taking her first steps, learning to talk. Her eyes would turn their own color.

"Pretty soon," said Penny, "she'll learn how to talk back to us."

Cora laughed. "Don't even get started on that."

Penny leaned forward on the hammock, her feet balanced in the springy grass. "Let's go to the lake today." The urgency in her voice made Cora look up. "I heard it's supposed to get cold soon. This might be our last chance."

16

BARBARA STIRRED a huge pot of simmering tomato sauce. Neatly laid out on the kitchen table were freshly sterilized canning jars, lids, and rubber rings. Everything was clean and ordered until the flies came pouring through a hole in the screen door, more flies than she had ever seen, their furry legs twitching down her arms, her sweaty neck, the back of her knees. Their bodies tumbled into the tomato sauce, plumping up like raisins. Flies covered the canning jars and lids. It was so hot in that kitchen, everything seemed to warp and collide, the flies swarming around her too fast to swat away. She became aware of someone standing behind her, breathing down the back of her dress with hot, measured breaths. Locked in her terror, she couldn't move. Her tormentor stepped forward. She could not see its face, could not tell if it was male or female. The faceless thing took hold of the bubbling pot of tomato sauce and tipped it. Barbara fell writhing to the floor as the scalding red sauce rained over her.

In the darkness, Barbara awoke with a cry and clutched herself. Nearly every night that week, she'd had dreams that wrenched her awake, shivering and sobbing. The night before she had dreamt, for the first time in years, of her father. Her father chasing her with a shotgun, hunting her down like a deer.

Climbing out of bed, she groped her way to the window. She could have turned on the light, but she was afraid of catching her reflection in the mirror, afraid of how ghastly she must look. Pushing up the sash, she let in a stream of frosty September air that made her shiver even harder. At least the fresh air made it easier to breathe. Some nights she dreamt she was suffocating, an unbearable weight pressing down on her, forcing the air from her lungs. She inhaled deeply before feeling her way to the dresser. Opening the top drawer, she rooted around until her fingers located the half-empty pack of Lucky Strikes and the box of household matches. In the past weeks, she had taken up smoking; on nights like these, a cigarette was the only thing that could soothe her nerves and slow her racing heart. She felt her way to the chair by the window, struck a match, and lit up. Her bare feet found the chipped old teacup she used to catch the ashes. Taking a deep drag, she filled her lungs with smoke and breathed out. Gradually her hands stopped shaking. She calmed down enough to pay attention to the night noises. The roof creaked and settled. Swaying elm branches scraped against the windows while her skin goose-pimpled in the draft. People used to have a lot of superstitions about elm trees. Her mother had told her it was the coffinmaker's tree. Nonsense, she told herself, sucking hard on her cigarette. As her eyes adjusted to the gloom, she caught herself staring at her daughter's empty bed. Something throbbed behind her temples until she looked away.

Hazel Hamilton used to sing ballads. Out of nowhere, Barbara recalled a snatch of melody and the words that went with it. *What cannot be cured, love, must be endured, love.* She commanded herself to take stock of her situation. She still had her beauty. She had the money she had saved. She could move on, forget this place, start a new life somewhere else, the way she had planned all along. It wouldn't be that difficult to find another man. But right now she couldn't imagine another man. She had thought her heart was a dead thing, yet now it pounded inside her, giving her no peace. She had come so close to leaving after the fiasco with Irene's bicycle. Slipping out the door with the suitcase would have been an easy escape. Except that she had fallen in love with him, breaking her own rules.

And how could she ever abandon Penny? Even though the girl lived twenty-one miles down the road and never spoke to her anymore, she was still her mother, would never stop being her mother. She couldn't bear the thought of leaving her behind. She wanted to keep track of her at least. Know that she was happy and getting an education. What if Penny missed her and wanted to come home?

She needed to go back to bed and try to sleep. Every morning she was up at six to fire up the stove and make breakfast for Laurence and the girls. Midmorning, when the girls were at school, he came home from the pop factory and led her upstairs. The affair had not ended, after all, even now that his girls were back in the house.

Then, like a passage in one of her less frightening dreams, her door opened noiselessly. He slipped into the room with the silent grace of a ghost. No floorboard creaked beneath his feet — it was as if he were weightless. Stabbing out her cigarette, she set her makeshift ashtray on the floor and sat up straight in her chair. His face was in shadow, but the moonlight silvered his hands. His beautiful hands. Neither of them dared to even whisper at first. He knelt so that his face was level with hers. The moon illuminated the planes of his cheeks and forehead, the curve of his mouth. He leaned against her, his lips to her ear. "I heard you cry out. Did you have another nightmare?"

She took his face in her hands. When he kissed her and rocked her in his arms, she bathed in the warm illusion of being protected. His hands moved over her breasts and under her nightgown. Between her thighs. She closed her eyes and let herself dissolve. The more tense and on edge she was, the more extreme her pleasure when she allowed herself to succumb to it. She half feared she would knock herself off the chair and sob aloud. He stroked her until she was sodden, the thin fabric of her nightgown sticking to her thighs.

She struggled to find the words to tell him it was time to put an end to this. He, more than anyone, knew that. Unlike her, he had so much to lose. They both knew it had to stop, but neither of them could make it stop. She had learned not to look at him when his daughters were present for fear that even little Ina would be able to see the love in her eyes. *Love.* She scarcely believed its force as it seized her. That it had taken her thirty years and the loss of her only child before she finally came to experience a man's love.

She touched his erection, but he gently pushed her hand away, signaling that it was time for him to return to his room. After silently kissing her, he crept out the door. She rocked herself and wept, for it was the first time a man had given her pleasure without asking for anything in return. The memory of his hands bloomed on her skin as she made her way to bed. What price would she pay if she allowed herself to be romantic, surrendering to the force of their love? It was always the woman who had to pay. But he had come to give her comfort. She embraced the pillow as though it were him lying beside her. Something stronger than fear unfolded inside her as she fell at last into an untroubled sleep.

Two doors down the hall, Irene lay awake. She had not detected her father's footsteps, but she heard the elm branches knocking against the windows and outside walls. And she smelled the cigarette smoke, which moved through the house like poison gas. That treacherous smoke made her throat so tight and sore, she thought she would start to scream and never be able to stop.

17

IRENE FOLLOWED her father and sisters down the corridor of the Sandborn Nursing Home. Usually she walked beside him, her long legs falling into pace with his stride. But this time she dropped behind to observe her family as they made their way along the hallway like blinkered horses, not turning their heads to look into the rooms with the senile old people and the veterans in their wheelchairs. Her father wore his Sunday suit of Harris tweed and carried a bouquet of her mother's dark red roses. Ina and Isobel trotted after him. Normally those girls would have been pushing and chasing each other one minute, then giggling the next. But in the nursing home they behaved like obedient little wind-up dolls, their patent leather shoes echoing faintly as they trod the waxed tile floor. They didn't even hold their noses at the smell of urine, especially strong that day.

Like a dutiful soldier, Father led them down that stinking corridor to Mother's private and dearly paid-for room. Before he could reach the door, Irene shot out in front of him and threw him a quick look, just to see the forbearance in his eyes. His gaze slid past her as he shuffled into the room and put the roses into the water-filled vase the nurse set out for their visits. Hitching up his trouser legs, he sat on the stiff metal chair at Mother's bedside. With pinched smiles, her sisters assembled at the foot of the bed, about as close as they dared to come to Mother, who lay utterly still. Her eyes were open but unblinking, her face a rigid mask. She smelled of urine, talcum powder, and her favorite perfume, which the nurse sprayed on her before their visits.

Irene watched her father take her mother's unresponsive hand. She listened to him talk to her with rehearsed cheerfulness. "Hazel, your roses are still blooming. All the way into September. Not bad, eh? I'm getting Lars Lilja to prune them again. He did such a good job last year." Father's wedding ring glinted in the weak sunlight coming through the narrow window that looked out on the red brick asylum next door. At his prompting, Ina and Isobel told their mother about their week in school. Their voices were strained and hushed. All the while Mother lay there, frozen like an enchanted princess in a glass coffin. Irene had to admit she felt sorry for Ina, who was only eight and could hardly remember Mother being well.

A stream of spittle ran down Mother's chin. Irene remembered the doctor telling them that excessive saliva was one of the symptoms of her illness. Father's hand trembled as he wiped it away with his handkerchief. Mother did not react to his touch. According to the doctors, she was unaware of the things and people around her. She couldn't recognize her own family, or so they said. Irene refused to believe that. Beneath her immobile face, Mother was still Mother. She couldn't be completely dead inside.

"I have to go peepee," Ina confessed, her eyes big and imploring.

"Me, too," Isobel said, a little more boldly.

"Irene," said Father, "will you go with your sisters?" It was against the rules to have young children wandering down to the washroom on their own.

"I want to be with Mother," Irene said icily. She glared at him. Then she noticed a long black hair clinging to his lapel. "Look," she said loudly, reaching over to pluck it off the tweed. She held the hair aloft for her sisters to see. "It's black. How did you get a black hair on you?" She and her sisters were blond like their mother.

Ina gave her a frightened look, then edged closer to her father.

When he finally met Irene's eye, he looked at her not in anger or shame but in bewilderment, as if she were a stranger and no daughter of his at all. A cuckoo who had hatched in his nest. "Well, come on, girls," he said, rising clumsily from his chair. Irene watched him put his hands on her sisters' shoulders, guiding them out the door. As though they were his children and she wasn't. The girls followed him unquestioningly.

Taking her father's place in the bedside chair, Irene clasped her mother's stiff hand and tried to warm it. "It's me," she whispered tenderly. "Irene." Did she imagine it, or did her mother's fingers move imperceptibly in response to her touch? She kissed her mother's cheek and stroked her pale gold hair, spread out on the starched pillow like an aureole. Mother was still beautiful, her skin translucent and rosy. She hadn't aged a day during the four years of her illness. Irene liked to think of her as Sleeping Beauty. Sometimes she asked the nurse to hold her mother upright so she could brush her hair, the way she used to when she was no older than Ina. When she was a little girl, her mother's loosened hair had swept over her like a golden shawl when she held her in her lap and told her the old Scottish tales. Irene's favorite had always been "Tam Lin," the story of how young Janet rescued the boy she loved from the Faery Queen. When Mother first fell into her long sleep, Irene had thought the fairies had stolen her away, too, and left this changeling in her place. There was a distant world where her mother lived in enchantment, drinking wine from acorn cups.

"This is your daughter, Irene." She delicately ran her fingers over her mother's brow until her persistence paid off. Mother blinked. The ghost of a smile played at her lips. That made Irene cry, her hand covering her mouth. She knew she was the only one who still loved her mother. Father and her sisters only pretended. Every Sunday afternoon they went through this ritual to absolve themselves for their lack of enduring love. Like Catholics going to confession, she thought spitefully. As far as they were concerned, Mother was already dead. When they returned home, they would go on with their lives, forgetting her until next Sunday. Father would go on with his filth and lies. He would be covered in black hairs. Irene grasped her mother's hand and confided to her what she would tell no one else. "I hate him."

Laurence hardly said a word to his daughters while he drove back to Minerva. He feared that if he started talking, he would break down in tears. They would think he was going crazy. Hands gripping the steering wheel, he kept his eyes on the road stretched out before them. The nursing home left such a chill on him. Each time he entered Hazel's sickroom, he felt something inside him die. He had never gotten over what had happened to her.

Today when he held her hand and talked to her about the roses, he had nearly choked up. The awful emptiness in her eyes did him in. She used to be a vital woman, always thinking up jokes to make him laugh. Then one morning in April, 1919, she hadn't woken up, despite his panicked attempts to rouse her. When she finally opened her eyes, she stared blankly without seeing him, as though she were in a trance. She could not speak. There had been no reaching her after that.

In the beginning Dr. Lovell said she was suffering from catatonia. Had she experienced some shock, he asked. He prescribed bed rest, saying she would probably snap out of it in a week or so. But Hazel had never snapped out of it. The illness had turned the wife he had cherished into a thing that was neither dead nor truly alive. When visiting hours were over, the nurses fed her with tubes, changed her diaper, turned her over to prevent bedsores.

Sometimes he feared the grief would turn him into a dried-out husk, the lifeblood drained from him. He would end up as vacant as Hazel. If it weren't for Barbara, he thought he would be trapped inside that vacuum forever. Barbara had raised him up like Lazarus; he had been dead until she gave him life again. He thought of the heat that rose from her body, the way that heat engulfed him when they made love. The strength in her grip when she took hold of him. The rich musk that rose from her skin, unmasked by perfume. The way her eyes softened when he spoke her name. His thoughts of her lifted him far and away from the nursing home. His skin tingled, blood pulsing beneath the surface.

Father parked in the garage off the alleyway. He and her sisters trundled through the back door into the kitchen, where Barbara Niebeck was keeping their dinner warm. If Irene turned her plight into one of her mother's old stories, it would go like this: Father had fallen under the enchantment of an evil witch. There she was, framed in the lit-up window and bent over some pot she was stirring like a cauldron. Her long black hairs slipped loose from her bun to fall in her face. With a red hand, she pushed them away. Irene imagined those hairs tumbling into the food she would serve them.

Steering clear of the kitchen, Irene cut through her mother's rose garden, where she paused to rub her nose into the last remaining blooms. Then she made her way to the front door and let herself in, only to be slapped in the face with the stink of roast beef and Brussels sprouts. She found Father and her sisters already seated in the dining room. Ina exclaimed how hungry she was, then squealed with happiness as Mrs. Niebeck carried in the plates. Her blouse, damp from the kitchen's steam, clung to her breasts. Irene saw the way her father gawked. Isobel and Ina might be too young and unsuspecting to notice, but Irene's eyes were sharp enough to observe the way Mrs. Niebeck leaned too close when setting his dinner plate in front of him. When she came with Irene's plate, Irene turned her head so she wouldn't have to look at her.

The food was getting worse these days. Mrs. Niebeck was slipping up. Slicing the meat, Irene discovered how rare it was, blood dripping from the dead flesh. And there was too much butter and cream in the Brussels sprouts. The rest of them went on talking and eating as though nothing were amiss while Irene cut her food into smaller and smaller pieces, lifting it to her mouth without tasting it, then putting it back on her plate and moving it around until it looked as if she had eaten something. She got up and asked if she could be excused, fleeing upstairs to escape the smell of undercooked meat. Hunger was a thing she could get used to if that's what it took to avoid the witch's cooking. Nobody complained about how thin she had grown. Dr. Lovell had just clucked approvingly and said, "I see you're losing your baby fat." It was the new fashion to be scrawny down to the bone, with gaunt cheeks and big staring eyes that popped right out of their sockets.

She stole into her mother's old dressing room to bury her face in her dresses. It was her mother's scent she longed for, the essence of her when she had been healthy and whole. Her mother who had rolled up her sleeves every Tuesday to bake shortbread. Mother had smelled of the rose bushes she planted, of spicy perfume and orange blossom hand cream. But when Irene nuzzled the folds of her blue voile tea dress, she breathed in something vulgar and rank — armpit sweat and household vinegar. Smothering a cry, Irene held the dress at arm's length. Then, with unsteady hands, she unfastened it to find a long black hair clinging to the inside.

She cornered her father in his study, where he sat at his mahogany desk with his papers from the pop factory spread out before him. On the wall behind him was her mother's photograph, a thin film of dust obscuring her face. That witch had let her mother's photograph go dusty. Irene held the dress out before him, showing him the black hair that dangled from the inner lining. It was evidence, just like the ruined bicycle. "Mrs. Niebeck has been trying on Mother's dresses!"

"Now Irene," he said, adopting his overly patient tone. "I think you're jumping to conclusions. Mrs. Niebeck has to air out the closet now and then, and move the clothes around so they don't go mildewy. You wouldn't want your mother's clothes going moldy, would you?"

"But she's been *wearing* them! And she's been inside Mother's writing desk. The stationery's all mixed up."

"Irene, I think you have an overactive imagination." Her father sighed. His face was so strange that she turned away to stare at his old hunting rifle locked in its glass case. "Sit down, sweetheart." His tone was gentler now. He pulled out a chair for her. "Those clothes have been collecting dust in the closet for years now. I think we should give them away, don't you?"

Eyes smarting, Irene hugged her mother's dress. "You can't."

"She's never coming back." His voice broke. Avoiding her gaze, he rubbed his forehead. "You know that. We have to stop pretending. She . . . she would have wanted us to give those clothes to the needy."

Irene rose from her chair. "Well, you're not giving them to Mrs. Niebeck!" It was hard to keep from screaming in his face. "You better not."

Slumped in his chair, her father looked weary. "I don't want to hear any more of this."

She was about to protest when Isobel tiptoed into the room. "The doorbell rang," she announced in an unnaturally quiet voice. "It's Miss Ellison. She wants to talk to you about starting piano lessons again."

"You girls go down and talk to Miss Ellison," said Father. "I'll join you in a minute."

As they went down the stairs, Isobel seemed half scared of her. "Why were you yelling at Daddy? We could hear you downstairs. Why do you have Mother's dress?"

Late that night Irene awakened to the smell of Barbara Niebeck's cigarettes. This time she heard her father's hushed footsteps. Head buried in the pillow, she trembled with hate. As much as she despised Penny, she longed to ride her bicycle out to the Van den Maagdenbergh farm so she could ask her the questions that no one would answer. Penny had known all along. Penny was the only one who had ever told her the truth about it, and now her absence proved that Irene's deepest fears were real. Her father had told her to stop pretending, so Irene decided to take him at his word. Instead of ignoring the clues or looking away, she would pay close attention.

. . .

160

The evidence that people knew about her father and Mrs. Niebeck was revealed in things like the way people gathered on the corner of Buchanan and Main. They whispered among themselves, only to straighten up, the men tipping their hats as Irene and her father walked past. It was reflected in the oily smile on Mr. Timmerman's face when they went into his hardware store to buy a new bicycle.

Hands in his pockets, Father whistled to himself while Mr. Timmerman wheeled out the ladies' bicycles and let Irene take her pick.

"Used to be if the hired help wrecked a bicycle, they'd be thrown out the door," Mr. Timmerman said, rubbing his mustache. "I guess your daddy's kinda soft, huh?"

Father had stepped outside, out of earshot.

Mr. Timmerman edged closer and winked slyly at Irene. She didn't like him standing right next to her. Only a year ago, she would have called for her father and backed away. Instead she commanded herself to stand her ground, stiff and unflinching as a soldier, while she made her choice. She pointed to the Schwinn with the white leather seat. Its frame was shiny dark green like a beetle's hard shell. Mr. Timmerman turned to take the bicycle out of the row and held it by the handlebars. He grinned, showing his teeth, stained brown from chewing tobacco. "Here, let me show you how the gears on this thing work." He lifted his hand, which would have brushed her left breast if she hadn't stepped back just in time.

Father wandered into the shop again, his eyes clouded and oblivious, and paid for the bicycle.

A few days later she was cycling at the edge of town one night after dinner. It was time to be heading back, but something inside her that felt dark and awful tugged her toward the Timmerman house. She could hear men's laughter and loud voices from the street, though she couldn't see them — overgrown bushes surrounded the yard. Crouching down low, she listened. Their talk held her captive. She couldn't help it, could only listen to their stories, which made her feel sick. They talked about things that girls like her were never supposed to hear. They discussed where to get dirty pictures. Roy Hanson knew of a mail-order place in Saint Paul. They went on and on about little Rosie Lansky, who was Father Bughola's housekeeper.

Just as Irene was about to creep away, they started in on Barbara Niebeck. About her new Sunday dress that was so short, it showed off her knees. When she sat down in church, you could see an inch or so of thigh. The men said it was a miracle the church didn't collapse when she stepped in the door. They talked about how she should sit in the raised back row of the picture house with her legs apart so the people in front could get a good view of her crack. They speculated what color garters she wore, if she wore panties or just went bare, her naked thighs rubbing together as she walked down Main Street in her high heels. They spent a good five minutes discussing how they all wanted to take her. But mostly they tried to guess what kind of antics she and Irene's father got up to. She probably went down on her knees, they said, to suck Laurence Hamilton off on the kitchen floor.

Irene forced herself to listen to their talk until she was ready to double up and spew. Knowledge is power. Some famous philosopher had said that. She couldn't remember his name, but it was one of Father's favorite quotes. Father always said that if you looked at things squarely, you had power over them and they couldn't hurt you.

But they could, she discovered, tossing in her bed at night as that hussy's cigarette smoke seeped under her door. Irene couldn't look at her anymore without thinking of her lifting her skirt and spreading her legs to show Father her crack.

During her piano lesson the following afternoon, Irene couldn't concentrate on what Miss Ellison was saying. The exercise book was open before her, but when she tried to play, her fingers slipped all over the keys as though she had lost control of her hands. "I can't do it," she said.

"What's wrong, dear?" Miss Ellison touched her arm. "I can tell something's on your mind."

Miss Ellison was Father's age. She lived alone in a tiny bungalow near the Civic Park and supported herself from the piano and voice lessons she taught. She was also the director of the church choir in which Father sang. Every year she somehow scraped together the money to go to the Chicago Opera. As a trusted family friend, she often stepped in to have female-to-female chats with Irene, telling her the things a girl usually heard from her mother. When Irene got her first period, Miss Ellison had explained everything to her.

"Isobel told me you quarreled with your father the other night." Miss Ellison spoke mildly, her fingers toying with the thin gold chain around her neck. A tiny jeweled cross hung from it. At first Irene couldn't speak. Miss Ellison touched her hair, smoothing it back from her face. "You don't look like yourself anymore. If there's something upsetting you, honey, you can tell me."

Irene looked down at the black notes jumping all over the sheet music. "I hear all kinds of talk about Father."

"Talk?" Miss Ellison stiffened. Everyone said she had a secret crush on him, that one day, when he was free again, she hoped to be the second Mrs. Hamilton. Sometimes Irene suspected she was only being kind to her as a way of getting closer to Father. "What kind of talk?" She sounded alarmed.

"About him and . . . and Mrs. Niebeck." She realized she couldn't say the name without her voice slurring in hate.

"Rumors." Miss Ellison seemed to regain her composure, her fingers stroking Irene's hand. "Don't pay attention to that kind of talk. People can be so mean-spirited."

"But what if it's true?"

Miss Ellison shook her head. "Irene, don't . . ."

"I have reason to believe that those rumors are true." Irene spoke decisively. Miss Ellison was sweet on her father. Maybe she had the power to make it stop, make him fire Mrs. Niebeck. Biting her bottom lip, she waited for Miss Ellison to say the words that would bring her solace. The parlor closed in around them. The knickknacks that had been there for as long as Irene could remember suddenly seemed sinister, as though the glass-domed anniversary clock could fly through the air, hit the family photograph over the mantelpiece, and shatter.

When Miss Ellison finally spoke, her voice was quiet but curt. "Your father's a good man," she said. "But he *is* a man." She held Irene's gaze with admonishing eyes. "It's not your business to be listening to those who speak ill of him."

Irene considered how those two statements contradicted each other. Then, with an angry swipe of her hand, she knocked the sheet music to the floor. "But it's *true*. You even *know* it's true." She stood up and shouted so loudly that her throat hurt. "You didn't say it's not true!"

Miss Ellison sat there tight-mouthed and unblinking. "Calm down, Irene. Your father's not hurting anyone."

Irene stumbled out of the room, then ran to the bicycle shed. Jumping on the new bike her father had bought her, she took off. Turning the corner from Lilac to Main, she saw Ned Fisk. Last year she had followed him around like a puppy and he'd hardly looked at her. Now he waved and called out her name, but she sailed right past him and cycled on until she was winded. That night at dinner, she told her father she was finished with piano lessons.

There would be no more heart-to-hearts with Miss Ellison. No more intimate discussion at all. There was nothing left of her old life. When her friends talked to her, their voices passed right through her head. To fill the hours after school, Irene joined the Minerva girls' archery team. She had wanted to join last year, because Ned Fisk was on the boys' team, but she hadn't been good enough to get in. So she had practiced all summer at camp, where she had discovered how calming it could be. Drawing her bow and concentrating on the target allowed her to empty her mind, the only peace she'd had during that whole strange summer. In the meantime, she had become so adept that everyone called her a natural. These days she had Ned's attention without even trying.

He liked to walk her home from practice, her archery bag slung over his shoulder, his arm around her waist. Once they kissed, his lips smooth and warm against her mouth. Yet even as she tried to kiss him back, it was hard to rekindle the crush she used to have on him before her father had sent her away to camp and her world fell apart. Now, when she examined her heart, she felt nothing for him in particular. The things that used to bring her joy left her empty and cold.

She still played piano an hour a day, every day except Sunday, when they went to visit Mother. After Miss Ellison stopped giving her lessons, she put away Beethoven and Chopin and started playing the Scottish ballads from her mother's songbook. "Prince Charlie Stuart," "The Bonny Boy," "I Live Not Where I Love," and "Sir Patrick Spense." Hammering the piano keys, she sang the odd lyrics she only half understood.

> *O lang, lang may the ladies stand,*
> *Wi their gold kems in their hair,*
> *Waiting for their ain dear lords,*
> *For they'll see them na mair.*

Everything was crumbling to pieces. Why could no one see that but her? Another Sunday dinner dragged on. They sat with dead slabs of pork on their plates, Irene not eating, Father lost in his other world, Ina and Isobel prattling on and on, pretending that everything was all right. Sometimes her sisters' trust in him just tore her up. The way they seemed to believe that he could do no wrong and that he would always be there to protect them. What would happen when they woke up to the truth? Who would save them then?

Drawing her knife through her mashed potatoes, Irene racked her brain. Somehow there must be a way, an opening in the stone wall, a way to bring Father back from the realm he had wandered into, abandoning them all. She had to work fast before he wandered too far away and was lost to them forever.

When she started speaking, she sounded younger than her

years, as young as Isobel. The innocence in her own voice jarred her. "Remember how we used to have sing-alongs on Sunday night? Back when Mother was here?"

Ina looked at her blankly. Isobel shrugged. Father smiled at her with that expression of unease he put on whenever she opened her mouth these days.

"We could do it again. We still have the songbook," she said.

Their expressions remained unchanged.

Pushing her plate away, she left the table without excusing herself and went to the piano. This time she left the parlor door open so they would hear. Opening the songbook at random, she chose "Fear a' Bhàta." Though she didn't understand Gaelic, she knew the plaintive melody and remembered how the words had sounded when her mother used to sing them. She played and sang as though she could summon back her mother's spirit from the dark forest she was lost in, calling her home. The piano chords made the floorboards tremble. She willed her song to fill the whole house — she knew her singing voice sounded just like her mother's. She was calling them to her until at last they stood in the doorway, Father with his arms around her sisters. When she caught his eye, he looked at her as though she was his daughter once more, a talented, intelligent girl who made him proud. The look he gave her said he was sorry for everything she'd had to go through.

They gathered around the piano and she played "My Bonny Lies over the Ocean," which was easy and familiar enough for her sisters to join in. Ina hopped up beside her on the piano bench and swung her legs excitedly as she began to sing. Isobel sang more shyly. Standing at Irene's side, she turned the pages of sheet music for her. In the second verse, Father joined in, singing in harmony as he had once sung with her mother. She had done it, drawn them back into the circle, her fingers dancing in perfect patterns over the keys. Mrs. Niebeck was banished to the kitchen, and Mother smiled in her photograph over the piano that Irene had dusted herself.

18

BARBARA WAS CUTTING soft butter into pastry flour when she heard the rap on the back door. Wiping her hands on a dishtowel, she drew back the curtain to see Miss Ellison, a curious event. Miss Ellison had never come to the back door before, only the front.

"Mr. Hamilton's not home," she said when she opened up. "The girls are at the matinee."

"It's you I came to talk to." Miss Ellison stepped into the kitchen.

Barbara smiled grimly. "Want some coffee?" She pulled out a chair, though neither of them showed any intention of sitting down.

"I think you know why I'm here."

"Do I?" Barbara folded her arms in front of herself.

"If you think people haven't caught on to your little escapades, I have news for you. Even Irene figured it out."

"Irene?" A blast of cool air swept through the open door and blew a dead leaf across the linoleum.

"I can only imagine," said Miss Ellison, "what your own daughter has to say about it."

"Watch what you say about my daughter."

"If you had any decency left in you, you'd get on the next train out of town."

Barbara laughed. "*You* think you can tell me to leave town?"

"If you haven't got the money," Miss Ellison said dryly, "I'll give you the money."

Barbara snorted. "If you think I'd take a penny from you . . ."

"Do you care for him?" Miss Ellison demanded. She sounded breathless and her face had gone red. "Even a little?"

For a moment Barbara was lost. She lowered her eyes and turned away. That gave Miss Ellison all the answer she needed.

"Because if you care for him," she said, "you'll get out of town before you ruin that man and his family." She put particular emphasis on the word *ruin*.

Barbara backed clumsily away, retreating to her bowl of butter and flour, the pastry cutter with its wooden handle. She was shaking, sweat collecting between her breasts. For the first time in her adult life, she had turned her back on an adversary. She shuddered when she heard the door click as Miss Ellison let herself out.

Barbara washed her hands. She climbed the stairs to her room and changed into her black crêpe de Chine dress. Careful not to snag the silk on her chapped fingers, she put on her good stockings, pinning them to her satin garters. She brushed her hair, put on her hat, her black kidskin gloves. Forgetting how brisk it was, she walked outside without a coat or even a cardigan. As she trudged down the sidewalk, she hardly felt the chilling wind that made the leaves dance across her path. When she passed the soda shop on Main Street, young Walt Nelson called out to her and made loud kissing noises for the benefit of his buddies. She didn't blink.

She walked until she reached the train station. The timetables were pinned up behind a grimy glass window. All the different destinations, the departure and arrival times blurred together. Chicago, Saint Paul, Saint Louis, Fargo, Seattle, Pittsburgh, Kansas City, Milwaukee. She told herself she was still reasonably young. She could go anywhere. Just disappear. He couldn't end it, so she would have to. Out of mercy for him. *Mercy*. She clutched at the comfort of that word while memorizing the timetable that promised her deliverance.

19

ONE RAINY SUNDAY, Cora brought her grandfather's gramophone down from the attic. Penny had found some old records in the parlor, mostly dance tunes and love songs. But the record Cora chose was Beethoven's *Moonlight* Sonata.

"Listen to it with your eyes closed," Cora said as she wound up the gramophone. "The music is meant to paint the picture of the full moon reflecting on a lake." Then she lowered the needle to the record. Irene Hamilton used to play Beethoven during her piano lessons, yet Penny had never heard anything like this. It sounded just like yearning. As the notes wove around her, the lake became a real thing, its dark rippling surface reflecting the radiance of the moon it adored. But at the same time, the calm mirroring water held secrets, fiercely protecting the sunken treasure hidden in its depths. Penny turned her face away from Cora as her eyes began to burn and a single tear moved over her cheek. Then Cora said something, her voice almost a part of the music.

"'The midnight moon is weaving her bright chain o'er the deep.'"

When Penny glanced in her direction, she saw that Cora had read those words out of a book. She had never seen her so peaceful, the way she leaned back in her chair, all the tight worry lines in her face smoothed away. This lull couldn't last long — Penny expected Phoebe to start crying any minute and shatter the spell. And yet the baby slept on and the music continued, each phrase of notes making her breathe deeper, the waters inside her unfurling in gentle waves that touched the shore.

"That was from a poem by Lord Byron," Cora said after a long pause.

"How do you know so much?" Penny asked her. "About music and poetry?"

"My father. He loved these things. When he was young, he wanted to be a pianist more than anything else, but his father wouldn't hear of it. He made him quit his lessons. Piano playing wasn't considered manly enough. My father was supposed to manage his family's slaughter yards."

"But then he met your mother."

"She fell in love with him when he first played for her. We kept a cottage piano in the house where I grew up. He played after supper. His face always changed with the music."

Penny imagined her as a little girl listening to her father. "Can you play?"

"I never had the patience for lessons. It was his gift, not mine. But my brother took after him."

"Didn't you get another letter from him?" Penny remembered the envelope with the foreign stamps that had come the previous week.

Cora smiled. "Yes. He says he's finally managed a sabbatical, so he can visit me. It sure will be nice to see him again." Her voice brimmed with hope.

"Your brother sounds nice," Penny said. "Your father, too. I always wanted a father." She spoke the last sentence so softly, she didn't expect Cora to hear.

"I know," Cora said. "Someone to be proud of you." She got up from her chair and sat beside Penny on the sofa, then touched the end of her braid, which had come undone. Without saying anything, Cora smoothed out the locks and began to braid it again. Penny turned around to make it easier for her. Closing her eyes, she surrendered to the gentle pressure, the tugging on her scalp. Her back was turned to Cora and yet she wanted to face her, wanted to pour into words the things that were hidden inside her. That she loved Cora and Phoebe more than anything, that she would stick by them forever, no matter what happened. But the words wouldn't come. Cora tied the ribbon at the end of her braid and the music washed over them both, music that was far more eloquent than her words could ever be. So when the sonata came to an end, she merely begged Cora to play it again.

20

Not much news from town reached the Van den Maagden-bergh farm. Penny was far more aware of the fall leaves and the brilliant purple fireweed that shot up all over the woodlot than of anything that transpired in Minerva. Cora dug the potatoes and planted the winter wheat. At the kitchen table, Penny worked on her lessons and read *The Odyssey*. At last she decided that maybe Penelope wasn't such a bore. She liked the way she gave Odysseus a run for his money in the end, was amused by the hints that she could see through his disguise, and admired the way she didn't automatically melt in his arms when he revealed himself to her. What Penny liked best was that, even after his twenty-year journey and their long-awaited reunion, Penelope insisted that he listen to her story and her dream of geese before allowing him to tell her of his adventures.

One November morning, Cora was napping upstairs with the baby, exhausted from a sleepless night. Phoebe was teething. Cora had been short-tempered recently, probably from lack of sleep. Penny hoped it was just temporary, but she found herself getting lonely sometimes.

She occupied herself with the messy work of hollowing out a pumpkin. She tossed the seeds and loose pulpy fibers into a pail for the geese, now confined to a pen for the cold part of the year. Thanksgiving was coming up — Phoebe's first — and Penny wanted to surprise Cora with a real Thanksgiving dinner. That meant making pumpkin pie, cranberry sauce, and scalloped potatoes. Instead of buying a turkey from the butcher's in town, she would finally work up the nerve to kill one of the nine geese she'd been fattening up during the five months she had lived here. They would have to slaughter at least one for Thanksgiving and one for Christmas, otherwise it would be too pricey keeping them fed all the way through winter when there was nothing for them to forage outdoors.

Her mother made roast goose for the Hamiltons every Christmas. One of these Sundays, she thought she would finally go visit her. It was hard, though. She hadn't seen her in so long, she didn't know what she would say to her anymore. Each Sunday came and somehow she put it off, fearful of what would happen if she knocked on the Hamiltons' back door. Maybe her mother would be mad at her for staying away so long. Maybe she would be indifferent. But she kept promising herself that she really would visit her, sometime before Christmas.

Lately she'd been trying to recreate her mother's old recipes by trial and error — her fried chicken and angel food cake. For Thanksgiving, she would try to remember the way her mother had prepared the pumpkin pies and roast goose. Following her memory, Penny took a freshly sharpened butcher's knife and cut the pumpkin into small segments to make it easier to remove the hard rind. She made herself remember how her mother had cut the raw pumpkin flesh into cubes, then simmered them in a pan of water with a cinnamon stick. Going into the pantry to hunt for cinnamon, she only found a jar of cloves.

She tossed some cloves in the pan as a substitute for cinnamon. Their scent filled the kitchen, and soon steam clouded the windows. Sitting at the kitchen table, she tried to write the remaining steps of the recipe. When the pumpkin flesh was cooked through, her mother had taken it out of the pan and mashed it with a potato masher. After letting it cool, she had folded in heavy cream, molasses, brown sugar, eggs, allspice, and freshly ground nutmeg. Then her mother had poured the mixture into a rolled pie crust and baked it.

Her mother's goose recipe, handed down from her grandmother, was even more elaborate. Penny found another scrap of paper and jotted down everything she could remember. Her mother had stuffed the goose with seasoned breadcrumbs, almonds, and raisins. Had she basted the goose with anything? How long did a goose have to cook? It would be pointless asking Cora, who knew even less about these things than she did. For a moment, she imagined her mother was in the kitchen beside her and could answer all her questions, take her through the recipes step by step.

Penny was clearing the pumpkin peels off the kitchen table when she heard the car come up the drive. She wondered who it could be. The ice deliveryman didn't come anymore now that the weather had turned cool. They kept the milk and eggs in the unheated pantry.

Rubbing the steam from the windowpane, she looked out and saw a touring car, its leather hood drawn up like a wrinkled bonnet. No one in Minerva possessed such a sporty auto — it looked like something out of a magazine. After giving her hands a quick wash, she tugged off her apron and stepped outside. The crisp air made her shiver, rubbing her arms as she watched a young man step out. He was hatless, the wind ruffling his chestnut hair. He wore a loose jacket and was carrying a box wrapped in pink gift paper under one arm. Squinting in the strong autumn sunlight, he shaded his eyes with his free hand and gazed at the house. When he caught sight of her, he waved. Then he stepped forward, his gait marked by a limp.

The faded image from those old photographs sprang to life. She could hardly quell her excitement as she went out to meet him, could barely resist the urge to shout out his name. He had Cora's hair, her green eyes.

"Hello, miss. You must be Penny." There was something curious about the way his tongue slipped around the words. He didn't sound American anymore after his years overseas.

"You know my name?" She couldn't hide her delight.

174

"My sister mentioned you in her letters. She said what a god-send you are. I'm Jacob Viney, by the way. Cora's brother."

"I know! I saw all the pictures of you."

"She showed you pictures of me?"

Penny bit her lip. There, she had given herself away for snooping. "When did you get here?" she asked, to change the subject. "Cora said you lived in France."

"I sailed over in October. I promised her I'd come and see the baby." He held out the pink-wrapped box. "This is for Phoebe."

"Oh, that's sweet." It occurred to Penny that Jacob was the first person ever to bring Phoebe a present. She wondered if he had brought it all the way from France. "Cora's taking a nap," she told him. Looking at Cora's bedroom window, she saw that the curtains were still closed. She must not have heard the car. "The baby kept her up all night."

A man appeared at Jacob's side, taking Penny by surprise. She hadn't seen him getting out of the car. "This is Penny," Jacob said to the man. "Penny, I brought a friend along. I didn't think Cora would mind. This is Adam."

"Hello there, Penny." Adam took off his flat-brimmed sports cap and shook her hand as though she were a fellow adult. A little older than Jacob, he was easily the handsomest man she had ever seen. His honey-blond hair was swept back from his fore-head. He had a thin mustache like a movie star's. It was impossible not to fall under his spell when he smiled at her like that. Jacob cleared his throat. Adam winked at her before letting go of her hand, which was warm and tingly from his grip. "Pleased to meet you."

"Come inside." She led the way. "Won't she be happy when she sees you." She flashed a smile at Jacob, who ducked his eyes.

"It sure smells good in here." When they entered the kitchen, Adam sniffed the air appreciatively, then lifted the pot on the stove where the pumpkin flesh and cloves simmered.

"I'm stewing pumpkin," Penny told him. "To make pumpkin pie."

"I love pumpkin pie," said Adam.

Penny showed them into the parlor and gestured at the velvet sofa. Jacob set his gift down on the side table.

"Well," said Penny, "I better tell her you're here."

But Cora was already thundering down the stairs.

Penny stepped in her path. "Cora, guess what?"

"You *idiot!*" She shoved Penny brutally aside, slamming her against the doorjamb so hard that Penny saw stars. Her legs buckled beneath her and she slid to the floor. Dazed, she watched Cora dash past her and lunge for the Winchester rifle, hanging above the parlor mantelpiece. But Jacob and his friend stood in her way, blocking her. When Cora saw her brother, she faltered. A gasp came out of her. He took hold of her arms.

"Cora, please. We just want to talk."

Penny sat up and raised her hand to her cheek. Her fingers probed her skin. There would probably be a bruise before it healed. She tried to catch Cora's eyes, but her face was a bloodless mask. Penny looked away from her and began to cry. "You're crazy."

Adam knelt beside her on the floor. "Did she hurt you, Penny?" His eyes were big with concern. After helping her to her feet, he took a handkerchief out of his pocket and pressed it into her hand. "Here you go, dear."

Struggling loose from her brother's hold, Cora made another attempt to get the rifle. This time Adam restrained her, holding her around the waist, her arms pinned to her sides as she kicked and fought.

"You bastard!" she screamed.

Penny stared at her without moving. Without feeling anything except the pain along her cheekbone.

Jacob took the rifle down from its perch. Edging quickly past Adam and Cora, he handed it to Penny. "Put this away somewhere safe," he whispered.

"Penny!" Cora was pleading. "Penny, help me."

For five months she had lived with Cora and taken care of her baby. After all they had been through together, Cora had called her an idiot and slammed her into the doorjamb. The hateful gossip about Cora came back to her. *That woman's dangerous, as crazy as they come.* Well, now she'd gotten a taste of it. Penny turned her head and walked away.

"Penny, come back here!" Cora's voice was hoarse with rage. "I *trusted* you."

Carrying the rifle, Penny escaped through the kitchen and out the back door. In Cora's bedroom, the baby was crying, screaming like her mother. She heard someone — Jacob? — running up the stairs while Cora went on cursing. Penny's hands shook so hard, she had to put the rifle down on the stack of firewood on the porch. Drying her eyes with Adam's handkerchief, she noticed the initials crisply embroidered in the corner: *AE.*

She thought her legs would give out. She had to sit down on the splintering porch steps. *Adam Egan.* The handsome stranger was the man Cora had cut out of the pictures. And she had let him into the house. But none of it made sense. He seemed so reasonable, so kind. That story about him breaking down the door and knocking down Roy Hanson — well, that was just gossip she'd heard at Renfew's. She had no proof that it ever happened. Cora herself hadn't mentioned it. None of the stories she had heard seemed to match up with the actual man. If he was so awful, why had Cora's brother agreed to come along with him? She thought about the cut-up pictures in the photo album. There was so much about Cora she didn't know.

Her face buried in Adam's handkerchief, she listened to their voices.

"Please don't go on like that, Cora." Adam spoke gently. "I just want to talk to you. We brought a present for the baby."

"Jacob, get him out of here!"

"Cora." Jacob's voice was anguished. "Please. It doesn't have to be this ugly. I swear to you, we only came to have a rational discussion."

"I don't see what there is to discuss."

"Don't you think it's normal that he wants to see his daughter?"

"Well, how did he even know about the baby?" Betrayal shot through her voice. "*You* told him. I never should have written to you. He wouldn't have known if you hadn't —"

"Cora, I'm not the one who told him."

"He's telling the truth," Adam said. "I heard about it from people in town."

"Who would tell you that?"

"I'm sorry, Cora, but some people here think you're strange and talk about you behind your back."

All the while, Phoebe cried. They talked around her, occasionally drowning her out.

"He asked me to come along," Jacob said. "To persuade you to talk to him. He wants to reconcile with you. You don't have to go back to him, just hear him out. Please."

"I want to make my peace with you, Cora. It's time we sat down and talked it through."

She laughed bitterly.

"We have the child's welfare to consider. Now that I know I *have* a child. I want to make things better between us. I love you, Cora."

"Some kind of love."

"We've come all this way," said Jacob. "Now I'm going to leave you and Adam for an hour. You can decide yourself what you want to do, but at least talk to him first."

"You are *not* leaving me alone with him. Jacob! Don't you dare walk out that door! Don't you dare . . ."

Jacob stepped out on the porch and shut the door behind him. He was carrying the crying baby. "Let's go somewhere and let them talk," he said to Penny.

"Jacob!" Cora yelled from the other side of the closed door.

He started walking away from the house while Cora kept calling his name, her cries pursuing him across the back yard. The faster he moved, the more exaggerated his limp became. When Penny caught up with him, she didn't know what to say. Hand on her face, she nursed her sore cheek.

Jacob looked at her sideways with eyes just like Cora's. "Did she ever hurt you like that before?" He was shaking. "I've never seen her like that. So full of hate. I nearly didn't recognize her." Balancing Phoebe's weight in one arm, he rubbed his eyes. "We used to be so close."

Penny turned her head so he wouldn't see her cry. "I never thought she could do that to me."

They reached the orchard of trees stripped of their fruit. Only a few shriveled leaves clung to the gnarled branches. Jacob regarded his niece, who had stopped crying and now stared up at him.

"She looks just like her mother," he murmured. "When she was a baby."

"She's been a real good baby." Penny tried to make herself sound normal. "Just a little colic now and then."

They reached the hammock, full of dead leaves.

"So her name's Phoebe." Jacob seated himself on the edge of the hammock. "She picked a pretty name for her."

"Phoebe Helena." Penny watched him rock back and forth with the baby in his arms. He held her so tenderly, his face softening. He must love babies, she thought. This was obviously not the first time he had held one. Phoebe seemed fascinated with him, too. She realized it was the first time the little girl had ever been held by a man.

"I didn't think Cora would be overjoyed," he said. "But I didn't think our visit would be like this, either." He bowed his head.

Penny took a deep breath. "She said she had to run away because he was cruel to her. She told you that, didn't she?"

Jacob laughed bleakly. "She didn't tell me a thing for the longest time." He paused. "I love my sister. I would never let anyone hurt her. If she had told me more, I might have been able to help her. But she had to do it all on her own."

Suddenly there were too many things crowding Penny's head, and none of them fit together.

"He begged me to come with him today. He thought I could coax her into being reasonable." Jacob shook his head. "I wish I knew what to do."

She sat down on the brittle autumn grass and hugged her knees to her chest. Jacob, she realized, was just as bewildered by all this as she was. "But do you believe her or not?" she insisted. "About Adam being cruel? She said her best friend wouldn't even believe her."

Jacob closed his eyes. "He swore to me that he never mistreated her. Of course, married people have their private problems. Something happened between them — probably a thing another woman could forgive. But Cora's not a forgiving person. She was always so extreme. Even as a child, she had the most terrible tantrums. She exaggerates things, flies into a passion."

Penny touched the sore skin around her cheekbone. She kept seeing Cora's face, that look of utter betrayal before she pushed her into the doorjamb. *I trusted you.*

"Once she has a grudge," Jacob said, "she holds on to it forever. Seems to forget that everyone is human just like her. Adam said that after she left him, he regretted every mistake he ever made. But she wouldn't even let him apologize."

"Did she tell you anything about why she left him?" Penny tried to imagine Cora writing out a letter to her brother.

Jacob was silent for a moment. "When he wrote to me saying that she ran away, I couldn't believe it. He was devastated. When he was a little boy, his mother abandoned the family and eloped with a lover. They never heard from her again. To have Cora run off like that was his worst nightmare. He really wanted children, too, so when he found out she had concealed the baby from him, he nearly fell apart. He told me he couldn't sleep at night thinking that Cora hated him and was here alone with the baby, living like some outcast. Then I wrote to her, wanting to hear her side of things. Six months went by without a word. So I wrote to her again."

She remembered the slim envelope with the foreign stamps

and the unreadable look on Cora's face when she told her the letter had arrived.

"When she finally wrote me back, she didn't sound like herself anymore. Her handwriting was different, too. It was as though she was taken over by something else."

Penny shivered. Suddenly the ground beneath her had grown too cold. Struggling to her feet, she rubbed her arms to get warm.

"She's changed so much." Jacob looked lost. "She used to be so clever and accomplished. Beautiful, too. She dazzled everyone."

The pictures in the album, Penny thought. The beautiful debutante in the flowing gowns.

"Now she's so full of hate," he went on. "How can anyone live like that? And what about the baby? It's a horrible thing for a child to be set apart from the rest of the world on account of her parents' mistakes."

Penny stared at the naked branches clawing the sky. She saw her breath in the air. "Phoebe's going to catch a chill. Wrap her in your jacket."

Jacob passed Phoebe to her before taking off his jacket. While Penny swaddled the baby, Jacob pulled a pack of cigarettes out of his trouser pocket. He tried to light a match, but the wind blew out the flame. Phoebe began to cry. Penny hugged her tightly, rocking and soothing her. She held out her index finger for Phoebe to grab and made funny faces until the baby smiled and started drooling on her uncle's jacket. Jacob shivered in his thin sweater.

"You fooled me," she said. "I would never have let him in the house if I'd known he was her husband. Now Cora thinks I did it on purpose." She paused as Phoebe latched on to her braid. "She'll never go back to him. If that's what you think, you've got another thing coming."

"She doesn't have to go back to him," he said. "He just wants her to be civil and to acknowledge him as the father of her child. He wants to support her. There's no reason why Cora has to struggle all alone. If she wants to stay here, I'll stay with her, help her out with things. Families need to stick together in times like this."

Cora isn't exactly struggling all alone, Penny wanted to point out, she has me. But maybe that didn't count in the big picture. Jacob probably thought she was just a kid, a hired girl, good for chores but not someone who could help and protect Cora, or ease her out of her bitterness. She wasn't her real family.

"Cora says you have a fiancée in France," she said instead. "Won't she miss you if you stay here instead of going back there?"

Jacob nodded soberly. "It's not an easy choice to make. But I have to do something for my sister. Take a look at this." Reaching into his pocket for his wallet, he took out a small photograph.

Here was the young Cora with her long tresses wound around her head, her smiling face beside Adam's. He gazed at her with absolute devotion, as though he could not bear to look away. Penny had to admit that they made a handsome couple. They looked so happy together. Cora seemed to glow. Once she had been smitten with him, all right. But even more obvious was how much Adam adored her. He was too crazy about her, she thought, to let her go without a fight. Perhaps he loved her far more than she had ever loved him. Maybe that was where the trouble had started. She remembered fragments of the shouting match.

"How did he find out about the baby?" she asked. Adam said he had heard about it from people in town, but that didn't make sense. People might talk in Renfew's, but who would bother writing a letter full of local gossip to some stranger in Evanston, Illinois?

Jacob seemed reluctant to speak about it. "He hired a private detective."

Penny recalled the man she had seen at the store back in summer. The one with the tanned face standing near the pyramid of apples. "Why did he do that?"

"It's not what I would have done. But Adam said he had to do something. Trying to conceal a child from the father is serious business. She lied on the birth certificate."

"How do you know she lied?" Penny's face went hot.

Jacob looked at her for a second, then laughed. "She said *unknown*. Well, unless another man steps forward and claims that he's the father, the baby will be legally seen as Adam's."

This was so complicated, she didn't want to start thinking about it. She snuggled Phoebe for comfort. It was too cold out here. Of the three of them, only the baby was warm.

Jacob moved his foot over the grass. "I have to say, some of the things they dug up about her sound far-fetched. I know she's unconventional in the way she dresses and acts, but it seems a little too much to say she's guilty of transvestism." He looked pale. "They said she served intoxicating liquor to the Mexicans at harvest time." He gazed at Penny, his forehead wrinkling. "And to you, too, and you're underage."

Penny shrugged. "The others might have had some wine, but I never touched the stuff."

Jacob looked at her intently. "Then they said she was cozy with one of the Mexicans. Supposedly they have a sworn witness saying he saw them kiss. That in itself is grounds to have the baby taken away." He shook his head. "Did that really happen, Penny?"

"No," she said firmly. "I never saw her kissing anybody."

Sworn witness? Suddenly she faltered, breathing hard. Gilbert. That rat. It was all her fault — she was the one who believed his sad story, let him in the house. She was the one who talked Cora into giving him work, a place at their table. An invisible cord tightened around her throat. *There aren't many people I trust. But I trust you.* Her hands were so unsteady, she feared she would drop the baby. "Here," she whispered, delivering her into her uncle's arms. "Take her."

She was an idiot, all right. Let Adam into the house. Invited him right into the parlor. She felt herself stagger again from the way Cora had shoved her aside in her mad rush to get the rifle.

"Penny." Jacob looked at her as he rocked the baby. "You have to understand."

Phoebe's eyes moved back and forth as she hypnotized herself on the bare twigs and branches. A bird perched above them and sang a few feeble notes before flying away.

"Cora's all the family I have left," he said. "We used to be best friends. She told me everything. Adam saved my life. He's like a brother to me." Jacob swallowed hard, the tendons in his neck tightening. "I don't know how she thinks she can bring up a child living the way she does. A baby needs a father. I've seen so much go to ruin." He paused. "I just want them to be happy. Marriage isn't easy, you know. It takes work . . . understanding. Both people have to keep trying. I gave him my word. I always worried about her. When she was nine years old, our parents gave her a pony."

Penny nodded, thinking of the photograph of Cora astride the shaggy pinto. *My Birthday, 1907.*

"She would ride it without saddle or bridle. Just hang on to the mane and then she'd be galloping away, breakneck, and suddenly she'd lift her arms and pretend she was flying. She'd be holding on to the pony with just her legs squeezing its flanks, egging it on faster. Our parents let her run wild. I was always afraid she'd get herself killed."

Penny squirmed. It was the cold sinking into her, going straight to her bladder. "Excuse me," she whispered, turning around.

"Where are you going?"

"I have to pee." She winced, saying it so plainly to a man.

"Don't go in the house," he said.

"I'll go to the outhouse," she muttered, already moving away from him. Phoebe began to cry. Left alone with a stranger. Penny wanted to turn back and hold her, but she was ready to burst. Walking fast, fists clenched, she made her way to the back yard, the clump of evergreen shrubs that hid the outhouse. She couldn't stomach that stinking hole, so she squatted in the grass, her skirt hitched around her hips. As she stumbled to her feet and pulled her underpants back up, she found herself peeking over the bushes at the house. An invisible tendril was tugging her. You couldn't live with someone for five months and take care of her baby without sharing something. Without loving her. *Penny, help me. I trusted*

184

you. If Cora had been exaggerating about her husband, then she wanted to find out for herself.

The back door was closed. Penny pressed her ear against it but heard nothing. Creeping around the side of the house, she made for the outside trapdoor that led down to the cellar. She tugged on the iron ring, pulling the blistered door slowly, inch by inch. The wind hid any noise she made. Then she stole down the stone steps into the cellar, which was as wide as the house above it. She tiptoed across the cold earthen floor until she stood beneath the parlor. Adam's feet creaked overhead. His voice rang out, calm and measured. Splinters of sunlight shone through the gaps in the floorboards.

". . . what do you say we wipe the slate clean?"

"You don't fool me."

"Come on, Cora." He let out a loud sigh. "Tell me how you're getting along out here. Give me an honest answer."

"I was doing just fine until you showed up." Venom flooded her voice.

He managed to respond without losing a beat. "You don't look fine. You look worn down. If you don't mind my saying it, you've aged."

"You mean I grew up," she said flatly. "I'm not some orphan girl you can push around —"

He cut her off. "Can you really handle this life?" He sounded genuinely concerned. "Running a farm and raising a baby on your own?"

"I told you, I just want to be left alone."

"What would happen if your hired girl got fed up and walked out on you? I think she just might do that, considering the way you belted her."

"I didn't belt her." Cora sounded as if she might cry. "I pushed her too hard . . . by accident."

He laughed sadly. "Oh, Cora."

"You're a fine one to talk," she said.

"Say this girl is afraid to go anywhere near you now. What happens if she leaves? You'd never manage on your own."

"I . . ."

"What happens if you get sick out here? Who'll take care of you and the baby? And what if the baby gets sick?"

"I'll get the doctor," she said tightly.

"You didn't even get the doctor when you went into labor."

Cora was silent.

"I think you'll agree that living alone out here isn't in your daughter's best interest. I think you know that deep down yourself." He waited for a minute, giving Cora a chance to speak. She did not reply.

"Have you ever thought what it's going to be like when she gets older? The way you dress and carry on, how are they going to treat her? Your daughter will be a pariah. You've turned yourself into a pariah. Well, you're condemning her to a life of hate and ridicule."

"How can you say —"

"You made a mistake, Cora. All right, I admit we both made our mistakes. But we can make everything better again. You have your brother back. He came all the way from Europe just to persuade you to come home."

"Your house is not my home." Her voice shook.

He ignored her remark. "We can be happy again." He sounded so seductive, like a movie actor who had the power to make any woman melt in his arms. "Don't you want to give your little girl a real family?"

"You're so full of lies."

"*Cora*. How can you say that? Everything I've told you is the honest truth. I think if you can be honest with yourself —"

She interrupted him. "If you really mean no harm, then turn around and go away. Now."

"It's not so simple, Cora. She's my daughter, too. I have a say in her upbringing."

"You have no proof of that," she said, a wicked satisfaction creeping into her voice.

"I told you we have all the proof we need. The detective gathered the evidence. The attorneys filed the papers."

"That's not what I'm talking about. You have no proof that she's your daughter."

It was the only time in the conversation that he faltered. Penny listened to Cora's footsteps. She seemed to be heading for the door. But then he must have stepped in her path and blocked her.

"You lied on the birth certificate." Something in his voice had changed. Penny took a step sideways and rubbed her cold arms.

Cora burst out laughing. "Oh, I'd like you to prove that I was lying."

Adam said something Penny couldn't catch. She heard his heavy footsteps and Cora's lighter ones backing away from him. He was pushing her into a corner.

"We can settle this among ourselves, Cora, or we can settle this in court. You decide. I think that even you have to admit we have enough evidence to have you declared unfit for motherhood."

"Why didn't you pay a visit earlier, then?" she asked. "If you already had all the paperwork in place in September?"

"I was waiting for your brother. You don't think I'd do this without his permission, do you?"

Penny felt something icy grip at her. *He was lying.* He had tricked Jacob, lied to him, too. Used Jacob to get his foot in the door.

Cora didn't speak. The silence stretched on for over a minute. Adam's feet moved forward, then Penny heard a sharp cry.

"Get your hands off me."

"I'm still your husband. I can touch you if I want."

The shuffle of feet overhead sent dust falling on Penny's face.

"I could have you put away. The detective says most people around here think you're insane. Even that little hired girl says you're crazy."

"She didn't say that."

"Oh, yes, she did. And your brother was there to witness it. Jacob's already signed the papers to have you committed."

Don't believe him, Penny wanted to shout. She wanted to run and get Jacob, but Adam would just twist her words around and say that *she* was lying.

"You're wrong. He would never . . ." Cora's voice trailed off into a choking sputter.

Penny couldn't breathe. A weight was pressing down on her, forcing the air from her lungs.

"So tell me what it was like when you kissed that Mexican. What's the matter, sweetheart? Wasn't I good enough? You had to do it with some wetback?"

"Stop it!"

Penny heard a body slam against the wall, then a drawn-out scream.

"Jacob!"

But off in the orchard, Jacob would never hear his sister crying his name. Penny heard a thud, a body falling to the floor. She listened to Cora struggle, then hit the floor again, sobbing helplessly. Adam was breaking her down, piece by piece.

"I'll do anything you want," she told him. "Just stop."

But he wouldn't stop.

Penny's feet made no noise as she climbed the cellar steps. Hired girls could be quieter than anyone, quieter than thieves. On the porch, she had to wipe the sweat from her palms and press them against her thighs until they stopped shaking. Then she took the rifle from the top of the woodpile and slipped in the door. She stole through the kitchen and into the parlor. His back was to her. He was bending over Cora, who thrashed on the floor.

"Let her go." Penny had meant to shout, but her voice came out in a whimper. He spun around in less time than it took her to draw breath. She wasn't braced to fire, hadn't remembered to cock the trigger. For a moment, he looked thrown. Then he jumped forward and wrestled the rifle away from her.

Cora came at him from behind, tried to get it, but he swung around and struck her in the face with the rifle butt. Penny watched her go down. It all happened so fast. While his back was still turned, Penny grabbed a vase and hurled it, hitting the back of his head. She watched him turn and stumble, then she sprang forward and wrenched the rifle from his hands. Cora was still on the floor. In a second, Penny had the rifle braced against her shoulder. She cocked to fire, her finger on the trigger.

When he staggered to his feet, his face was taut with rage. She no longer recognized him as the smiling man she had shown into the house. His eyes met hers with a force that made her tremble and nearly drop the rifle. She was standing between him and the door, blocking his escape. Her mind moved fast, trying to figure out what a man like him would do when he had been caught knocking his wife around. Some stupid hired girl had witnessed how he behaved in private.

"Penny, watch out!" Cora shrieked, but then her voice was lost.

Be fast, be fast. A voice inside ordered her to step aside and let him out. She only had to let him pass. Even with her as Cora's witness, no one would take a hired girl's word over a surgeon's. She was just Penny Niebeck, no threat to this man. Nothing she said or did would have the power to hurt him. But, clumsy in her terror, she couldn't step away fast enough. The image of a pressure cooker flashed through her brain. The parlor was a pressure cooker with Adam and Cora trapped inside. She was the lid. Now the temperature was so high, the whole thing would explode unless she . . .

She stepped back, but not soon enough. He was coming straight at her. Cora was face down, no longer moving.

"Look what you did to my wife. Look what you *did*. We were just having a conversation."

Coming straight at her. The force that had moved Cora's hands when she pushed her against the doorjamb, that had moved her mother's hand when she slapped her, now screamed in her body. Something ignited inside her, telling her to pull the damn trigger. She would miss, of course she would. It was just to keep him from taking the rifle away. Who knows what he would do if he got the rifle again? She told herself, Just shoot and miss. Then he would run past her out the door, run to Jacob in the orchard and tell him that the fool girl nearly shot him.

He was coming at her with a face so frightening it made her cry out. It was something automatic, some instinct that moved her finger on the trigger. She forgot to brace. The impact threw her back against the wall. She screamed at the roar of it, a Winchester rifle going off in a parlor. Outdoors the sound would have rung out over the fields, echoing away, but here it had nowhere to go. It could only ricochet against the walls with their faded paper, that pattern of blue morning glories. A pressure cooker. She was the lid and then it had blown.

She had never thought what happened if you shot a man in the chest at such close range. The force knocked him against the far wall. He slid to the floor, his pure white sweater ripped open from the single bullet, his wound like raw meat. His blood puddled on the oak floorboards. No amount of scrubbing and bleach would ever make that stain disappear. His eyes were frozen wide open.

A noise wrenched out of her throat. If she telephoned Dr. Lovell, he would come with the police. He would open his black book and make her sign her name with his silver fountain pen. It would go on record. A minute ago, that man had been alive. Now he was . . .

"Cora."

Rising from her broken huddle on the floor, Cora stared at her, then at her husband. Her face was white as candle wax. His white sweater had gone red. Saturated. Penny couldn't look anymore at what she had . . .

"Cora, here." She held out the rifle. "Take it." When Cora reached for the Winchester, her hands were shaking hard.

"I'm sorry," Cora whispered, her face twisting to the side. "Penny, I'm so sorry." Her jaw was puffy from the blow with the rifle butt. Her nose was bleeding.

They heard footsteps, the baby's wailing. Jacob appeared in the parlor doorway. His face went papery when he viewed the body on the floor and then his sister with the rifle in her hands. He looked at Penny, who covered her face and began to cry. Before she could say a word, Cora spoke, each word loud and distinct.

"I shot him."

Penny uncovered her face and shook her head. Jacob only looked at his sister, who wiped the blood from her nose on her shirtsleeve.

Jacob's eyes were red. He started blinking hard. "My God. Cora."

Cora set the rifle down and, skirting past her husband's body, went to take Phoebe from Jacob's arms. Without the baby's weight to anchor him, Jacob seemed to collapse, leaning against the doorjamb. He breathed in quick and shallow puffs. Penny watched his collar go up and down, up and down.

She had to say something. If she didn't speak up, she would be guilty of something even worse. "No. Cora didn't do it."

Cora cut her off. "You are my witness," she told her brother. "I shot him. Penny came in when she heard the shots. Penny, this is between me and my brother. Take the baby upstairs." She pressed the baby into Penny's arms, then pushed her out of the room.

"But Cora." Penny was faint, the inside of her mouth so bitter she feared she would vomit. "I did it." Her words were lost as Cora closed the parlor door in her face.

"She's in shock," she heard Cora tell Jacob on the other side of the door. "She's just a child, and look at what she saw."

Phoebe thrashed in her arms. The baby had wet and soiled herself in her uncle's jacket. On weak legs, Penny forced herself up the stairs to Cora's room. She laid a towel on Cora's dresser, then set the baby down, stripping the stinking layers off her. It was the messiest diaper she had ever seen. Wetting a cloth at the washstand, she wiped Phoebe's bottom clean. Wiping a baby's bottom with the same hands that had just shot a man.

"We have to call the police," she heard Jacob say. His voice came from directly beneath her — they had moved to the kitchen.

"None of this would have happened," said Cora, "if you'd just left me alone."

"He swore he would never hurt you."

"I bet he told you all kinds of things."

What Jacob said next was too muffled for Penny to make out.

"Listen to me, Jacob. He fooled you. Just like he fooled everyone."

Penny managed to pin a fresh diaper on Phoebe and find fresh clothes for her. A clean blanket to wrap her in. Although the baby wanted to be held, she put her in her quilt-lined basket, which she had nearly outgrown. Bundling together the soiled diaper, blanket, and Jacob's ruined jacket, she stepped out into the hallway. She should go down right now and soak the whole mess in the laundry tub, but she . . .

"I'm sorry," he said. "Cora, if I had known, I would never have come out with him. I'm so sorry."

"Are you going to turn me in?" she heard Cora ask. "You know, they could put me in the electric chair."

The smell of scorching pumpkin began to overpower the stench of baby shit.

"All I'm asking is twenty-four hours before you tell anyone," said Cora. "Just give me a chance to escape."

Someone downstairs began to weep in hoarse jagged gulps. It wasn't Cora, Penny realized after a few seconds. She heard Jacob ask his sister if there was anything to drink in the house.

"There's wine in the cellar," Cora said. "Just sit down. I'll get it for you." She heard Cora go out. Penny remembered she had left the cellar door wide open.

This was completely out of hand. Jacob thought his sister had killed the man who had saved his life in the war. She had to go down there, tell him the truth. Call the police herself.

She stood at the top of the stairs, about to take the first step down, when she heard Jacob sobbing again. Cora returned to the kitchen and tried to comfort him. She, too, was weeping. *I'm sorry, I'm so sorry.* Their voices blurred together. Turning around, Penny retraced her steps to Cora's room, scooped the complaining baby out of the basket, and sat on the edge of Cora's bed.

Phoebe wouldn't stop crying. After a while she started screaming. It had been hours since Cora had last nursed her. Finally, after the room had turned golden with the light of early evening, Penny heard Cora come up the stairs. She looked different; the swollen skin on her jaw had turned sickly yellow. Something in her eyes looked glassy and haunted, as though she really had been the one to fire the rifle. It hurt just to look at her face. Without a word, Cora took the baby and opened her shirt. Penny walked to the window and looked out at the touring car with its leather roof. It seemed to rest lower on the ground somehow. It had to be a trick of the light, of the long shadows cast by the low, blinding sun.

"Did you take the pot off the stove?" Penny asked. "It was burning."

"Yes, Penny. I took care of the pot."

She turned to look at her, a woman with a worn-out, beaten face and a baby at her breast. Cora was in tears. "I hurt you, didn't I? When I pushed you like that. I never meant to hurt you."

Penny's hand automatically found the sore spot on her cheekbone. "Why did you lie to your brother? I did it!"

"Honey, don't shout like that. We'll talk about it later. I promise."

"But —"

"Penny, please. I have to stay calm while I'm doing this. Could you start packing your things?"

She had to breathe in fast to keep the blackness from rushing into her head. "Pack?"

"We can't stay here anymore. You know that."

Penny went across the hall to the room with its shelves of books that had been her world for the past five months. Avoiding the mirror, she tore off her dress. It must be marked with blood. She put on an old winter dress of scratchy wool that was too tight across the chest. Pulling out her flimsy wicker suitcase, she packed her clothes and squeezed her schoolbooks in around the edges.

She packed Javier's carved wooden bird. When she set her suitcase in the hallway, she saw that Cora, too, was packing, working fast, with fierce concentration. Phoebe lay in her basket, lulled into a milky sleep.

"Take your suitcase down and put it in the back of the pickup," Cora told her. "Put your bicycle in there, too."

"Where are we going?"

"I'm not driving through Minerva, but I can take you to Sandborn."

Something cold washed over Penny. Sandborn, where the county court and prison were. The county asylum, where they'd sent Sadie Ostertag for axing her four children.

"Penny, we need to hurry. When you go downstairs, don't talk to my brother. Just leave him be."

Penny found him slumped in the rocking chair, facing the wall. A drained glass and an open wine bottle rested beside him on the floor. Had he passed out, she wondered, or was he in a state of shock? Either way, it didn't matter. She slipped out the door. After she had loaded her suitcase and her bicycle into the pickup, she remembered the animals — if she wasn't there to feed them, they would die. There was so little time. She ran into the barn to fork down hay for the cow, then raced to the poultry pens and opened the doors so the chickens and geese could escape. There were still late berries in the woodlot for them to forage. The chickens probably wouldn't survive the winter, but the geese would. She was convinced they would turn wild. They were fierce enough to thrive, to defend themselves from bobcats and foxes. Even when the snow lay thick on the ground, they would endure somehow — they were that tough. Their clipped wings would grow back and they would fly away.

She crept past Jacob and back up the stairs. "Did you pack all the clean diapers?" she asked.

Cora was holding a thick winter coat of royal-blue wool. "This was meant to be your Christmas present." She handed the coat to Penny. "Put it on and button up. It's supposed to snow tonight." Then she gave Penny the basket where the baby slept. Picking up her suitcase, Cora led the way down the stairs, stopping to get her rifle. Jacob still sprawled in the rocking chair, his face turned to the wall. Penny noticed an envelope on the kitchen table, the words *To Whom It May Concern* made out in Cora's elegant script.

"We have to go." Cora stepped between Penny and the kitchen table, blocking her view of the envelope.

"What about your brother?" Penny whispered.

"Leave him be."

When they climbed into the pickup, the sun was low in the sky. A sharp crescent moon hung over the horizon — a new moon. Penny knew it was setting, not rising. Tonight the moon would set along with the sun.

21

Penny held the baby as they drove down the darkening road. Phoebe's head rested against her shoulder, a thin trail of drool dampening her new winter coat. Cora drove fast, gravel flying against the fenders. A rabbit darted across their path, then leapt to safety on the other side of the road.

"Where will you go?" Penny asked, turning to catch Cora's face in the last of the fading light.

"I can't tell you. It's safer if you don't know."

Penny's heart thudded with a hollow sound. The baby's weight was so solid and substantial in her arms. It seemed impossible that anything could separate her from Phoebe and Cora.

"Later on I can write to you," Cora said. "Maybe in a few years. I'll write in care of your mother at the Hamiltons' address."

"But *why* do you have to run away? I'm the one who did it." She shouted so forcefully that Phoebe began to cry. "Hush," she whispered, kissing her. So many things were flying through her head. She imagined great flocks of birds circling in chaos. "What about your brother?" She remembered how still he had sat in that rocking chair. Unnaturally still.

"I asked him not to report the crime for a day or so. Just to give me a head start." Cora spoke evasively.

Something awful plucked at Penny when she recalled the drained wine glass beside him on the floor. "Did you . . . did you *do* something to him?" She couldn't frame the word *kill*.

"Remember my grandfather's sleeping powder? I mixed two packets in with his wine. He'll sleep for a while, that's all. It seemed my best chance of calming him down so I could get away."

Penny's thoughts began to race again. "But what happens when he wakes up? He'll call the police."

"He can't. I cut the phone wire. And I slashed his tires. He won't be going anywhere unless he starts walking."

"You did that to your brother?"

Cora bit her lip. "He was so upset, I didn't know what he would do. He might never forgive me for it, but I couldn't take any chances."

"Why didn't you tell him that I did it?"

"Oh, Penny." She took a quick swipe at her eyes. "You think I'd let them put you away?" She paused, breathing deeply. "I want you to listen to me. When we get to Sandborn, I'm going to let you off, and that's the last we'll see of each other — for a very long while at least. So please pay attention."

Penny hugged Phoebe tighter, allowing the baby to close her hand around her braid and pull hard. It hurt, but she made no noise.

"I've left a letter behind for the police. I've taken full responsibility for . . . for the shooting. I signed my name, and said that you and Jacob had nothing to do with it."

"But why? Why do you have to run away because of what I did?"

"He . . . Adam would have put me away. Taken Phoebe away. I don't know if I could have done it, even if I had gotten the rifle away from him." Beneath the urgency in her voice there was something fragile and raw. "He just broke me down, Penny. Broke me until I was the same way I'd been before I left him. But you did it for me. What I couldn't do. Deep down I just wasn't brave enough."

Penny sobbed aloud. She saw Adam Egan, lying on the floor, painted in his own blood, his dead eyes staring at her.

"You're too young to get dragged down in my mess. Let me be the criminal. I was on the run from him anyway." Cora paused to steady her voice. "There will be a police inquiry. They'll call you in to give evidence. I want you to promise me that you'll tell them I did it. Say you came in when you heard the shot, saw me with the rifle. Then you got on your bike and fled because you were scared."

"*No.* It's wrong. I'm going to go to the police and tell them the truth."

"Honey, please listen to me." Cora pulled over to the side of the road. "Your life is brand-new. You could be anything you wanted. I want you to go out and be a heroine. Live your life and be someone great. I ruined my life when I was only twenty-one, married a man I didn't even know very well. I don't want your life ruined. You should get an education. Sometimes I think you're my true soul, Penny. You're so strong and unspoiled. I want you to be a heroine for both of us."

Penny wept while Cora stroked her hair.

"Promise me, Penny. Promise me you'll do all those things you talked about. You said you wanted to be a nurse. It would make me so proud. Just think. We would share the same profession."

The sun and moon had vanished, but the truck's headlights provided enough illumination for her to see Cora's eyes as they reached deep inside her, drawing forth her dreams like jewels. Everything she had ever longed for. A road stretching before her into an unknown landscape with mountains and towering trees.

"If you're my friend," said Cora, "do this for me."

Penny threw her arms around her neck.

"You still haven't promised me."

"I promise," Penny said faintly.

"A friend is someone you never lose," Cora told her. "One day when everything is better, our paths will cross again. Who knows?"

She clung to Cora until Phoebe, squeezed between them, began to protest. Then Cora started driving again. Penny looked to the horizon, where she could already make out the distant lights of Sandborn.

"There's one thing I want you to do," Cora said, "as soon as you've had a chance to calm down. I want you to go see your mother."

Penny said nothing.

"She loves you. Believe me, Penny. I saw it on her face. When she came out that time. Just go and have a talk with her." Cora switched off the headlights and cut the engine. "If Phoebe ever turned away from me, it would break my heart."

"You're going to Mexico, aren't you?" The thought came to Penny with marvelous clarity. Cora spoke Spanish. Maybe she could join Antonio — she wondered if it was too late to ask if Cora had really kissed him. "Once you're across the border, they can't get you anymore. Can they?"

Cora was silent.

"Or Canada." As long as she kept talking, she could make time stand still. Keep Cora with her a little longer. "That's even closer." If Cora drove all night and day, she could cross the border before anyone caught up with her. "Can I come with you?" For a moment, it seemed not only possible but necessary, essential, the thing Penny wanted more than anything else. "I want to go with you."

Cora spoke sternly. "That's crazy talk, and you know it."

She winced, turning her head to the passenger window. She could just make out the streetlights, a string of houses with lit-up windows.

"I think it's best if I let you off here. It's better if no one sees you getting out of my truck." Cora let herself out and went around to the back. Penny could hear her hauling out her bicycle and suitcase. But she stayed where she was, holding Phoebe securely on her lap, running her fingers over her downy head.

Cora opened the passenger door. "Come on, Penny." She took her daughter and walked a few paces away. Penny stumbled out of the pickup. The black sky swam with stars. When her eyes adjusted to the darkness, she made out the shape of her bicycle.

"I put your suitcase in the rear basket," Cora told her. "You're about a quarter of a mile from town. Go to Swenson's Ladies' Guesthouse on Main Street. I've heard it's clean and respectable. In the morning, you can take the train to Minerva. Once you're back in town, you can start going to school every day like a regular student. Here." She placed an envelope in Penny's hand. "Put that away carefully. Your wages are in there. I put in a little extra to tide you over for a while. There's a pocket with a zipper inside your coat. Stick it in there." Cora hovered close until Penny tucked the envelope safely away.

"Good luck," Cora whispered, hugging her, Phoebe nestled between them. "Remember our promise. You're going to live a good life." She kissed Penny's cheek and then stepped away. It was over so fast. The pickup started up and drove off. Penny swung her leg over the bicycle seat. Her feet found the pedals and pushed off, letting the distant lights of Sandborn draw her into town.

22

PENNY REACHED Sandborn Main Street as the snow began to fall, large sticky flakes coating her shoulders and hair. The cold didn't matter — if it sank deep enough inside her, it wouldn't hurt anymore. After setting the geese free and after Cora had dropped her off in this town where no one knew her, she decided that she was turning into something feral, too. Just a stray that didn't belong anywhere. She couldn't imagine returning to Minerva to go to high school, any more than she could picture going back to her mother. And when she located Swenson's Ladies' Guesthouse, she couldn't bring herself to write Penny Niebeck in the register. That girl didn't exist anymore — she had died along with her innocence and the man whose life she had taken. *Hazel Leith*, she wrote instead. That had been Mrs. Hamilton's maiden name. If she couldn't be Penny anymore, she would be Hazel. Maybe it would bring her better luck. Someone named Hazel probably wouldn't do what she had done.

The guesthouse was as respectable as Cora had promised, the sheets on the bed immaculate and freshly ironed. She stood in front of the long narrow mirror on the door and examined her face from all angles. Her cheekbone was still tender, but apart from some puffiness, there was no mark, no sign that a bruise would form. So that was one less thing she would have to explain. Her mother always told her that she was the tough kind of girl who didn't bruise easily. She fingered her braid snaking over the front of her snow-dusted coat. Tomorrow she would go to a beauty parlor and get her hair cut. The braid was part of Penny, so it had to go.

As she stepped out of her heavy new coat, she heard something rustling in the inside lining. Unzipping the inner pocket, she took out the envelope Cora had given her. It was much thicker than she had realized. When she tore it open, she found a fat wad of twenty- and fifty-dollar bills bound together, more money than she had ever seen. There was also a folded note.

Dear Penelope,

This is for your education, so spend it wisely. I hope you can put this behind you. You are such a promising young woman. You're not going to be foolish like I was; you're going to be brilliant, much better than I could ever be. Think of me sometimes and know that I wish you well. I will always remember you.

Your friend, Cora

She sat for a long time reading and rereading that note. If she closed her eyes, she could hear Cora's voice as clearly as if she were standing just behind her chair. She was talking about Patagonia. "We lived on the edge of a long fjord. There were swans that were half black, half white. White swans with black necks. They swam in salt water. Here, if you talk about salt-water swans, people think you're lying."

She could see Cora driving down the endless moonlit roads. Would the snow block her way? If she drove south, heading down to Mexico, maybe then the roads would be clear. Perhaps she would ditch her pickup, hop a freight train like a hobo, her baby tied to her back with a shawl. She could do it if she had to. She was a swan, half black, half white, that could survive in a cold salty fjord. *Ave, ave.* On the inside of her closed eyelids, she saw silver feathers brushing air, long necks stretching. She heard beating wings, the wind rushing past. Flying, soaring, and far below, the snowy spines of mountains, their peaks like the white caps of storm waves.

When she lay down and finally slept, she didn't dream of

Cora or of the man she had shot. She dreamt of her mother hanging up wash on the Hamiltons' clothesline. Her mother turned to her and smiled. "Penny," she said, opening her arms, and then Penny jolted awake, feverish and cotton-mouthed as the wind rattled the windows and whistled down the chimney with a haunted sound. Burying her face in the pillow, she tried to go back to sleep.

She woke up with the chills, her throat sore, her forehead burning. When she tried to get up and get dressed, she felt so weak that she crawled back under the covers. What did she have to get up for anyway? For the next three days, she drifted in and out of fever, shivering and then sweating until the bedsheets were clammy and sour. Mrs. Swenson, the landlady, brought her hot tea with lemon. "Oh, poor Hazel," she said. "Would you like me to call the doctor?"

"No, ma'am, please. No doctor. I'll be all right."

When her mind was clear enough to concentrate, she read *Great Expectations*. She had promised Cora she would keep up with her schoolwork. And Cora had promised her she would love the book. So she read about Pip, Estella, and Miss Havisham while the snow kept falling, covering the town in dazzling white crystals. Frost etched her windowpanes in a landscape out of a fever dream. On a tree outside, a blood-red male cardinal perched and sang.

It would not let her go, the vision of the bullet exploding in his chest. His dead eyes staring at her. She kept reliving that scene. If she hadn't been blocking the door. If she could have protected Cora without killing him.

Mrs. Swenson stood over her bed, her face a haloed blur in the lamplight. "Hazel, if you're not better tomorrow, I *have* to call the doctor."

23

ON HER FOURTH MORNING in the boarding house, Penny made herself go down to the dining room to eat her breakfast with the other guests. She sat next to a middle-aged woman who wore steel-rimmed spectacles. "Hazel Leith," the woman said. "I've never heard the name Leith before. What kind of name would that be?"

"Ruby, don't pester her," said Mrs. Swenson. "Can't you see she's been sick?"

Penny swallowed a mouthful of weak coffee. Lethe was a river in hell, she wanted to tell her. Its water had the power to make you forget everything, wiping your memory clean.

"A shame you were sick," Ruby said. "You missed our Thanksgiving dinner. Mrs. Swenson made a real nice turkey."

The landlady laid her plate in front of her. "It's a Spanish omelet. I thought you'd like something special to help build back your strength."

Eggs smothered in tomato sauce that looked like blood congealing on the plate. Her stomach twisted up.

"She's going green around the gills, Mrs. Swenson."

The landlady snatched the plate away. "Sorry, Hazel. It looks like maybe toast would be better."

"Toast is just fine." Penny tried to smile.

"You give that Spanish omelet to me," Ruby told Mrs. Swenson. "I hate to see something so nice going to waste."

After breakfast, she took a long hot bath, then got dressed and went to sit in front of the radiator in the parlor, where she brushed out her hair until it was dry.

"Nice head of hair you got." Ruby plunked herself on the sofa with her knitting. She was working on a man's sweater. In the old days, Penny thought, she would have asked her whom that sweater was for and how she came to live in this guesthouse. But now she wasn't interested in hearing anyone's story.

"I want to get it cut." She spoke in a dull monotone. "I want to get one of those new dos."

"Try Kretsky's Barbershop on Second Avenue," said Ruby. She ran a hand over her own hair, which was short but too thin, with patches of bald scalp winking through the lank blond strands. "He does a good job on ladies' hair, and you don't have to pay. He'll pay you."

"How's that?" If her voice sounded sharp and suspicious, Penny was too tired to care.

"He sells the hair to a wig company. I reckon he'd give you a good price for yours. Your hair sure looks healthier than the rest of you, if you don't mind my saying."

Wrapped in her new winter coat with her old winter hat pulled down over her ears, she plodded down Sandborn Main Street where she had once walked with Cora and Phoebe. The cold kept her face tight and rigid. When she passed the photographer's studio with the baby pictures displayed in the window, her eyes remained dry. Like some frozen gutted thing, she turned a corner and arrived at Kretsky's Barbershop with its red-and-blue-striped pole, its golden scissors painted on the big front window. The inside of the place smelled of men's hair oil and the special disinfectant soap they used to clean the combs and brushes. When she sat in the barber chair and loosened her braid, Mr. Kretsky gathered up a hank of her hair, gauging its length and thickness. She tried not to shrink from his fingers.

"How much will you give me for it?" she asked. She didn't even sound like herself anymore, but like a hard rough girl who smoked cigarettes and went with the wrong kind of men.

"How does three dollars sound?"

"Sounds fine. Cut it short. I want one of those new bobs." She tilted her chin up so her reflection in the mirror wouldn't look so helpless and lost.

"You been sick, missy?"

"There's been a death in my family. I'd rather not talk about it." She really had turned into someone else. Penny Niebeck would never have lied like that. She narrowed her eyes so she would not have to look too closely at her bloodless face in the mirror, the face of a girl who had committed a mortal sin. She would go straight to hell. The only way to save her soul would be by going to confession, taking her penance. She had promised Cora she wouldn't tell the police, but Cora hadn't said anything about priests. *Don't think about that now.* She tried to find solace in the rhythm of the clicking scissors. Bit by bit, the long tresses fell away, exposing a startled new face. A woman's face and not a girl's.

"Didja hear the news?" a man was saying in the background. "There's been a murder over in Minerva. A real humdinger, too. It's so bad, they want to keep it out of the papers."

Penny watched her face in the mirror turn red. She wanted to tear the barber's cloth off her shoulders and run out on the street, even though her hair was only half cut.

"Shut yer mouth, Clarence!" Mr. Kretsky called out. "Can't you see we've got a young lady present? Don't fret, miss. He'll keep his trap shut."

Penny met his eyes in the mirror and saw the kindness there. She was nothing to him, just a strange girl who had come in to sell her hair for three dollars, and he was being nice. Just like Mrs. Swenson bringing her tea and making her a Spanish omelet when she didn't deserve it. How would they treat her if they knew what she had done? Her lip began to tremble. She bit down hard to make it stop.

"Now, now, miss. I see you've lost a loved one. My missus passed away last year."

"I'm sorry," she said.

His eyes met hers in the mirror again. "You're not from Sandborn, are you?"

"No." She sat up straight as he clipped the last long strands of hair, which fell to the floor in a heap. Her head felt so light now without the hair to weigh it down. "Mr. Kretsky, do you know where I can find a Catholic church?"

"We have two Catholic churches in town, the Polish church and the Bohemian. Which do you want?"

"I just want to go to confession."

"You go to the Polish church." He smiled. "That's where I go. Follow Main Street down to Sixth Avenue, then turn right and go about four blocks."

She left the barbershop with three dollars in her fist and a picture in her mind of what she had to do. She would kneel in the dark confessional and pour out her crime. The priest would tell her what prayers she had to say, what penance to make. It would be a relief, really, just to tell someone. Of course, he would tell her to go to the police. She kept thinking of Cora and Phoebe stranded somewhere in the snow. If she confessed her crime, they would stop hunting Cora. Maybe going to prison would be less awful than living the rest of her life with this weight hanging on her. What good was her promise if it made her hate herself? She was a killer, no different from Sadie Ostertag.

Heading back down Main Street, she searched the horizon for church steeples, but the two- and three-story shop fronts blocked her view. The streets were clogged with automobiles, and the sidewalks were full of people come into Sandborn to do their Saturday shopping. The crowd was so dense, she felt like a fish struggling against the stream. People were looking at her. A young man met her eye and winked. Catching her reflection in a shop window, she saw she looked older now with her short hair and her new winter coat, more experienced, not like those ruddy-cheeked farm girls with shawls tied over their heads.

Passing a newspaper stand, she ducked her eyes, not wanting to catch a glimpse of the headlines. Murder over in Minerva. It would take a lot of doing to keep it out of the papers. Jacob must have asked them to keep quiet about it. Maybe he had told the police that Cora killed her husband in self-defense. Would they believe that? There was only one right thing to do — first she would go to the priest and then to the police. Set the record straight.

She still couldn't see any church steeples, and in the press of the crowd had forgotten Mr. Kretsky's directions. Where did they hide the churches in this place anyway? In Minerva you could see the church steeples from everywhere in town. Maybe most of the people here were like city people, who never went to church. If you didn't have religion, where did that leave you when you committed a mortal sin? Cora had told her once that she didn't believe in hell. And Penny had read in the Chicago paper about people who were turning away from religion and embracing science and psychology instead. The power of human intelligence.

"Penny Niebeck!" A man's voice jumped out of the crowd. A doctor's voice, full of authority. Penny shook her head, not believing any of it, even when he took her arm and peered into her eyes. "Penny, my Lord, it *is* you." Dr. Lovell was carrying parcels of the things he had bought in the fancy-goods shops. His wife stood just behind him, gazing at Penny over his shoulder. He looked so pale, so anxious, and wouldn't let go of her arm. "When I heard what happened, I feared the worst. They couldn't find you. I went over to examine the body and the scene of the crime."

Her eyes blurring, she tried to bolt, but he held her fast.

"I thought she must have killed you, too. Or taken you hostage."

"Dr. Lovell, she didn't do it. It was me. I shot him."

"Now, dear, calm down."

"He was trying to hurt her. I didn't mean to kill him. I . . ."

"She's upset." Mrs. Lovell stepped out from behind her husband and put her arm around Penny's shoulders. "Honey, why don't we go somewhere and have a nice cup of cocoa?"

"But I . . ."

"It's a natural reaction, Penny." Dr. Lovell spoke in a comforting tone. "I know you were very loyal to her. But don't blame yourself. I blame myself for making you take care of her. I should have known better. She's a dangerous woman."

Penny raised her voice and kept telling them over and over what she had done.

"Now, now, dear," Mrs. Lovell murmured. "Don't cry." She took Penny's arm and steered her into a café where people clustered around tables covered in red-checked oilcloth. The air was thick with cigarette smoke. Penny wanted to turn and run, but Mrs. Lovell held her steady.

Dr. Lovell slipped a fifty-cent piece to one of the waitresses. "See if you can find us a quiet table, miss." The waitress led them to a back room where the air was a little easier to breathe. Dr. Lovell ordered hot chocolate for the three of them, then pulled out a chair for Penny. Mrs. Lovell wouldn't let go of her hand.

"You poor girl," she said. "All this and now your mother."

Penny looked at her blankly. "My mother?" She tried to get up, but Mrs. Lovell pulled her back down in her chair. Her head began to hurt. The Lovells looked so nervous, even Dr. Lovell, who was never nervous. He took his hat off and cleared his throat. Penny watched his face turn color.

"So you haven't heard the news."

Baffled, she shook her head, gazing from Dr. Lovell to his wife, who had something glistening in her eyes.

"They wanted to keep it out of the papers," he said. She saw his lips move and listened to his words, but the things he told her were simply preposterous. She heard the words *murder*, *mother*, and *shot*. That couldn't be possible.

She kept saying, "No, that can't be true." Dr. Lovell had to repeat his message several times before she could take it in.

24

Gradually the story sank into her, eating into her bones. Dr. Lovell was too prudent to spit out the whole uncensored report — he fed her only the bits and pieces that he seemed to consider fit to disclose to the girl whose mother had been shot. It was up to Penny to fill in the blanks.

It might not have come to this. Barbara Niebeck had her suitcase packed. She was ready to leave, having made inquiries at the station about taking the train to California. She had enough saved up to start a new life. But nothing could happen in a town that small without word getting around. The morning she intended to vanish, he was waiting for her. He begged her not to go. Not even if it was for the sake of his family. Never.

For the first time, they went into the parlor to talk. "We'll find a way," he said. "Just don't leave." They stood in front of the mantelpiece she had forgotten to dust that week. "Hazel won't live forever. One day, maybe sooner than we think . . ." He seemed to shudder at this admission, at all that it cost him. The very walls of the house seemed to lean close and press in on him, registering his betrayal. Outside, rain fell, the wind beating his wife's rose bushes against the windows. He said, "When that day comes, we won't have to hide anymore." He clasped her arms. "I don't want to hide always."

For her, it seemed that everything came apart at once. The parquet floor beneath their feet turned to liquid. *Don't you understand*, she wanted to say. *We'll never be able to love each other in the open. Not as long as we stay in this town.*

"Are you sure you know what you're saying?" she asked him instead. "Your girls . . . what would they think?"

"Ina and Isobel would be just fine. But Irene . . ." His head fell forward. He looked so defeated that she wrapped her arms around him. She watched his eyes move around that room, so thick with family memorabilia. The wedding portrait and the honeymoon plate from Santa Barbara, the family photographs and Irene's sheet music in disarray on the piano bench.

"You're doing your best with her," she whispered. "It's not easy when they get to that age. I didn't do very well with my girl, either. Did I?" Her voice broke.

"Maybe it's just a matter of patience." The lines in his face eased. "In two years she'll be off at college. She'll have her own life."

"That's right." Barbara nodded, a curious relief stealing over her. She hadn't thought of that. Irene was nearly grown up.

Monday morning, November 17, around ten-thirty, some of the pop factory employees noticed Mr. H. slipping out. His daughters were at school. Back at the house, Barbara was waiting. That morning they made love not in the back bedroom but in the master bedroom, in Mr. H.'s broad marriage bed with its real linen sheets. She tasted the sweat on his neck, arched her body over his. He told her that only she had the power to make this cold sleepless bed sweet again. She smoothed back his hair, her capable hands stroking the length of his body. Her kisses fell on his skin like rain, and the November sun poured through the lace curtains to cast intricate patterns on their faces. They didn't speak, because they didn't need to. They were beyond words, Barbara straddling him, blinding him with her loosened hair.

The house was still, a fortress that protected and concealed them. On the dresser, his brass alarm clock ticked away the seconds while downstairs the grandfather clock tolled the hour. Eleven o'clock on a Monday morning. Love was a realm they could step into at will, shutting the door to the outside world. How were they to know their secret world could turn into a trap?

211

The November wind throwing the elm branches against the bedroom windows swallowed the noise of the back door opening, then closing. The measured footsteps mounting the stairs. She had come to investigate just like any professional detective in the crime novels she borrowed from the library. She had come to see what she could see. It was an experiment in testing how strong her nerves were. At first she stood outside the closed door and listened. If she had heard them together in the back bedroom, it might not have come to this, but to hear them moaning and sighing in her mother's own bed, in which she and her sisters had been born, was too much for any girl to bear. Something inside her shattered in a cold burst.

Backing away noiselessly, she found herself in her father's study. Her eyes moved across the room until they rested on the glass case that enclosed his neglected hunting rifle. An unnamable impulse possessed her as she walked over to the case and discovered it was unlocked. How careless of him! She had never held a rifle before, didn't even know if it was loaded. What she did know was that it would give them a good scare and show them a thing or two. After this, her father wouldn't be so quick to disgrace her.

She crept back to the bedroom door, then slowly turned the knob and pushed it. There was Barbara Niebeck riding her father like a horse. She thought of her mother, wasting forgotten in the nursing home while this went on. Assuming the position she had seen in so many pictures and movies, the butt against her shoulder, her finger poised on the trigger, she nearly screamed *Stop!* Only a choked sob ripped loose from her throat. Her father saw her before Mrs. Niebeck did. He pulled her mother's hand-sewn quilt over his and Mrs. Niebeck's nakedness. He shouted in anger, but soon he was pleading. Mrs. Niebeck just looked at her, too white-faced to scream. When she aimed the rifle, she thought she would finally put that bitch in her place.

Although she had never fired a gun, her archery practice served her well. The butt kicked back against her, but she leaned against the doorjamb, which kept her upright. She cocked the lever and squeezed the trigger while Barbara's screams went on and on. The blood welling up from her father's chest stained the white linen sheets from her mother's wedding trousseau. It reminded her of a line from one of her mother's old tales: *red roses in white snow*. And that shrieking whore, well, she'd have to shut her up, too. So she kept firing, but Barbara was thrashing around too wildly for her to aim well. One bullet shattered the bedside lamp; the next lodged itself in the mattress; the next struck Barbara in the shoulder. When she squeezed the trigger again, nothing came out. Dropping the spent rifle to the floor, she fled. Barbara's screams chased her down the stairs, ricocheting inside her, red roses bursting inside her head.

Though Irene Hamilton shot her father three times in the chest, Barbara Niebeck inexplicably escaped with a flesh wound, something Dr. Lovell could treat in the Hamilton kitchen. When she telephoned for help, she didn't mention her own wound, just begged him to get an ambulance to rush Laurence Hamilton to Sandborn Hospital.

"I'm afraid it's too late for that," Dr. Lovell told her when he examined him. "No pulse. His heart stopped. You're damn lucky you didn't wind up dead, too." After bandaging her shoulder, Dr. Lovell filled out Mr. Hamilton's death certificate, which Barbara, as a witness, had to sign. The sheriff and police came to take fingerprints and to write a report of the mussed and bloodstained bed. In the kitchen, they interrogated Barbara, prodding her for the more prurient details about her affair with her employer, until Dr. Lovell stepped in and told them to stop.

And Irene? She ran. If it had been a summer day with clear roads, she might have escaped on her bicycle and disappeared. But the streets were clogged with slush, so she stumbled through them in her kelly-green knee socks, her mouth open as she choked on the cold air. In her haste to flee her father's house, she had left her coat behind.

She still couldn't grasp that those were real bullets she had pumped into his flesh. She had only meant to frighten him, shock him out of his indifference, but she kept seeing roses, blood-red roses blooming in her mother's white bed. Words from her mother's ballads wove around her. *Mother, mother, make my bed, make for me a winding sheet.* When she reached the place where the railroad tracks curved around the back of the lumberyard, she knew what she had to do. The westbound train was coming. Shivering in the strong wind, her shoes and socks sodden from the melting snow, she threw herself down, clutching at the cold dirty iron. A red explosion danced behind her closed eyes as the train whistled and shrieked in its tracks, too fast and close to stop in time. A pair of hands wrenched her away just before the train hissed past in a rush of smoky air, the conductor screaming out the window.

"Goddamn crazy girl!"

Irene's deliverer was Lester Nilsson, a maintenance man for the Minerva railway yard. She wasn't the first would-be suicide he had dragged off the tracks. Although it was a subject even the most brazen gossips in town considered unlucky to discuss, it happened a few times each year. Usually bums or workingmen down on their luck, or girls who got themselves in a bad way. It took Lester Nilsson by surprise to discover that Laurence Hamilton's daughter was so eager to end her life.

"Miss Irene," he said, drawing her away from the rails. "Does your father know where you are?"

She could only weep and tug at her hair, so he kept his voice calm and patient, the way his brother did when gentling a spooked horse.

"C'mon, honey. This is no place for a girl like you. Let's get you out of here."

She offered no resistance when he took her arm and led her away. In these situations he always followed the same procedure: quiet them down, get them to the doctor. "Life's hard, ain't it? When you're a kid, nobody ever warns you how hard it's gonna be."

Since Dr. Lovell was at the Hamiltons' house talking to Barbara and the police, Mrs. Lovell was the only one home when

214

Lester and Irene appeared on her back doorstep. The look Lester gave her told the whole story. *Oh boy, here's another one I had to pull off the railway tracks.* Inviting them into the kitchen, Mrs. Lovell served scalding cups of coffee. The unfocused glint in Irene's eyes and the way her hands trembled too violently to hold the cup made the doctor's wife fear that this was more than a case of common despair. Lester met Mrs. Lovell's eye and shook his head, as if to say, *It can happen to the best of them.*

In the next room, the phone rang. It was her husband, telling her how Irene had shot her father. When Mrs. Lovell whispered that the girl was in their house, the doctor told her what to do.

"Here, honey, why don't you have a glass of blackberry cordial?" Mrs. Lovell said to Irene after hanging up the phone. She served it in a pretty cut-glass goblet, gently coaxing the girl while she tipped it back into her mouth. Mrs. Lovell had laced the cordial with laudanum, which Dr. Lovell kept on hand for treating patients suffering from hysteria and other ailments of the mind. Helping Irene to the parlor, Mrs. Lovell watched her slump slack-mouthed on the hard chintz sofa, covered in a pattern of dark red roses, which began to burst and implode in a dizzying cloud. Irene drifted off to another place as the Faery Queen swept her away. She sailed downstream into a twilit world where her dim-eyed mother abandoned her narrow bed and wrapped her in a moist embrace. Roses grew everywhere, arching their bloody faces over the glass coffin in which her mother enclosed her.

Irene awoke in a high-ceilinged white room, an old woman strapped down on the next bed. When she tried to speak, someone gave her a glass of pinkish fluid, which made her head go fuzzy again, forcing her back into that dark shuddering place. If her head were clear, she could have sat up in her bed, looked out the barred window, and seen her mother's window in the nursing home directly across the barricaded lawn, which skirted the asylum like a moat. However, only the less dangerous patients were permitted to stroll in that garden below. Irene was in the ladies' ward on the top floor, where they kept the criminally insane. Sadie Ostertag was two doors down the hallway.

25

PENNY SILENTLY repeated the information to herself, over and over like an incantation. *Not dead, your mother's not dead, only injured.* She stood outside the boarding house and waved goodbye to Ruby and Mrs. Swenson while Dr. Lovell put her suitcase in the back of his Durant sedan.

"You better get inside the car, Hazel," Mrs. Swenson said. "You're shivering."

When Penny climbed into the back seat, Mrs. Lovell turned around to give her a funny look. "Why did that lady call you Hazel?"

Penny could only shake her head.

Mrs. Lovell shrugged. "Well, I s'pose it's hard to keep track of everyone's name if you run a boarding house. She must see new faces every day."

Dr. Lovell got into the driver's seat and started the car. "Your mother will be so happy to know you're safe." His voice seemed to come from miles away.

The Lovells had explained that her mother had been staying in their guest room since the day of the shooting. In less than an hour, Penny thought, she would be with her again. Yet whenever she tried to recapture the dream of her mother opening her arms and calling her name, she only saw Irene's bone-white face. As soon as she reached the Lovells' house and saw her mother, she hoped those ugly visions would disappear.

. . .

When they reached Minerva, Main Street was reduced to a bottle-neck with all the automobiles parked in front of the Commercial Hotel. "Folks from out of town coming in for the funeral," Mrs. Lovell said. "His sister Blanche came over from New Hampshire yesterday. Took the whole top floor. She has Ina and Isobel staying there with her. After the funeral, she's taking them back east."

Those poor girls, Penny thought. If this hadn't seemed so un-real, she would have said those words aloud.

"Never seen so much traffic," Mrs. Lovell mused. "The whole town will be out for the funeral." She nearly sounded ex-cited. "This will be the biggest funeral we've ever seen."

The Lovells lived on Elm Street, two blocks from the Hamiltons' residence, but Dr. Lovell made an elaborate detour to avoid driv-ing past that house. "Your mother's been very upset," he said after he had parked the car. "She's really fragile. Keep that in mind."

Penny nodded, although even now she couldn't imagine her mother being fragile. Anything but fragile.

He unlocked the front door and carried Penny's suitcase in-side while his wife trotted up the stairs ahead of him. "Oh Mrs. Niebeck!" she called. "Guess who's here?"

Penny followed her into a narrow room with a slanted ceiling, a single dormer window, and a collection of garishly mismatched furniture and ornaments. The guest room was where Mrs. Lovell stuck the things that had grown old but that she wasn't quite will-ing to part with. There was a watercolor painting of a cactus out-lined against a desert sky. An old pincushion shaped like a giant tomato. But nothing of her mother's in sight.

"Well, where can she be?" Mrs. Lovell turned around in a cir-cle. "Maybe she's downstairs."

"No." Dr. Lovell set Penny's suitcase down. He nodded toward the empty closet with its wide-open door. "Her things are gone."

Penny's stomach clenched in a hollow ache.

"Let's look downstairs," he said. "See if she left a note."

A thin girl appeared in the doorway. "I think she left because of the news, sir. She was in the kitchen with me, listening to the radio."

"What news?" Dr. Lovell asked.

"The business at the Maagdenbergh farm," the girl said with a nervous blush. It was Ruth Zimmer, the Lovells' housekeeper, two years older than Penny. Once they had played together at a Fourth of July picnic in the Civic Park, Ruth pushing Penny on a swing. But now Ruth didn't seem to recognize her.

"Well, she knew all about that," Dr. Lovell said. "That's been in the paper for days."

Penny's eyes wandered to a dusty yellow vase filled with faded strawflowers.

"But they say her girl's gone missing." Ruth stared at her shoes. "Sheriff says that Maagdenbergh woman probably shot her, too."

Penny's legs caved in.

Mrs. Lovell caught her before she could hit the floor. "Oh, honey."

Fighting to regain her balance, Penny wriggled out of Mrs. Lovell's arms.

"Her daughter is right here." Impatience crept into Dr. Lovell's voice. "Did Mrs. Niebeck tell you where she was going?"

"She didn't tell me anything, sir. Just went upstairs after the news. Said she wanted to be alone. Then I had to go to Renfew's. When I came back, she was gone."

Through blurred eyes, Penny stared at a picture of an insipid angel guiding two children over a bridge.

"We should never have left her alone," Mrs. Lovell murmured.

"But she has nowhere to go." Penny looked bleakly around the room. "Where would she *go?*" Outside the dormer window, snow was coming down, darkness falling. Somewhere out there her mother was all alone, thinking Cora had done her in.

"She couldn't have gone far." Dr. Lovell laid his hand on

Penny's shoulder. "The funeral service is tomorrow at two o'clock. You'll see her then, if not before."

"I'm going for a walk," she told him. Before anyone could stop her, she was down the stairs and out the door, dashing along sidewalks made treacherous with new snow concealing glassy ice. On the corner of Elm and Madison, she fell and banged her knee. But she didn't feel any pain, merely emptiness as she picked herself up and dragged herself on to the Hamiltons' house, cordoned off with rope. On the front gate, a sign was posted, the big red letters still visible in the twilight: NO ENTRY BY ORDER OF THE SHERIFF.

She had always imagined that the house and her mother were somehow inseparable, her mother as permanent a fixture as the Hamiltons themselves. But who would live in that house now? The door was locked, no way back. A new pain in her belly burrowed so deeply it hurt to breathe, hurt to look at that abandoned shell of a house with its ice-glazed rose bushes.

When she returned, the Lovells were waiting for her in the kitchen. A place had been set for her at the table. There was a pot of tea, a basket of bread. Ruth filled her bowl with navy bean and bacon soup that tasted like her mother's. It was so hot, it burned her tongue.

"You have to eat, dear." Mrs. Lovell watched her closely until her bowl was empty. Only when Ruth had cleared the dishes away did they show Penny the evening's *Minerva Reporter*.

"I'm surprised they printed it," Dr. Lovell said. "Thought they'd at least wait until after the funeral. We've had enough trouble as it is."

So this was what her mother had heard on the radio. What startled Penny most was the photograph printed alongside the article. A young woman posed in a tiered white dress, loose and flowing like the Greek robes Penny had seen in her illustrated copy of *The Odyssey*. The woman hardly seemed familiar. A slender ribbon was tied around her brow. Her hair fell in waves over her shoulders, and her bodice was cut low enough to reveal the shadow between her breasts. The only part of her face that she even faintly recognized was the tilt of her chin. *Mrs. Cora Egan, 1921.* It must have been the only picture they had been able to dredge up on such short notice, probably supplied by her Chicago in-laws.

WOMAN WANTED FOR MURDER
$5,000 REWARD

Nov. 30 — Sheriff E. S. Tanner issued an all-points bulletin yesterday for Mrs. Cora Egan for the brutal shooting death of her husband, Dr. Adam Egan, of Evanston, Illinois.

Estranged from her husband, Mrs. Egan had been living on the Van den Maagdenbergh farm outside Minerva with her infant daughter. She was known to local residents for her anti-social temperament and her habit of wearing male attire.

The slain body of Dr. Egan was discovered in the farmhouse by postman Ed Magnusson when he came to deliver registered mail. Dr. Everett Lovell, who examined the body, attested that Dr. Egan had been shot with a rifle at close range and had been dead for at least five days before discovery.

In a letter dated November 20, written and signed by Mrs. Egan and left at the crime scene, Mrs. Egan claims full culpability for the shooting. She also states that she drugged her brother, Mr. Jacob Viney, who accompanied Dr. Egan on his visit. A wine bottle and a wine glass with traces of sleeping powder were found in the kitchen.

No trace could be found of either Jacob Viney or Miss Penelope Niebeck, Mrs. Egan's hired girl. "It is possible that Mrs. Egan might have harmed or killed these two people," Sheriff Tanner told the *Reporter.* Mrs. Egan's 1920 Dodge pickup was missing from the scene. It is believed that she fled the state.

After his wife's desertion of him in November, 1922, Dr. Egan had employed private detective Vernon Ward, who over the past year had collected a significant amount of evidence proving that Mrs. Egan was unlawful, antisocial, and thus unfit for motherhood. Elliot Baxter, Dr. Egan's attorney, had drawn up a summons to take Mrs. Egan to court. The charges Dr. Egan intended to bring against her include aiming a firearm at him and threatening to kill him on November 3, 1922; concealing the existence and whereabouts of Dr. Egan's daughter, Phoebe; and lying about the child's paternity on the birth certificate.

Attorney Baxter believes that Mrs. Egan deliberately drugged her brother before proceeding to murder her husband with both malice and premeditation.

The warrant for Mrs. Egan's arrest was issued yesterday by Sandborn County Judge Charles Flint. Mrs. Egan is believed to be armed, dangerous, and mentally disturbed. In the interest of the safety of her infant daughter, she must be approached with extreme caution.

Mr. Paul Egan of Chicago, brother of the slain man, has offered a $5,000 reward for any information or assistance leading to the arrest of Cora Egan and the safe return of his niece.

Description: age, 25 years; height, 5 feet 7 inches; green eyes; auburn hair cut very short; light complexion. She was last seen wearing overalls, a flannel shirt, and heavy work boots. Her daughter, Phoebe, is five months old.

Wire all information to E. S. Tanner, Sheriff, Sandborn County, Sandborn, Minnesota.

After supper, Dr. Lovell called the sheriff's office. Penny sat at the kitchen table and stared at Cora's picture while she listened to him talk on the telephone.

". . . I want to let you know that Penny Niebeck is safe and unharmed. She's staying with me and my wife at the moment. Yes . . . yes, of course . . . Look, I know you want to question her, but give it a few days," he said quietly. "Now her mother's missing, and we don't know where to find her. Miss Niebeck is in no state to give evidence right now."

. . .

There was nothing left to do but climb the stairs to the cluttered guest room and lie down on the bed where her mother had slept the past few nights. Penny drew back the covers hoping to find some trace of her, if only a forgotten handkerchief. Under the pillow she discovered a small wooden statue she vaguely remembered seeing before, long ago, when she was very young. A stern-faced woman with a dark blue mantle. In her outstretched hand she held a miniature tower with three windows. Penny turned the statue over and found the name Barbara carved on the bottom in clumsy letters.

She was turning into a child again, the way she cried for her mother and cradled that statue. She remembered her mother's smell of sweat and vinegar with something else underneath it, some baking scent. For the first time in half a year, she began to pray, stroking the saint's black wooden hair with her finger. *Bring her back, please bring her back.*

The next morning, they dressed for the funeral. Since Penny didn't own anything black, Mrs. Lovell lent her a black cloche that completely covered her short hair and shaded her eyes. She imagined that if her mother saw her now, she wouldn't recognize her. She would remember her as a girl with a long braid, dressed in Irene's castoffs.

It felt strange to follow the Lovells into the Presbyterian church. The walls were so plain, the altar so bare, it hardly seemed like a church at all. There were no statues of saints, there wasn't even the smell of frankincense, but it was packed to bursting with the best families of Minerva. She spotted Miss Ellison and the Fisks. Everyone from the Jaycees and the Rotary Club had turned out. A stout woman done up like a battleship in rippling black veils led Ina and Isobel down the aisle to the front of the church. Aunt Blanche, the girls' new guardian — Penny had met her once before and hated her — talked as if she had mothballs glued to her tongue. Decked out in matching black hats and coats, Ina and Isobel looked like grim little china dolls. Workers from the Hamilton

Creamery and Pop Factory squeezed into the outer aisles. Some of them wept openly. With Mr. Hamilton dead, they didn't know what the future of the factory would be, or if they would still have jobs.

Everyone in Minerva seemed to be here — except her mother. Penny clasped her hands over her belly as the pain returned, much worse than it had been the day before. Numbly she sat back and regarded the coffin. Barely visible under its load of hothouse flowers and ribbons, it looked like some morbid carnival float. A few minutes later a red-eyed Miss Ellison began to play the organ. Everyone sang the spare Protestant hymns, then the service began, the minister going on and on about what a good man Mr. Hamilton had been, a shining example for the community. Maybe that's why her mother wasn't here — someone had warned her to stay away. But what if something had happened to her? What if she had lost her, after all? It was all her fault for being so hard and unforgiving. By now the pain was so bad, Penny doubled over, her forehead pressed to her knees.

"What's the matter?" Mrs. Lovell stroked her neck in a motherly fashion. Penny swallowed a cry.

"I need air." Stumbling over Dr. Lovell's feet, she squeezed her way through the crowded aisle and out the door.

Shivering, she made her way across the adjoining cemetery and climbed the artificial hill made over the years with earth dug up from the graves — or at least that was the story Irene had told her once. As the pain racked her, she imagined leaving her body behind, rising weightlessly like a ghost. The pain sank in so deep, she wondered if this was the way Irene had felt, the unspeakable wretchedness that had made her reach for her father's rifle.

When the service came to an end, men from the Rotary Club carried out the coffin and set it down beside the freshly excavated pit. From where she stood on the hill, Penny could see the entire crowd. Aunt Blanche looked so staunch and severe that Penny could imagine her happily murdering her mother, finishing off

Irene's botched attempt. Ina and Isobel huddled to one side of her. On her other side stood Miss Ellison, her face nearly disfigured from crying. If her mother was here, Penny imagined that she was watching from a distance, her face hidden behind a black veil.

As the minister began to read the last rites, a commotion started at the back of the crowd. With an air of astonishment, the pop factory workers moved aside, allowing Barbara Niebeck to step forward, her unveiled face exposed to everyone. Penny's breath caught. The tight cluster of family and friends refused to surrender an inch. Her mother forged on, fighting her way forward, making a path between their unbudging bodies. When they elbowed her, she pushed back. Miss Ellison raised a hand to her mother's face. For a moment, Penny thought Miss Ellison was going to smack her. Dr. Lovell took her mother's uninjured arm and tried to shield her from the crowd, but her mother yanked free. Before anyone knew what to do, before even Aunt Blanche could block her way, Barbara had emerged at the front and taken her place beside the coffin. She reached into her black overcoat and drew out a single white lily. With infinite tenderness, she laid it on top of all the other gaudy flowers that smothered her lover's coffin. As the sobs shook her, she held herself steadfast, taking her place beside him like a widow, not a mistress.

When they lowered the coffin into the pit, she threw down the first handful of earth, then clutched her handkerchief to her mouth and wept. The ceremony came to a close. Still she would not move from the grave. Eventually even the Hamilton relatives retreated, heading for the funeral dinner in the church banquet hall. But her mother remained, as though she had become a part of that dead winter landscape. Penny's insides throbbed with a pain that made her dizzy. Hands thrust into her coat pockets, she made her way down the hill and around the headstones until she stood by her side. Her mother's eyes were so clouded, she didn't seem to notice Penny was there. Penny reached for her hands, blindly kissed her salty cheek.

"Penny?" Her mother's eyes moved over her face as though

Penny weren't real anymore. "I thought I lost you, too." Then she hugged her so fiercely that Penny started crying with her, hiding her face in her collar. "I heard on the radio . . ."

"That's all lies. She would never do that to me."

"I know. I didn't believe it when I heard it."

She looked at her mother in amazement.

"But they said you were missing. I thought you'd gone away with her." Her mother's words were so simple, and Penny saw that she understood everything. Then she doubled up in pain, rocking in her mother's arms beside Laurence Hamilton's grave. The cramping in her belly tore at her with a force that would have knocked her to her knees. Her mother's embrace was the only thing that kept her standing. "I know," her mother whispered. "Shh, I know. It hurts something awful, doesn't it? You really cared for her and that baby. Honey, I know." She held her, not like a child but a woman, her equal now. "I talked to her once. You weren't there. I knew right away she'd take care of you and not let you come to any harm. If there was one comfort, I knew she was making you happy." Then she broke off and held Penny by the elbows, looking her up and down. "You seem so grown up." Her expression changed. "She had to shoot him, didn't she?" Her mother pressed her lips together. "I'll bet he tried to take the baby away."

Penny struggled to find words, but her throat hurt too much.

"Come on." Barbara wrapped her good arm around Penny's shoulders and guided her over the dirty, trampled snow.

"Where are we going?"

"I rented a room at the Pig 'n' Whistle." Her mother couldn't stop staring at her. "You're so peaked-looking. I've never seen you like this."

"I had the flu pretty bad." It was the easiest thing to say and sounded like the truth, even though she couldn't name the thing that was tearing her insides to pieces.

Tucked in a side street on the other side of the railroad tracks, the Pig 'n' Whistle was a rickety three-story wood-frame building with a faded blue façade. Downstairs was the café, upstairs were the rooms, which could be rented for ten cents a night.

"Where's the bathroom?" Penny asked.

"Down off the second-floor landing. Knock on the door to make sure no one's inside."

When she sat on the toilet, she saw the blood on her underpants. So that's what it was. She gazed in the mirror to see if she looked any different. Her face was very pale, almost waxy, her eyes swollen from crying, an angry pimple in the middle of her chin. After washing her hands, she climbed the stairs to her mother's small, spare room.

"Do you have any old rags?" She tried to sound calm. "I'm bleeding." But then her voice caught.

"Your first time?" Her mother gave her a careful look before fishing through her suitcase. "Does it hurt? Dr. Lovell gave me a bottle of aspirin. Here, why don't you take some?" She got a few clean pieces of padded cotton and showed Penny what to do. When that was done, she lifted her daughter's cloche off her head and ran her fingers through her hair. "I see you got one of them bobs." Her voice was so gentle. "That's a nice sweater you're wearing."

"Cora gave it to me. The skirt, too."

"Well, she knows what suits you. Real angora." Barbara touched the soft wool. Penny closed her eyes as she felt her mother's hand on her shoulder, the warmth of her fingers seeping through to her skin. Bit by bit the pain in her belly eased as she imagined her mother's strength flowing into her.

A gold ring set with a ruby glinted on her mother's hand. She wore it in place of her old fake wedding band.

"What's that?" Shyly, Penny took her mother's hand.

"He gave it to me." For a moment her mother looked like a girl. Then her face twisted in grief. Penny caught her in her arms and held her until her mother pulled away and briskly dabbed her eyes with an already sodden handkerchief. "Why don't we go downstairs and get ourselves some dinner?"

They ate their supper of chicken à la king and coconut cream pie with grave discipline, even though neither of them was hungry. Penny glanced at the surrounding tables. The other customers were all men. She guessed that to have ended up at the Pig 'n' Whistle, they were probably hired men between jobs, traveling men down on their luck. She picked out a few hoboes, who must have traded chores for their meal. Her mother was staring at a slender man in the corner with thinning reddish hair. At least in the dim light, he looked like Laurence Hamilton. Her mother bunched her napkin in her fist and squeezed hard before she could pick up her fork again.

"There's going to be a trial in two weeks." Barbara spoke quietly. "For every murder, there has to be a trial." She sucked in her breath.

Then there would also be a trial for Dr. Egan's death. Of course, they couldn't bring Cora to trial until they found her, but if Penny stepped forward and made her confession . . .

"I have to stand witness," her mother said. "Blanche Hamilton wants to hush it all up as much as she can. I don't think she'll let them drag me through the mud any more than they have to. It would just make her family look bad. As soon as the trial's over, we have to leave town. Both of us."

"We can't live here anymore." Penny warmed her hands on her cup of boiled coffee.

"I've got some money saved up to get us out of here."

"So do I," Penny said. Her mother looked at her questioningly, but didn't ask for details.

"I was thinking we could go to California," her mother said. "Once we're settled, you should go back to high school. I want you to get your diploma and go to college. You have to rise above this life."

At first Penny could not believe she was hearing this from her mother's mouth. When she looked into her eyes, she saw how much love and grief had changed her. There was more to her mother than she had ever guessed.

"You're pretty smart. I want you going places."

Penny began to cry, right there at the table, tears spilling onto the oilcloth. "But I *can't*. Not after what I did."

Her mother put down her fork. "What are you saying, Penny?"

"You heard the news. There's a reward out for her. Five thousand dollars. I can't let her go to jail for what I did. She has a baby."

"What do you mean, for what *you* did?"

Penny lowered her head over her plate. "Cora didn't shoot him," she whispered. "I did. She took the blame so I wouldn't have to go to jail."

Barbara scanned the room, as though to see if anyone was eavesdropping. "We better talk about this upstairs."

"Cora made me promise not to tell." Hunched on one of the narrow beds, Penny cried into a spare pillowcase that her mother had handed her. All their handkerchiefs were used up. Penny told her how she had picked up the rifle and hadn't believed the bullet would really hit him.

Her mother's skin was so drained of color, Penny thought she could look through it and see the skull beneath. Her mother's eyes shone with something like dread. She flinched, her hand automatically moving to her injured shoulder. It was as though her mother were looking at her and seeing Irene staring back.

"I'm sorry," Penny whispered. "Please don't hate me. I let him in the house. I wasn't supposed to, but he had me fooled. Then he started hurting her. I didn't mean to do it." She couldn't say anything more.

Her mother balled her white-knuckled hands in her lap. "You made a promise to Cora." Her voice was so quiet, Penny had to lean forward to hear. "Now I want you to make a promise to me."

Penny nodded. "Any promise you want."

"I never want you touching a rifle again, do you hear?" Her mother swallowed. "Not as long as I'm alive. I never want to see another gun in my life."

"I promise." Penny watched her mother's face change, the color flowing back into her skin.

Her mother took her hands and squeezed them. "But you did it to save your friend." Her voice broke when she said the word *save*.

"But I . . ."

"Listen up. Nobody ever tried to save me. I was your age and . . ." Her mother closed her eyes. "You know your grandpa tried to drown you."

Now it was Penny's turn to flinch. Whenever she heard this story, she felt as though insects were crawling over her skin.

"Nobody tried to stop him. Not even my ma. I had to run away." Barbara held fast to Penny's hands. "But you stood by your friend. I wish I'd had a friend like that. My life would have been so different if someone had stood by me the way you stood by her."

Penny looked closely at her mother's face. She imagined the worry lines melting away until her mother was a girl no older than she was. A hurting girl who was too pretty for her own good. The work-roughened hands that held her own were the same hands that had pulled her out of the rain barrel. Suddenly she saw her mother's long journey, all she had suffered just to keep her. Her mother's life was as heroic as anything she had read about in *The Odyssey*. Very few people did anything as courageous in their entire lives as what her mother had done when she was fifteen years old.

"Penny, why are you crying like that?" Her mother took her face in her hands.

"You saved me," she said. "You didn't let me drown."

Her mother embraced her. Penny closed her eyes. All at once, it was so overwhelming — the thought of being saved.

Her mother stroked her hair. "Always remember that you stood by your friend. You didn't let him hurt her." She spoke fiercely. "Now she wants to save you from going to jail." She took her daughter by the shoulders, pushing her slowly until Penny sat erect, her spine unbowed. "You saved her," Barbara said. "And now she wants to save you."

26

DR. LOVELL insisted on being present, along with her mother, when the police questioned Penny about the shooting at the Van den Maagdenbergh farm. When she stuttered over her answers, the doctor broke in, his voice ringing with unshakable authority. "Officer, you can see she's innocent. She nearly lost her mother, and she's only fifteen. How can you think she had anything to do with that mess?"

Dr. Lovell also drove Barbara to the Sandborn County Courthouse the day they both had to testify in the Hamilton murder trial. Penny insisted on coming along to Sandborn, even though she was not allowed inside the closed courtroom.

"Wait for us in the library," her mother told her. The Sandborn library was across the street from the courthouse.

"It shouldn't take longer than two hours," Dr. Lovell said. "That Blanche wants this to be finished as fast as possible."

Penny watched them climb the courthouse steps. Her mother was dressed in the same black clothes she had worn to the funeral. Dr. Lovell opened the heavy door for her mother to step through, then the courthouse swallowed them both. Penny turned to the street, waiting for a lull in traffic so that she could cross to the library, a pillared building that reminded her of the mausoleum in the Presbyterian cemetery. Her mother had been going to visit Laurence Hamilton's grave every day.

When Penny reached the bottom of the library steps, she found she could go no farther. The building repelled her. It was so cold and severe, like a big stone idol condemning her. Carved in the masonry over the double doors were the words *Truth Is the Highest Thing That Man May Keep*. She turned again to look back at the courthouse. The sheriff's office was somewhere in that four-story building. The county jail was only a few blocks away.

Tugging her hat low over her eyes, she began walking up the sidewalk, pointing herself away from the library and courthouse. Dr. Lovell said that they didn't need to worry about the outcome of the trial. There could be no dispute that Irene was her father's killer. Although Barbara Niebeck was the only surviving witness, the police had found Irene's fingerprints on the hunting rifle she had thrown to the floor before running out of the house. When the police had questioned Irene, she confessed her crime, albeit in garbled and confused language. She had meanwhile been declared mentally unfit to stand trial. It was better that way, less humiliating for her aunt and the rest of her family. Surely Ina and Isobel had been through enough without their sister making a spectacle of herself in the courtroom. After the trial was over, Aunt Blanche was returning to Hanover, New Hampshire, with Ina and Isobel in tow. She wasn't the maternal sort. Penny had heard she would be sending the girls to boarding school. And she would be leaving Irene behind in the asylum. A woman of her wealth and position wielded special power. She would not have her niece sent to prison for murder, or even for manslaughter. But neither, according to gossip, did she want to bear the responsibility of having Irene re-leased again into the world. It was easier to have her committed. Dr. Lovell said that at the asylum, it was a simple matter of signing a declaration. Penny imagined Aunt Blanche would be happy enough to let her niece rot there. Now Irene and her mother shared the same fate — life in an institution, no more Sunday visits.

Penny thought again about the words carved over the library entrance. *Truth Is the Highest Thing* . . . She had let her mother and Dr. Lovell lie for her. Especially Dr. Lovell. He knew, she realized, from the moment she had offered up her flustered confession, when he and his wife had run into her on Sandborn Main

Street. His wife must have chalked up her admission to the confused ramblings of a shook-up girl. He had recognized the truth, yet he would not allow her to turn herself in. Her mother had told her, "You can't do it. You're all I have." Penny had promised Cora, promised her mother, and now she was free to walk down the sidewalk in the crystalline winter sunlight while Cora was on the run and Irene locked up.

Penny's gaze rested on the tall roof of the asylum, visible from everywhere in town. It looked like a castle with its sheer walls rising straight into the sky, its narrow barred windows. Razor wire wreathed the high brick wall enclosing the grounds. The asylum drew her toward it, a vacuum sucking her in. Her mother had bought their train tickets. They were leaving Minerva tomorrow. This was her only chance.

When she knocked on the front entrance, the nurse at first did not want to admit her. "Only relatives are allowed to visit." The nurse had a broad peasant face and wore her hair in thick flaxen braids pinned around her head. From her sensible low-heeled shoes and the blunt cut of her fingernails, Penny guessed that she had grown up on a farm, that her life had been full of responsibility even before she came to work here. Maybe she was the oldest of ten children, used to getting up early and staying up late to take care of everyone else.

"Please," Penny said. "We grew up together. I'm catching the train out west tomorrow." She tried not to cringe under the nurse's scrutiny. If she were asked to give her name, the nurse would figure out that she was the daughter of the woman Irene shot.

The nurse just shrugged and rubbed her hands together. "I can give you fifteen minutes." Penny followed her bulky white form down a long passage and then into a narrow brass cage of an elevator.

"Can't we take the stairs?" Penny's head began to pound as the door clanked shut, blocking her escape.

The nurse grinned, revealing a gold-capped tooth. "You ain't never been in an elevator before? Oh boy. It sure beats climbing all them stairs."

When they reached the top floor, the nurse ushered her through several locked doors, opening each with a key she kept on an iron ring. Guarding the last door was a thickset young man who could have been the nurse's brother. "Hey, Clem," she said. "This is a friend of the family coming to visit Miss Hamilton." She nodded toward Penny.

The young man unlocked the door, only to lock it again the instant they stepped through. A tremor crept up the back of Penny's legs as she heard the heavy bolt sliding into place.

"This way." The nurse showed her into a windowless room. "You wait here, and I'll get the patient." She disappeared through another door.

Penny sat down on a hard metal chair, which faced a thick glass wall reinforced with iron bars. At first she didn't recognize the shockingly thin, sharp-chinned girl who appeared on the other side. Her hospital gown hung as loose as a flour bag on her bony frame. She wore black canvas shoes that looked too big for her.

"Irene?" She could only speak to her through a small opening in the glass. "It's me. Penny."

The creature on the other side regarded her with blinking mole's eyes. Penny's empty hands itched. It was wrong for her to visit without a gift. She should have thought of flowers or chocolates.

"Irene." She tried to sound patient and kind, though the urge seized her to slam the glass with the flat of her hand and shout, *It's me, Penny. Your enemy, the girl you pushed around for eight years. The girl whose mother you tried to kill.*

How could this quivering bag of bones be the tormentor who had plagued her since she was seven years old? Viewing Irene through the wall of glass was like looking into a dark mirror and seeing a lost self reflected. They were guilty of the same crime, except only Irene was being punished. Irene, who had always had everything in life given to her without having to fight for it, without having to work or earn a penny. We could have been sisters, she thought. If your father had married my mother.

The nurse joined Penny in the visiting room while another nurse hovered in the shadows on Irene's side. Aware of their eyes on her, Penny reached through the window. Irene would not take her hand. Still, Penny called out to her. And what she felt as she tried to reach her was no longer rage nor even pity but a horrible familiarity. The truth was that they were more alike than she wanted to admit. As fear took her by the throat, Irene finally sprang to life, her eyes locking on Penny's, her face assuming its old scowl as she threw herself at the glass and began to shriek.

"She did it, she did it! It's *her* fault. Let me go. She's the one who did it." Irene sank her fingers into Penny's wrist. And now Penny began to understand what it was like to hear voices — Irene's taunting voice raised to full pitch. "Look at her face! She's the guilty one!" she was yelling at the nurse. "Even someone as dumb as you could figure it out. Ow! Let me go."

The nurse on the other side caught Irene in a grip that made her loosen her hold on Penny, who staggered away from the glass and stumbled against the nurse who had shown her in. "Don't cry, miss." She guided Penny to the door. "They get like that sometimes. Don't take it personally." She rapped on the door, signaling the guard to unlock it. "Ain't by accident that she's on the criminal ward. Ya, she's a dangerous one. Can't trust her. Once she threw her dinner tray at a nurse. Hit her smack in the face. Poor gal needed stitches." The nurse kept speaking calmly as she guided Penny through the labyrinth of doors and down the shuddering cage elevator. "I don't like that Hamilton girl a bit. I like the quiet ones. They're the ones who stand a chance of getting better. The quiet ones can be real sweet."

Penny found her mother and Dr. Lovell in the library lobby.

"Where were you?" her mother asked at once. Penny could tell she had been worried. And she must have had a grueling time in the courtroom, too. Her face had taken on a sickly tinge. She had grown so thin, she resembled a brittle stalk.

"I went for a walk." Penny could hardly confess that she had just gone to visit Irene. She was still shaking, could still feel Irene's fingers latching on to her, hear that mad voice screeching inside her head, accusing and ravenous, a hungry beast that had to draw blood.

"I think both of you should eat something." Dr. Lovell, who looked rather sunken and weary himself, led them in the direction of a quiet café. Following a few paces behind, Penny observed the way he took her mother's good arm and guided her around the slippery patches on the sidewalk. When she saw the way he looked at her, she had to wonder if he, too, had fallen under her mother's spell. Was that why he had been doing all of this for them? If so, her mother seemed too deadened to notice. And Mrs. Lovell? Penny bit her lip. It was a good thing they were leaving tomorrow.

"What you both have to realize," Dr. Lovell told them in the café, "is that it's over now. You both have to put this behind you."

Penny swallowed a spoonful of lukewarm soup. She was careful not to appear ungrateful, but he was mistaken. It wasn't over, would never be over for as long as she and her mother lived. Her mother would never forget what had happened — a part of her would linger forever by Mr. Hamilton's grave. And Penny would carry Irene's voice and Adam Egan's face, his frozen eyes, inside her always. How easy it would be to let that dead man force her down into the world of shadows where Irene lived. He was dragging her there now, to that place where Irene's hot breath hit her face, her hand latching on to Penny, never to let go.

For her mother's sake, Penny finished her soup and bread. When they left the café, she drew her shoulders back and tried to walk calmly even as they headed straight into the wind, which was so strong and bitter it brought tears to her eyes.

27

IN JANUARY 1924, when the snow drifted deep over fences and railway tracks, Mrs. Deal and Mrs. La Plant warmed themselves by the stove at Renfew's and took tiny sips from their cups of hot chocolate.

"Well, they sure left town in a hurry," Mrs. La Plant said. "That Niebeck woman and her daughter."

Eyeing the basket of hard peppermint candies on the counter, Mrs. Deal nodded. "Yep. We sure won't be seeing them anymore."

"Rosie Lansky's leaving town, too."

"Father Bughola's housekeeper?" Mrs. Deal perked right up.

"They say she's . . ." Mrs. La Plant mouthed the words *in trouble*.

"She's got relatives in Silver Lake. She'll land on her feet." Mrs. Deal shrugged. "No doubt she got some money off him in exchange for keeping her mouth shut."

"I hear they got a lovely Polish church in Silver Lake."

"Speaking of money," said Mrs. Deal, "that Niebeck woman sure made out well. Did you hear, he included her in his *will*? Can you believe it? And the hussy had the nerve to take it! Now she's off to California like some movie star. Who does she think she is, anyway?"

"That's sure far to go," said Mrs. La Plant. "And they have no family there or anything."

"She'll find a new man to pay her dress bills." Mrs. Deal rolled her eyes. Her hand snaked out and snatched one of the peppermint candies from the basket. They only cost a penny, but

Mrs. Deal peeled off the wrapper and popped it in her mouth without Mr. Renfew noticing. "What about the Maagdenbergh woman?" she asked languidly, rolling the candy in her mouth. Her peppermint breath hit Mrs. La Plant's face, making her friend titter uneasily and draw an inch or so away. "Think they'll ever track her down?"

With an anxious flourish of her hand, Mrs. La Plant gave her cup a stir. "Newspaper said they looked everywhere, even searched around with dogs." She took a sip of her hot chocolate and discovered it had gone cold. "But it's hard trying to find someone when the snow keeps falling and covering their tracks."

SEARCH FOR MISSING WOMAN
CONTINUES

JAN. 14 — The search for Mrs. Cora Egan, née Viney, missing from her farm near Minerva since November 20, continues. In a letter to the authorities, Mrs. Egan confessed her culpability in the shooting death of her estranged husband, Dr. Adam Egan, formerly a surgeon at Evanston Hospital in Evanston, Illinois. The extensive search led to people being questioned as to Mrs. Egan's whereabouts as far away as Kansas, Missouri, and Texas. Mrs. Egan continues to elude law enforcement officers, who have discovered no further trace of her or of her now six-month-old daughter, Phoebe.

Mrs. Egan's brother, Jacob Viney, present at the shooting, has also been missing since November 20. Police are seeking him for questioning. Any knowledge of Mr. Viney's whereabouts should be reported to the authorities.

Mr. Paul Egan, the slain man's brother, has raised the reward for information leading to Cora Egan's arrest and the safe return of his niece to $10,000.

28

The most popular song of 1924 was destined to be "California, Here I Come," a thing Penny and her mother had no way of knowing when they boarded the Northern Pacific train to Portland, Oregon, in December 1923. From Portland, they planned to catch a Southern Pacific train to Oakland.

In the dining car, Penny watched her mother struggle to finish her chicken potpie. Barbara had grown so haggard and depleted. She was clothed completely in black, from her low-heeled shoes to her high-necked blouse. To Penny, it seemed that her mother wanted to hide away somewhere, never stick her neck out again.

At the next table, two young couples were talking in loud, animated bursts, laughing back and forth as though they had never tasted grief. One of them related a story he'd heard about a gang of outlaw rumrunners — "and they pumped that copper's chest full of bullets."

Penny watched the fork fall from her mother's hand. Barbara rose from her seat and walked stiffly away. Getting up to follow her, Penny glared at the next table. "What's the matter with you? Can't you see my mother's in mourning?" She stood so tall they ducked their eyes and mumbled apologies as though she were their senior and not just a kid who was going on sixteen.

She found her mother back in their sleeper compartment, her face turned to the window. Penny sat across from her. "You didn't eat much." She opened her satchel and took out a bar of chocolate. "Want some?"

Her mother shook her head.

Following her listless gaze back toward the window, Penny watched the snow-crusted fields race by. "Do you think we crossed the state line yet?"

The landscape no longer looked familiar. Farms were sparser. There were fewer towns. The dull white horizon met the gray sky in one long monotonous blur. Leaning back in her seat, she tried to let the train's motion soothe her. She had never been so far from home, but she didn't feel any excitement or expectation. The future still seemed unreal, a thing that belonged to someone else. Not her. She knew they would look for an apartment in Oakland, her mother would look for a job, and she would go to high school. She would spend the rest of her life pretending she was a normal person who had never killed a man.

If she ever confessed her sin to a priest, he, at least, could be practical about it. He would give her a suitable penance to bear. So many prayers, so many good deeds, and her sin, with the mercy of God, could be absolved. Yet what penance could possibly make up for taking someone's life? When she looked out the window, she thought that the emptiness of the landscape would claim her, make her its own. She would wander there her entire life and never find her way back again.

She wondered what had happened to Jacob. What had he done when he had awoken from the sleeping powder, alone in the house with his brother-in-law's dead body? She liked to think he had found the old pair of cross-country skis in the barn and escaped that way, taking off over the frozen fields. It was so easy for a young man like him to disappear from sight. He could hitch a ride, hop a freight train, and be gone. Perhaps he was back in France now, or maybe he was wandering around in this country, as lost and desolate as she was.

Penny raked her hands through her hair. The rhythm of the train seemed to chant *there is nothing, there is nothing*. She kept going over the facts. She had delivered her friend. She had killed a man. These two truths slammed around inside her head like wrestlers trying to hurl each other to the floor. If she was a killer who went unpunished by the law, then she was also a savior of

240

sorts, as her mother had insisted over and over. But she couldn't call herself a savior, couldn't embrace the one noble deed without admitting the other, the dead body splayed by the bullet she had let loose. What penance would she take on, what gift could she give back to the world to both keep her promise to Cora and redeem herself?

What was the opposite of a killer? Someone who saved lives. A doctor, like the man she had shot. If she became a nurse and dedicated her life to helping sick people, to trying to save as many lives as possible to make up for the one life she had taken, would that remove the stain? She imagined Dr. Lovell's face hovering in front of hers. *You've got nurse written all over you.*

Her mother dug her knitting out of her bag and began to work with vacant-eyed abstraction. Penny opened *Great Expectations*, which she still hadn't finished. Then it got dark, and they had to switch on the light. Later they pulled the seats flat into sleeping bunks. The porter came by with sheets, blankets, and pillows. Her mother seemed to fall asleep at once, her head buried in the bedclothes, stamped with the Northern Pacific logo.

Overnight the sky cleared. In the morning, there were mountains. It was just like looking at Cora's photographs, except these peaks were real, right in front of her, rising like a crown. How the sun dazzled on the alpine snow, which had never been stepped on, at least not by humans. Penny decided that only wild creatures could live on those summits and crags. The train carried them higher and higher, the sky blazing a darker blue than she had ever thought possible.

"This is like the place where Cora grew up," she told her mother shyly. "Way down in Patagonia."

Her mother nodded, as though she understood her daughter's wonderment and pain, which wrapped around each other like twin vines. Barbara took out the chocolate bar, tore off the crisp wrapper, broke off a small piece for herself, then handed the rest to Penny.

· · ·

When the train finally wound down the other side of the mountains, they left the snow behind. The skies were overcast, rain falling on evergreens. When they reached Portland the next day, it was as if winter had been replaced by an early and tenuous spring. The rain had stopped. Stepping off the train, they could walk around with their winter coats unbuttoned. They had four hours to kill before boarding the Oakland train.

"Well, I s'pose we could check our suitcases and stretch our legs a little," said Barbara. "Take a look around."

As they strolled along the riverfront, Barbara's eyes were busy scanning the tall, spruce-clad hills enclosing the city and the snow-covered mountains beyond. They watched the timber barges and fishing boats move up and down the Willamette. The fresh air brought out the color in her mother's face.

"I'm sure hungry," Barbara said. "The food on that train tasted like pasteboard. I wonder where we could go."

Penny decided that her mother was afraid of going to some swank place where they would have to lay down too much money for a slab of gray meat. "We could go here," she said, pointing to a riverside café. From the outside, it looked like little more than a shack, but there were green gingham curtains in the window, and the smell of something delicious drifting out the door. "Let's see what they have."

The menu was written on a blackboard hanging over the zinc counter.

"Look!" Penny clutched her mother's arm. "They have fresh oysters." She had read about them in books, but never imagined actually eating them.

"Take a seat, ladies." The olive-skinned man who emerged from the kitchen spoke with a melodic accent. So they sat down at a table near the window to eat their plates of oysters, fried and served with a spicy red sauce.

"Ever tasted anything like this before?" Barbara asked her after the first cautious forkful.

"No. They're really something." Their flavor was salty and foreign, like the ocean she had never seen.

"I s'pose if we're going to live near the coast, we better get used to eating this sort of thing," her mother said between bites. In a few minutes, her plate was clean.

"Want some more?" Penny asked.

"Well, it wasn't a very big plate, was it?"

Penny caught the cook's eye. "Another plate of fried oysters for my mother, please."

They slept on the train heading south to California. When they opened the curtains the next morning, dense fog shrouded everything. Rain beaded the window. While her mother went to the washroom, Penny took out the photograph of Cora that she had clipped from the newspaper before leaving Minerva. Her image in the newsprint was grainy, already beginning to fade. It didn't seem fair that this was the only picture she had to remember her by, that she had no real photograph. If only she had remembered to ask her for a more lasting keepsake — a photo from her album, a lock of Phoebe's hair. She wondered if Cora, in her haste, had packed the pictures she had taken of her and Phoebe in the orchard.

As she studied the blurred smile on Cora's face, the deceptive sweetness in her downcast gaze, Penny finally figured out why Cora had not allowed her to take that snapshot of her in the overalls with her daughter in her arms. Some people said a camera could steal a person's soul. Cora had taken the safest route — the only picture of herself in public circulation was this illusory portrait of a society lady and wife who didn't exist anymore.

The only authentic images of Cora were those childhood photographs in her album. The nine-year-old on her pinto pony, her chin sticking out in happy defiance, her blinding smile. That girl who rode her pony at full gallop without saddle, lifting her hands high in the air and terrifying her big brother. Maybe the real Cora, her essential spirit, had been trapped somehow in those early pictures. Ever since the death of her parents and the long journey to Chicago, all the photographs of her had been false. Maybe she had learned to hide her true self away where no one could find it and break it.

Now that Cora had disappeared, Penny believed that she understood her at last. From the age of thirteen, Cora had lived her life veiled and camouflaged, taking on one disguise after another. The overalls and work boots were as misleading as the flowing dresses had been, merely outer armor to protect her true identity, the hidden face she saved for her daughter. And that she, for a time, had shown to Penny. *Shape-shifter.* Penny allowed herself to remember Cora's transformation at Lake Griffin, the way she had shed her men's clothes and revealed her true skin before plunging into the lake, her strong woman's body weaving through the water.

What new disguise would she think up? She must know that the police were hunting a woman dressed in overalls. But Cora would fool them, hide her short hair under an old poke bonnet if she had to, conceal her muscled body under a shapeless calico housedress.

At what moment had Cora turned herself into a legend? The Maagdenbergh woman. Once Cora had told her that the name Van den Maagdenbergh meant "from the mountain of maidens" in Dutch. Penny could still hear her proud laughter when she told her that. When Penny thought about Cora's name, she imagined her friend living on top of some impossibly high mountain. She lived at the very peak, where no one could reach her or do her harm. The sheer slopes were glassy with ice, too slippery to get up unless you had wings or special powers.

But there were no mountains in view when she looked out the window, only rundown logging towns, ghostly in the fog. She opened *The Odyssey* to a page she had marked, whispered the words she had underlined in ink.

> *Do not detain me longer, eager as I am for my journey;*
> *and that gift, whatever it is your dear heart bids you give me,*
> *save it to give when I come next time . . .*
> *So spoke the goddess gray-eyed Athene, and there she departed,*
> *like a bird soaring high in the air.*

In the old myths, a warrior goddess could take up weapons, go to battle, fight whole armies, and even win, emerging whole and victorious. Like a wild bird, Cora had taken to the sky, her whole being bent on freedom and escape. While I'm stuck here on earth, Penny thought. She told herself she wouldn't cry, but she did, quietly, her face to the glass.

Because now she understood Penelope, too. Understood what it was like to be the one left behind to mourn and remember. She was left with Cora's picture in flimsy newsprint, a fragment of an interrupted story. If she had a loom, she could gather the fragments together and weave them into an unending tapestry that she would then unravel and weave anew. Weave and unravel for the rest of her days.

When she heard her mother's footsteps, Penny held the open book over her face so her mother wouldn't see her tears.

"You sure like that book a lot," Barbara said. Penny could feel her mother's eyes on her. "Why don't you read some of it to me?"

"It's a long poem." She spoke evasively. Right now she wanted to be left alone. "And it's real old, about a bunch of Greek heroes. I don't think you'd like it."

"What makes you think I wouldn't?" Her mother sounded offended.

Penny could hear her knitting needles clicking together. "Well, all right, then." She turned to a new page and began to read a few lines at random, something neutral and tedious that would bore her mother, put an end to her curiosity. But when she began to read, it was hard to keep her voice from shaking.

> *How I wish chaste Artemis would give me a death so*
> *soft, and now, so I would not go on in my heart grieving,*
> *all my life . . .*

"What kind of foolish talk is that?" her mother interrupted.

"I told you that you wouldn't like it." Penny then found herself trying to explain the plot to her mother, how Athena was so moved by Penelope's anguish at her separation from her husband

and son that the goddess had come to her in a dream, appearing in the guise of Penelope's sister, to comfort her. The peace of that dream had been so overpowering that Penelope had prayed never to awaken again.

Her mother's face twitched. "Dreams aren't enough." She turned to stare out the window.

Penny put *The Odyssey* away and looked out into the fog. There was book wisdom, but there was also her mother's wisdom, won from her hard battle with the world. In the light of her mother's scrutiny, her daydreams rang ridiculous. She wasn't Homer's Penelope, and there had to be more to her life than waiting and remembering. How could anyone spend her whole life weaving? Cora wanted her to be a hero, not just some hero's wife. The train's rhythm seemed to mock her, saying *you'll go on and on and on and on*. At last she closed her eyes and dozed off. She dreamt of geese, a wild meadow full of them. One by one, they took to the sky, until nothing but a dusting of white feathers remained to mark the place where they had been.

"Penny, wake up!" Her mother was shaking her shoulder. "Look!"

The sun had burned through the fog to shine on trees that rose like towers, their uppermost branches lost in a high canopy of needles. The girth of their trunks was so immense that if they were hollow, an automobile could have fit inside. A family could have made their home there. How the trees gathered like a tribe of giants sprung from the mossy, ferny earth.

"Those are redwoods."

Penny tried to hide her awe, but her voice was nearly lost as she craned her neck to try to see the tops of the trees. She had read about them in her school geography book. Now it came back to her, the paragraph that said each mature tree contained enough wood to build thirty big houses.

"Some of those trees are as old as that story." She pointed to *The Odyssey*. "Three thousand years old."

She realized she was exaggerating the life span of the trees by a thousand years, but she wanted it to be true, wanted to believe that the saga had been conceived when those mammoth redwoods had been seedlings. Their roots sank deep into the memory of a lost and golden age.

"Those trees," she told her mother, "can survive forest fires. There's something special about the bark. That's how they can live so long."

A voice welled up inside her like a voice in a dream, full of wisdom and comfort. Cora wanted her to be a hero, and now she had come to live among giants. If her friend had disappeared only to emerge again in another guise and another landscape, then so had she. With her eyes wide open, she began to dream her future. Dreamt she would graduate from high school, then go on to study not nursing but medicine. She would become a doctor. Before leaving Dr. Lovell's house, she had paged through his medical textbooks, seen cadavers sliced open to reveal the secret organs and vessels. Only in medical school would a girl like herself be allowed to take apart a human body, dissecting each organ, so that she could learn to put the severed pieces back together again. She had already touched death. What did she have to fear? If she had brought down a man twice her size and saved her friend, then she could also do this.

Penny saw her destiny as she traced those trees to their uppermost branches, brilliant against the deep blue sky. She pressed her hands together, feeling their strength.

EPILOGUE

I GREW UP in a town at the bottom of a valley enclosed by rocky hills burnt yellow and brown in the summer heat. Sometimes the streets seemed deserted, with the young men gone away to find work in the cities or north of the border. The young women remained to weave rugs of dyed wool from the sheep that lived in the hills. The old women made lace. In the cobbled central plaza there was a single trickling fountain; a white colonial church that my mother and I never entered; and the Hotel La Paloma Blanca, abandoned since its proprietor went bankrupt in the Revolution. It became an ornate ruin, its broken windows cloudy with cobwebs and dust. When I was a child, I believed it was haunted — when I was young, ghosts were very real.

My mother was the town's busiest midwife. She hardly ever spoke about her past. We lived on the outskirts in a stone house surrounded by a walled garden full of pepper and bean plants, tomatoes and squash. Our front gate, door, and shutters were all painted blue, the color that the old people claimed could ward off evil. The inside of our house was as spare as the garden was lush. The front room contained the blue-painted table where we ate our meals and where my mother gave me lessons in English and Spanish, Latin and Greek, geography and mathematics. The back room held our narrow beds. Our house seemed quiet and empty compared to our neighbors' houses, bursting with children, aunts, and grandparents, pictures of husbands and fathers who had gone away to find work. There were no pictures of men in our house, no relatives who came to visit. Just the picture over the mantelpiece of the young girl holding the baby.

When my mother was off attending births, I stayed with the old woman next door, who told me stories. Once she told me the tale of a princess grieving the death of her twin sister. She set out on a long journey to find a land where neither age nor death existed, thereby abandoning her parents and breaking their hearts. The princess journeyed to the edge of the earth, leaving all living land behind, until she came to a barren place that was the Palace of the Winds. Because the winds blew and blew so constantly, they kept age and death away. So the princess decided to make this bleak outpost her home. The winds roved the globe and brought back all manner of things — birds' feathers, pages torn from books, beads from broken necklaces, strands of hair, buttons carved from bone. Everything on earth that had been lost, never to be found again, ended up in the Palace of the Winds. And the princess spent her days sifting through the pile of lost things until one day she found her father's broken signet ring and realized that far away, in the land of the living, her parents were long dead.

I never stopped dreaming of my lost father. I imagined him having red-gold hair like mine. The only thing my mother would tell me about him was that he was deceased. For the rest, it was as though he had never existed. She seemed to want me to believe that I had sprung from her alone. She wouldn't even tell me how we had come to live in this town where my strawberry-blond hair made me stand out like a dandelion. I had always known we were different, from El Norte, and that for some unspoken reason my mother could never return. She never revealed the reason for her exile but told me it was simply so. A thing we had to accept.

My mother was respected and had many friends, for she had found her place in our town with the work she did. The women loved her, swearing she was the best midwife in the entire valley. They said that no matter how much a woman screamed or cursed in her labor, my mother stayed calm, never raising her voice. She mopped her patient's forehead, wiped her tears, lifted her shoulders, and urged her to hang on and keep pushing. They called my mother La Piedra, the stone, because she never lost control of herself.

La Piedra. What could be more solid — and more silent — than a stone?

When I was very young, I imagined that the Palace of the Winds was just beyond the hills that enclosed our valley. If I could only make my way to that place, I would find that heap of lost things and sift through them until I found my father's photograph. Some memento of him. A key that would unlock the door to the past and unravel my mother's secrets. The talisman that would show me where we came from and who we really were.

I knew she was hiding something from me, a secret too awful to speak of. It was common knowledge that criminals from El Norte found refuge south of the border. They lived among us, pretending to be innocent when in fact they were outlaws. Sometimes when I looked at her out of the corner of my eye, I wondered what she had done. Was she a murderer, a bank robber? No one in our town could imagine living so cut off from their relatives and home. Even the people who went away to work came home to visit. They sent money and photographs, and were remembered in their families' prayers.

Yet as wild as my imagination sometimes was, it was hard to cast my mother, the careworn midwife, as a villainess. This was my mama, who hardly ever raised her voice to me no matter how I sometimes tried her, who taught me to love Shakespeare and Beethoven. Besides, in the movies, gangster women were always glamorous and had perfectly coifed hair and cigarettes hanging out of their lipsticked mouths. My mother never wore lipstick or rouge, never painted her nails. She wore her shoulder-length hair tied back under a bright orange scarf that one of her patients had given her as payment. She never did anything to make herself look fancy.

Sometimes I thought she had been framed. That happened to

good people in the movies. Whenever a gringo came to town, which didn't happen very often, I stood warily at attention, fearing it would be someone from my mother's past who had come to settle an ancient score. She seemed to have this scenario at the back of her head, too. When I was ten years old, she taught me to shoot her Winchester rifle so I wouldn't be defenseless if a bad person came. No one in our town dared to give my mother any grief. She had an aura about her, a way of fixing people with her eyes that said she meant business. She had the power to make even rough men look away.

My mother had admirers, too. When I was six, a young schoolteacher courted her. He brought her candied fruits and white gardenias. In the cool evenings, after she had put me to bed, she sat with him in the garden. Sometimes I spied on them through a crack in the shutters and saw them kissing. I prayed that they would get married so I would finally have a father. When he presented my mother with a ring, however, she told him no, it could never be. She couldn't give up her midwifery for marriage; the women needed her too much. In addition, she was older than her suitor. She told him he was too young to settle down. The young man's parents had their own reservations about my mother, competent midwife though she was. How could they welcome her into the family when they didn't know anything about her past? Obviously my mother was concealing something scandalous.

After my mother declined his proposal, the young man moved away. If he could not have the woman he loved, then he would see the world. Now and then a letter from him arrived. Once he sent us a postcard from New Orleans. Meanwhile the rumor went around that my mother had refused him because she had a husband still living. There he was again, my father's ghost. How that invisible man haunted me.

I was worldly enough to know that not all fathers were good. I'd seen wives and children with bruises they tried to hide. In our town there were fathers who drank, and worse. I don't know which possibility was more chilling — that I had lost a good father or that I was descended from a bad father whose bad blood ran in my veins.

My mother's silence made it even worse. I loved her more than anything and knew it hurt her when I asked about her past. She never cried, just covered her face and looked so sad that I learned to leave the subject alone. Images of what might have been filled the silent void as I tried to guess what unspeakable thing in her former life had closed up her throat. I sensed that she planned to tell me one day when she decided I was old enough, yet with each passing year she grew more reluctant to speak of what was past. My questions burned inside me until I thought that they would make me burst into flame.

In July 1936, I had just turned thirteen. It was a hot day, the arid hills lost in a haze of dust. The winter rains were long past, forgotten as a dream. I had gone to feed the hens and gather eggs when I heard someone knocking at our back gate. Eggs still warm in my loose pockets, I stuck my head over the stone wall and saw a stranger standing there, a woman in trousers. One glance was enough to tell me that she wasn't from anywhere around here. She addressed me in shaky, hesitant Spanish, asking if my mother was home. And she looked at me in the most curious way. All the hairs on my body pricked up at once. My eyes traveled to the bolt on the gate, then traced the path to the back door. It would take only a matter of seconds to run in and get the rifle.

"My mother's out," I lied. "She won't be back for the rest of the day." In truth, Mama was fast asleep, having come home at seven in the morning after attending a difficult breech birth.

The stranger's face wrinkled in confusion as I addressed her rapidly in our local dialect. Although it was becoming clear that this woman was a gringa, I refused to speak English. If she had come here to make trouble for my mother, I wasn't going to make it any easier for her. "Go away, why don't you?" Obviously this stranger was not a pregnant woman in need of my mother's services. Being rude to her would do no particular harm.

I turned my back, about to return to the house and lock all the windows and doors, when she started pleading with me in broken words like a child, asking if she could wait in the garden until my mother returned. She said she had come a long way in the heat and that she was very thirsty. Looking at her again, I noticed for the first time that she had a leather rucksack strapped to her back. Her face was beaded with sweat. I let out a long breath. What if she had come for no good reason? How would I be able to tell? But it was so hot. If I let her wander until she collapsed of heat stroke, the neighbors would never let me hear the end of it. Her face and mouth were so pale. I was half afraid she was going to faint right there.

So I opened the gate for her. Her trouser legs were powdery with dust, making me wonder if she had walked all the way from the train station in the next town. But I didn't ask. Even a tourist from a cooler climate should know better than to walk so far in the midday heat.

"Sit," I told the stranger, addressing her like a dog and pointing to the stone ledge against the wall. So she took a seat there in the shade, easing her rucksack from her shoulders. The back of her white cotton shirt was dark with perspiration. Meeting my eyes, she repeated her request for a glass of water. I kept an eye on her as I worked the iron pump that brayed like a donkey until the water ran clear. As I filled the iron bucket, I watched her shake out her sweat-laced hair. Then she took something from her backpack and turned it over in her hands. It was an object too small for me to see.

My bucket overflowed, cool water gushing over my sandaled feet. I found the tin cup on the garden table, rinsed it out, and dipped it into the water. "Here." I slapped it down next to her on the stone ledge.

She didn't pick up the cup, didn't drink, just stared at me. Then she said my name. "Phoebe."

My throat closed. I had to fight to get out the words. "How do you know my name?"

She opened her palm and showed me a carved wooden bird with its wings outstretched. And then she gave me a look that made me think she was a bruja, a witch. Her eyes said that she had known me from the beginning of time. I took a step backward and called out in a loud shrill voice for my mother.

When she flew out the door, my mother's face was as pale as her wrinkled nightgown. I shouted at her in warning, but she didn't seem to hear. The stranger spoke instead, drowning me out. She said my mother's name. My mother began to blink rapidly and said something in a voice too low for me to hear. The stranger rose from the bench and went to her. For a moment they just looked at each other. I had never seen my mother at such a loss. And then they embraced, my mother weeping in the stranger's arms. My mother, La Piedra. It was the first time I had ever seen her cry.

They were oblivious of me, though I kept gawking, bewildered and fearful of this foreigner who knew my name and had such power over my mother. Cramming my fists in my pockets, I crushed the eggs, and the yolks burst from the broken shells, staining my skirt a sticky gold.

"Phoebe." Tears in her eyes, my mother held out her hand to me. "This is her, darling. This is *her.*"

Now I understood. That sweet-faced girl whose picture hung over our mantelpiece, that girl with her braid pinned around her head, holding a baby in her arms. She had found her way back to us, our angel.

Our guest, who was no longer a girl but a woman with a face as grave and life-worn as my mother's, drew me into her arms. When I looked into her eyes, I saw the same tenderness that was in the old photograph.

Penelope was the key. She took me to the place where all the lost things were gathered. She showed me the photographs, the pictures of Minerva. The faded newspaper clipping of my mother as a lovely young lady in a white flowing dress. Penelope told me the story that my mother hadn't been able to put into words. She revealed as much of it as she thought my thirteen-year-old ears could bear. That she loved us and had never forgotten us. That she had become a doctor, one of three women in her graduating class. That she had been searching for us all along. One summer she had worked at a charity hospital near Tijuana and spent her free hours combing the surrounding villages, asking people if they knew of a gringa with striking green eyes who was raising a girl on her own. Finally, in a hospital in Los Banos, California, she had treated a man from our town who had told her where she could find us.

Over the years, when she returned to visit us each summer, I learned the whole story. She told me about my father and then about the shooting, confessed that it was her finger on the trigger, not my mother's. She opened herself to my reprisals. After my shock died down, I at last came to understand the mystery behind my mother's silence. Penelope proved to me that I was my mother's daughter, not his. I was my mother's child, sprung from her body, her fierce longing and love. It was on account of Penelope that I learned who I was and where I came from.

In that summer of 1936, I watched Penelope and my mother playing chess in our garden. The intense sunlight streamed through the dancing eucalyptus and olive branches and shone on the orange nasturtium and blazing red hibiscus. The sun poured down on my mother's chestnut hair and on the garden table, painted deep turquoise. I watched their hands move the kings and queens across the board. Penelope, the real outlaw, who had lived her life disguised as an innocent. My mother, the innocent, who had taken on the guise of an outlaw, choosing a life of exile in order to protect her friend. Looking through Penelope's eyes, I learned to see my mother as beautiful and courageous, a woman who could not remain earthbound but who had sprouted wings and flown farther than anyone had thought possible. Sometimes the Gods disguise themselves as mortals and walk among us, at least for a time, before they disappear.

ACKNOWLEDGMENTS

The lines from *The Odyssey* are from the great Richmond Lattimore translation (Harper Perennial Library).

A historical note on Mrs. Hamilton's illness: in the wake of the Spanish flu pandemic, sleeping sickness (encephalitis lethargica) struck five million people worldwide between 1918 and 1927. The illness was the subject of Oliver Sacks's book *Awakenings*.

The first draft of this novel was completed while I was a visiting fellow at Hawthornden Castle International Retreat for Writers in Scotland. I am indebted to Dame Dru Heinz for her generosity.

Wendy Sherman, my wonderful agent, and Jane Rosenman, my brilliant editor, helped bring the book to fruition.

The following people gave me support and inspiration. My mother, Adelene Simons Sharratt, provided details on Minnesota farm life. Ellen Cooney told me I needed to have balls. Greg Hyduke taught me all about Winchester rifles. Sandra Gulland gave me fabulous criticism and career advice. I am deeply indebted to Susan Ito, Gayle Brandeis, and everyone in my on-line writing group. I also wish to express my gratitude to the Munich Writers Workshop, my friends at Readerville, the two California groups that welcomed me, the Monday Night Group, and everyone at Womenswrite in Manchester, England, especially Cathy Bolton. Cath Staincliffe, Jane Stubbs, Margaret Batteson, and Julia Brosnan read my manuscript with great care and delivered valuable feedback.

Finally I would like to thank everyone who read *Summit Avenue* and asked me when my next book would be available. Her readers are a writer's great love.